Kings of the Roundhouse

Kings of the Roundhouse

JOHN PRESTON

VIKING
an imprint of
PENGUIN BOOKS

This is a work of fiction. Names, characters, places and incidents are either entirely the product of the author's imagination or are used fictitiously. In particular, the only resemblance between the Roundhouse described in this work and the Roundhouse in Camden, London, is the name and the geographical location and everything else is entirely fictitious

VIKING

Published by the Penguin Group
Penguin Books Ltd, 80 Strand, London WC2R ORL, England
Penguin Group (USA) Inc., 375 Hudson Street, New York, New York 10014, USA
Penguin Books Australia Ltd, 250 Camberwell Road, Camberwell, Victoria 3124, Australia
Penguin Books Canada Ltd, 10 Alcorn Avenue, Toronto, Ontario, Canada M4V 3B2
Penguin Books India (P) Ltd, 11 Community Centre, Panchsheel Park, New Delhi – 110 017, India
Penguin Books (NZ) Ltd, cnr Rosedale and Airborne Roads, Albany, Auckland, New Zealand
Penguin Books (South Africa) (Pty) Ltd, 24 Sturdee Avenue, Rosebank 2196, South Africa

Penguin Books Ltd, Registered Offices: 80 Strand, London WC2R ORL, England

www.penguin.com

First published 2004
1

Set in 12/14.75 pt Monotype Dante
Typeset by Rowland Phototypesetting Ltd,
Bury St Edmunds, Suffolk
Printed in Great Britain by Clays Ltd, St Ives plc

A CIP catalogue record for this book is available from the British Library

ISBN 0-670-91489-4

Contents

PART ONE
Edmund

ROUNDHOUSE ACCOUNTS FOR YEAR ENDING 3 APRIL 197–

	BUDGET (£)	ACTUAL OUTGOINGS (£)
Maintenance of building	24,730.00	78,500.00
Cleaning (see also below)	18,600.00	0.00
Disinfecting fluid (chemical toilet)	420.00	7,612.00
Bar staff	16,448.00	64,996.00
Food staff	8,401.00	5,694.00
Insurance	8,777.00	44,602.00
Miscellaneous purchases	235.00	1,263.00
Magazine subscriptions	57.00	412.89
Office costs	240.00	8,662.00
Wages	49,000.00	64,664.00
TOTALS	126,908.00	276,405.89

The disparity in the 'Maintenance of building' figures refers to the new roof, work on which was completed at the start of this year. Serious structural damage was also discovered in the basement, due principally to the corrosive effects of sewage. These repairs

3

have yet to be carried out. There are no records of any cleaners being employed anywhere in the building during the whole of the preceding twelve months. Possibly this is due to loss of paperwork.

The considerable jump (1,800 per cent) in the expenditure on disinfecting fluid is a particular cause for concern. The provision of mains sanitation to all areas of the building, including the dressing rooms, remains a priority. Also of great concern is the loss incurred on sales of alcohol and soft drinks. Although three of the bar staff were convicted on embezzlement charges in May of last year, their removal appears to have had little effect on the scale of the deficit. Unauthorized use of telephones is believed to account for the massive leap in office expenses. This too is a major cause for concern.

Both insurance payouts refer to cases of botulism traced to the Roundhouse kitchens by Public Health Inspectors. Following the second of these cases, a stomach pump was purchased on the advice of the Public Health Inspector for use inside the building ('Miscellaneous purchases'). Regrettably, this stomach pump has now gone missing.

I

An Unfavourable Impression

A lodging house in Finsbury Park. An Edwardian villa of unusual drabness, with sharply pointed gables and bricks the colour of dried blood. Eight-thirty on a Thursday morning in March. The mid 1970s.

A young man opens the door of his bedsitting room. Immediately he clamps his hand over his nose, then shrinks back into the doorway. There is a terrible smell out there. A dank airless stink that's piled up in the stairwell over many generations; a smell of burning fish bones and broccoli boiling away to nothing in small, unventilated spaces.

Taking a deep breath, the young man lowers his head and charges down the stairs. On his way he passes a blur of other doors leading off to left and right. The house has been divided up into a bewildering number of bedsits. Rooms split vertically, horizontally – any way you can imagine. The place is a warren of plasterboard partitions and tiny hutches. Everyone packed together; stacked up on top of one another, like bodies in a mausoleum. Some of the residents have a single pane of glass to look through – although they may have to stand on a cupboard or lay down on the floor to do so. Others have no window at all.

The young man's name is Edmund Crowe. He is twenty-one years old and takes no pleasure in himself. In the ten days that Edmund has lived here, he hasn't seen any of his fellow residents. They are a shy lot, scuttling back to their hutches at any sign of human presence. Even shyer than him, and that takes some doing. At night, though, he can hear them: hear the hiss of their gas cookers; hear them rolling over; snoring and crying out in their sleep for lovers real or imagined. All this just inches away from where he lies wedged in his iron crib.

Edmund could, of course, have chosen to live somewhere else. A flatshare perhaps. Hundreds of these are advertised every day in the evening paper. But the thought of being scrutinized and evaluated by other residents – that would have been agony to him. So instead he has come here, to this plasterboard labyrinth in Regina Road, N4. To this lodging house full of other stragglers and misfits: immigrants, out-of-towners, night-shifters and fugitive au pairs. Or newly qualified young professionals like himself, of modest means and rudimentary social skills.

Still holding his breath, Edmund lets himself out of the front door and stands on the step, snorting through his nostrils – trying to expel the smell of the place. Then he walks to his car. Usually he takes the Tube to work, occasionally the bus. But today, when both Tube and bus unions have joined forces in a hitherto unprecedented show of solidarity and called a combined strike, he will drive the pea-green Austin Allegro that his parents bought him recently to celebrate his passing his final auditing exams.

Edmund is as self-conscious about this car as he is about everything else in his life. And not without reason. Although it goes efficiently enough, it's not the sort of car that anyone would wish to be seen driving – no one under pensionable age anyway. Its unsuitability for speed, for movement generally, being emphasized by its having a square steering wheel. Once again British designers have surpassed themselves, creating a perfect fusion of unsightliness and impracticality.

Settling into the driver's seat Edmund grips the steering wheel by its two bottom corners. Although there are more cars than usual on the roads today because of the various strikes, there are hardly any lorries or commercial vehicles – and no buses, of course. Almost everyone is on strike. But then the entire country has collapsed. The cost of living has risen by 20 per cent in a single year. Unemployment is higher than it has been since the 1930s; bankruptcies are at their highest level ever. In an attempt to cut down on costs, a three-day week has been declared. However, it hasn't made much difference – no one has worked for more than three days a week in years.

A haze of sloth has settled over the land. The British worker is officially the laziest, the least productive, in Europe. He's a clodpoll, actually phobic in his attitude towards employment. A number of scientific studies have proved it. Britain is finished. That's the truth. We have become an international joke.

According to the Scandinavians, we've brought it on ourselves. It's all to do with our being repressed. There may be something in this. Unfortunately, being repressed is about the only thing we're still any good at. Although the French are in almost as bad a state as ourselves, that hasn't diminished their delight at our difficulties. For a while the Germans even toyed with buying us up – the whole country – at a knockdown price. In the end, though, they decided there was more sport to be had from watching us being eaten by the giant rats that now throng the streets.

A few weeks earlier, the existence of a new mutant rat was reported. At first this rumour was dismissed as scaremongering, but it has rapidly become accepted as fact. This new rat is much larger than usual, being the size of a cat – even a small dog. It's also well-nigh indestructible, being immune to any normal forms of poison. There is a theory that this new mutant rat has evolved at double-speed in order to take advantage of all the waste, all the decay. It is a symbol of our shortcomings; nature's way of telling us that something has gone terribly wrong.

Nothing works any more. Light? There is no light. Power cuts happen frequently and without warning. Large sections of the city are plunged into darkness at the flick of a switch. Coal? Certainly not. None of that either. Everywhere the sweet tang of something rotting hangs in the air. Old people probably – they're dying so fast that the mortuaries can no longer cope.

But then it could be rubbish. The rubbish collectors went on strike at the same time as the power workers. Now, in London squares, refuse sacks are stacked high above the tops of the railings. There's a sound of rustling that never lets up. If you look closely enough you can see the sacks quivering as the rats scamper about in the polythene.

Meanwhile the country's petrol reserves are running dangerously low. Motorists who do manage to find petrol guard it carefully. At night thieves sneak about with lengths of hosepipe and suck it out of people's tanks. Sometimes these thieves suck too hard and swallow mouthfuls of petrol. Then a few hours later they light up a cigarette without thinking and burst into flames. Soon they too start to stink – and so it goes on . . .

Edmund continues on his way into work. Past shuttered schools and empty petrol stations. Past understocked shops and teeming off-licences. Past posters proclaiming that we have just been over-taken by Chad on all major indices of economic prosperity. Past colonies of giant rats frolicking among refuse sacks containing the charred remains of self-incinerated petrol thieves; past queues of people waiting dazedly beneath enormous bubble perms for buses that never arrive.

Four miles later, Edmund turns off the Chalk Farm Road, bumps up an untarmacked track, through a set of rusting iron gates and into a car park. This car park is just a cordoned-off area of waste ground, dotted with pot-holes, separated from another, larger, patch of waste ground by a few clumps of scrub. Edmund parks and turns off the engine. Ahead of him is the domed roof of the Roundhouse. Beyond it, a broad stretch of railway line that carries trains north – up to Newcastle and the Scottish Borders.

For a while he simply sits in his car, his eyes roaming across the Roundhouse from top to bottom, from side to side. With its windowless walls and its domed roof, the building looks as if it has erupted from the ground like an enormous boil. Built almost exactly a century earlier as a maintenance depot for locomotives, it still has rails inset in the floor where early steam engines were once shunted in for repair – and then sent back out to haul passengers and rolling stock through our newly industrialized nation.

Once, only a few years beforehand, the Roundhouse was the most fashionable venue in London. Everyone – everyone who was anyone – wanted to perform here: fashionable rock bands, shrill visionary poets prophesying nuclear winter; children's circuses; shadow puppeteers from the Andaman Islands; and wandering Breton minstrels in stupid hats. In the foyer opposite the main entrance to the building there is a wall made up of bricks auto-graphed by people who have either appeared on the Roundhouse stage, or else given money to the place. This wall is like a Counter Culture *Who's Who*, a nonconformist roll of honour. Here are all the great figures, the Titans of the age.

But now only the children's circuses and the rock groups are left. Once these children's circuses were huge and awesome spectacles; meticulous re-creations of ancient folk pageants. Not any more; now they're just the cheapest ones available. The jugglers drop their balls; the sword-swallowers perforate their lungs; the unicyclists swerve into the audience and leave tyre marks all over the children.

As for the rock bands, they are in an even worse state. The successful groups have all moved on – to early burnout, violent feuds or tax exile. The only ones left are the has-beens and the no-hopers, all of them struggling to come to terms with their lack of fame and money; all trying to convince themselves they have managed to hang on to their integrity by not selling out. All crushed beneath the weight of disappointment and self-pity.

Most of the Roundhouse staff have gone too. Just a few people have been kept on to maintain the fabric of the building – or rather to ensure that the place doesn't fall down completely. Even here in Chalk Farm, in a building once associated with everything that was joyous, experimental and free from economic forces, even here the winds of change have begun to blow.

Still Edmund continues to look at the Roundhouse through his car windscreen, gazing at it with unconcealed distaste. This is not – in normal circumstances – the sort of place that he would ever go anywhere near. It is a white elephant, a blot on the landscape, an absurd leftover from a bygone age. The sooner it is swept away, the better. Worse still, it's full of the very lowest kind of people; people with no moral fabric or standards of personal hygiene.

However, Edmund's attitude is complicated by the fact that he believes himself to be a ridiculous person. Doesn't his car proclaim it for a start? But there's more. When he looks in the mirror what he sees strikes him as far from comely. Take his throat. Here a certain amount of spare skin can be seen. At moments of high tension – of any tension, really – it starts to vibrate like the wattels on a turkey.

Then there are his surges; torrents that course through his arteries like rivers in flood. It's not easy for him to feel a little of anything. Instead he finds himself tossed by great waves of emotion – anger, resentment, suspicion. And very occasionally gratitude. Back and forth they go like shingle flung down upon a beach.

Sometimes these surges manifest themselves visually, with a dangerous flush suffusing his grey, indoor complexion. And sometimes audibly, with a low snarl that slides out of the corner of his mouth. Either way, over-stimulation is a constant danger for him. If he's not careful he can easily become carried away. Hence his outward caution – he bruises far too easily.

Yet viewed objectively he doesn't look so strange. No worse than countless others, anyway. He doesn't have a crackpot perm. Nor does he smell of petrol. Nor have his clothes been gnawed by giant rats. And yet he remains convinced that he belongs on the margins – or out beyond the margins – where sticky, awkward people are rounded up and held in stockades for their own protection.

More than anything else, Edmund wants to fit in. He wants it so badly that it makes his chest pound with longing. The trouble is he has no idea what social or professional niche he could possibly fit into. Nothing feels remotely suitable. For all his eagerness, all his yearning, he seems doomed to remain an outsider.

The Roundhouse. 10 March 197–. Nine-forty on a Thursday morning.

Two men are carrying a large metal drum across the reception area towards the main entrance. This drum is full of blue disinfectant. Every so often liquid slops out over the rim and on to the floor. One of the men is black and has long dreadlocks that dangle down over his face. The other man has tangled brown hair and a sleepy look that suggests he's just woken up – or perhaps never made it to bed the night before.

Slowly they stagger across the floor. Every so often, and with no warning, the man with tangled hair puts his side of the drum down. This causes the other man to jerk back and almost lose his footing.

'Hey!' he cries angrily. 'Hey! What the hell are you playing at, Barney?'

The other man takes no notice of this. He rubs his hand where the wire handle has dug into his palm, and then, when he is ready, picks up the drum again. Every week these two men do this: carry the chemical toilet from the rock musicians' dressing room and empty the contents into one of the pot-holes in the car park. If the rock musicians' cocaine has been cut with baby laxative – which has been happening more and more lately – then the chemical toilet gets filled up in no time at all and has to be emptied more often.

Bent in a low crouch, they carry the drum towards the main entrance, blue disinfectant sloshing over the rim. As they do so, the main doors of the Roundhouse swing open. With his briefcase tucked under one arm, Edmund Crowe heads towards them. When he sees the puddles of disinfectant on the floor in front of him, Edmund tries to adjust his stride and walk around them. But his rhythm has been disrupted, his poise disturbed. For a moment he seems about to panic. Then he gathers himself back together and continues on his way – across the reception area, past the wall built of bricks signed by the Heroes of Counter Culture, and up the stairs at the far end.

Behind him the two men carry on for another few yards, until the man with tangled hair sets his side of the drum down again. This results in further spillages – along with more infuriated cries from his companion.

'Not again. Jesus! What it is now?'

Again the man with tangled hair takes no notice. Instead, he asks, 'Do you know who that guy is, Ron?'

'What guy?'

'That guy. The one who just walked past.'

The man with dreadlocks looks at Edmund as he climbs the stairs. 'Never seen him before.'

'I have. Several times now.'

'So what?'

'So nothing – necessarily.'

'Then why bring it up?'

'No reason, Ron. Got a big arse on him, though, hasn't he?'

'Hadn't noticed.'

'Come on. Just look at it.'

'I guess . . . I seen bigger, though.'

'Not in captivity.'

'OK, Barney.'

'He looks very straight too, doesn't he?'

'Kind of. It's hard to tell from the back.'

'Not that hard. So what do you think he's doing here?'

'How the fuck should I know? Now, are you going to help me with this thing, or not?'

'I'll help you, Ron. I gave you my word, didn't I? Just take it nice and slow. Like I showed you.'

'You don't want to take it at all, Barney, that's the trouble . . . OK? Now – one, two, three – and up.'

Together, the two men lift the drum of disinfectant and stagger towards the main entrance. As they do so, a trail of blue puddles slops out on to the floor behind them.

Edmund's Secret

Edmund continues up the stairs to the next floor. This is where the Roundhouse's administrative office is situated. It's a large room overlooking the broad swathe of railway track, full of desks and filing cabinets. The walls are covered in posters dating from several years earlier – tattered, luridly coloured reminders of when the going was good.

When Edmund arrives only one other person is there. This is Clive Beasley, the Roundhouse's Chief Administrator. A former Chairman of the Egg Marketing Board in Harold Wilson's first government, Clive was responsible for introducing the red lion that's still stamped on all eggs as a guarantee of freshness and quality. Or would be if there were any eggs to be had. These too are in short supply, due to the road hauliers' strike and the power cuts, which have played havoc with the chickens' egg-laying routines.

Previously an efficient, if not especially able, civil servant, Clive has undergone a big transformation since taking over the Round-house. Whereas once he used to dress in conventional suits and ties, now he favours far more casual clothes. Usually he is to be seen in a sheepskin-lined jerkin decorated with various embroidered symbols. These symbols, he believes, represent Indian deities. In fact, they denote various foreign currencies, executed by an unusually inept hand.

On his size-six feet he wears white plimsolls. These are always immaculately white, as if straight out of the box. His trousers, though, are a hangover from the old days – carefully pressed and with the waistband hitched over his small protruberant belly. He has fussy, precise movements, like a ballroom dancer. His hair has been allowed to grow. Now it is luxuriantly coiffed; while his forehead remains exposed, his ears are covered by thick, white muffs.

Mentally too he has undergone some big changes. Once a stickler for discipline, known in the Civil Service for his dry, almost obsessive, rigour, Clive is far more relaxed in his attitude these days. Among his former colleagues, whom he no longer sees – whose narrow-mindedness he now dismisses with scorn – he is reckoned to have gone native and lost his mind.

This is not unusual. Clive was only one of a number of civil servants appointed to jobs in arts administration by the former Prime Minister. Jobs for which they possessed no relevant expertise whatsoever. It was never made clear if Harold Wilson was rewarding them for good work, or punishing them for previous incompetence. No one liked to ask.

In the five years since Clive took over the Roundhouse, its reputation and its fortunes have gone into a steep, almost vertical, nosedive. Yet nothing in Clive's manner suggests he is remotely bothered by this – or has even noticed.

As he has been every morning when Edmund arrives, Clive is standing by the window, gazing across the railway tracks to the craggy silhouettes of terraced houses beyond. Sometimes he stays there for hours without moving, as if he's fallen into a trance. Occasionally, he walks around for a while, then returns to the same spot. All the desks are piled high with newspapers, piles of litter, stacks of dusty papers, bills, court orders, eviction notices . . . Some of these have been opened and stacked up, to be attended to at a non-existent later date. Others – the vast majority – are still in their envelopes.

In the whole office there is only one tidy spot – one still point amid the chaos. This is the cage of Clive's pet canary, Pippa. Clive lavishes an enormous amount of care on this bird. He's always changing her water, her food, the newspaper lining the bottom of her cage. Always sticking a new treat between her bars as he bends down and puts his lips very close to Pippa's beak.

On his first day at work Edmund was shown up to the office

and introduced to Clive. They shook hands – Clive's handshake, Edmund noticed, being soft and spongy in texture, like a partly inflated rubber glove.

'So you're the one,' said Clive, then shook his head sadly. 'I never thought it would come to this, you know.'

Edmund said nothing.

'If I were you,' Clive went on, 'I wouldn't tell anyone else why you are here. I won't tell anyone either. Best keep it as our secret.'

This suited Edmund fine. All his instincts tended towards secrecy. Besides, there were all sort of reasons for not telling anyone what he was doing in the Roundhouse. Not that anyone showed the slightest interest in him during his first few days – not as far as he was able to tell. The place was as unwelcoming, as impersonal, as his lodging house.

And so Edmund had set to, going through what books – what records – he could find. Always, Clive hovered about, looking through the window, padding around the office in his white plimsolls and talking to Pippa, the canary, in a hushed, singsong voice. Much of what Clive said was inaudible. Occasionally, though, Edmund made out stray phrases.

'He thinks he'll be able to find what he's looking for, doesn't he? He thinks it's all here. But he won't, though, will he? No. Of course he won't.'

On this particular morning Edmund was working through an inventory of staff. While a column of names had been entered in a reasonably legible hand, there was no record of any wages being paid to them – nor any National Insurance contributions. Nor was any indication given as to whether the employees listed were still working there.

Edmund asked Clive if he could help.

'Obviously, I'll do what I can, won't I, Pip?' said Clive. 'Fire away.'

'Eric Ostersund,' Edmund read out.

'Yes, indeed. Eric. He came to visit us from Sweden. Blond, of course, like so many of those Northern races. Broad-chested, and with an unusually dimpled chin. Not unlike Kirk Douglas, although with the dimple set fractionally off-centre.'

'Yes, but is he here anymore?'

'Here? Eric? Goodness no. Hasn't been for ages. He still sends the occasional postcard, though. You've no idea how much that sort of thing means – but then how could you?'

Edmund paused before going on. If he lifted his arms up as high as they could go, then brought the ledger down flat on the top of Clive's head, he was pretty sure he could drive it some, if not all, of the way into his neck cavity. And even if he failed, surely the effort alone should count for something?

'Sophie Beach?' he asked.

'Poor Sophie' – Clive's voice dropped – 'I remember her. Yes . . .'

'Where is she now?'

'In some sort of sanatorium, I believe. All desperately sad.'

By the time Edmund had reached the end of the list, it was lunchtime. Clive took his lunch downstairs in the bar. Edmund, however, preferred to continue working – not that he'd been invited to join Clive.

As Clive was on his way out, Edmund said, 'I wonder if I could talk to you about the staffing rotas some time?'

Clive stopped and executed a small jiggling motion with his feet.

'Staffing rotas?'

'Yes.'

'What on earth for?'

'Well, to work out who is being paid to do what.'

'I don't really have anything to do with that. You'd best talk to Barney.'

'Who is Barney?' Edmund asked.

'Who is Barney? You don't know who Barney is?'

'No,' said Edmund, 'I don't know who Barney is.'

There was a pounding in his temples that might indicate the onset of a headache, or possibly a more major seizure.

'Who is Barney?' repeated Edmund.

Clive giggled. 'I daresay you'll find out soon enough. Oh yes, he'll find out who Barney is. Won't he, Pip?'

Again Clive prepared to go, brushing some fluff from the hem of his jerkin and draping a jacket over his shoulders.

'There was one other thing . . .' said Edmund.

'Another one? What is it now?'

'Just that I noticed this morning that the lead appears to be missing from the roof.'

'The lead?'

'Yes. It was there last week. But now it seems to have gone.'

'All of it?'

'I believe so.'

'Well, what do you think has happened?'

'I assume it's been stolen.'

Clive now gave a braying, head-tossing laugh, both casual and dismissive, like an elderly donkey shrugging off clumsy attempts to dupe it into wearing a bridle.

'No, no, it won't have been stolen. I'm sure there's a quite innocent explanation.'

'I don't see how there can be.'

'That's because you have a suspicious mind, Edmund. Not an attractive feature in someone of your age. Especially when taken with the . . . with the . . .'

'All right then. Look for yourself.'

'I might very well do that.'

Clive walked away, his jacket draped over his shoulders and his hands holding on to the lapels. When he returned from lunch – hands and jacket still in much the same position – Edmund asked him if he'd had a chance to do so.

'As a matter of fact, I did. Certainly, the lead does appear to have gone,' Clive conceded. He paused momentarily. 'But I daresay someone has just borrowed it.'

'Borrowed it?' said Edmund, managing to keep his voice from breaking.

'That's right,' said Clive. 'Borrowed it. No doubt they'll put it back soon. Besides, it'll be spring in a week or two. With luck, we won't have much rain before then.'

That night Edmund lay in bed listening to the creaking of the plasterboard partitions, the moans of his fellow residents, the eddies of stale air gusting round the stairwell. Feeling his blood rush heedlessly round and round his extremities.

Every night it was the same, as he twisted about in agonies of frustration. It was like being boiled alive in his own testosterone; the stuff was like battery acid, leaking out of his pores and bringing him out in angry red weals. What could he do to relieve his suffering? To bring himself any sort of lasting relief? Nothing! Nothing!

The sound of a voice came through the wall. A man's voice; so close that Edmund could hear it quite clearly. A thin, plaintive sound, like a prayer, or an entreaty. For a moment he even wondered if it had come from him. Then, realizing with relief that it hadn't, he switched off the bedside light and closed his eyes.

3
Enter a Free Man

Excerpt from 'Your Kitchen on Wheels' – a pamphlet jointly issued by the Ministry of Transport and the Central Office of Information.

This pamphlet contains advice for those motorists who still have access to petrol on how they can save on domestic fuel costs by cooking in their cars. With a little ingenuity, the heat generated by a car engine can be put to productive use. If motorists wrap pieces of meat, or fish, in tin foil and place them on their exhaust manifold, then the contents will be cooked through in a surprisingly short time. Commuters can therefore make useful savings by preparing their evening meals as they drive home.

Obviously, cooking times will depend on the length of a particular journey. Fish – e.g., cod or coley – will cook through on a ten-minute journey. However, drivers should allow at least half an hour for steak – although adjustments should be made to suit personal tastes. For their own safety, as well as for that of other motorists, it is important that food should be securely fastened to the exhaust manifold. For this purpose wire is strongly recommended. String or raffia should never be used.

Motorists are advised to confine themselves to simple dishes for one or two people. The method is not appropriate for larger groups. Likewise, it is recommended that larger cuts of meat such as legs of lamb or poultry should not be cooked in this manner, for fear that they might become dislodged and cause a traffic hazard. Under no circumstances whatsoever should meat be marinaded in alcohol before being cooked.

At six o'clock the next evening Edmund stopped work. However, he couldn't face going back to his rooming house – the single gas ring, the moans of his invisible neighbours, the bubbling cauldron of testosterone . . . No, he thought, not that. Please. Not for as long as possible, anyway.

In the end he went down to the Roundhouse bar for the first time. He'd wished Clive goodnight, but there was no reply. Clive was busy crooning at Pippa, pressing his nose up to her cage while rocking himself back and forth on the balls of his feet.

The bar resembled a big Yukon cabin with its tables and partitions made from roughly hewn railway sleepers. Despite the fall in the Roundhouse's fortunes, deadbeats from all over North London continued to congregate here. As well as alcohol, drugs of any type were available from the bar staff. For those with strong stomachs, there was also food – a variety of coagulated dishes, all bursting with roughage, all made from flour that both looked and tasted as if it had been collected from the hopper of a sawmill. The food was served at a separate counter next to the toilets by consumptive-looking girls in stained aprons.

After buying himself a pint of beer Edmund sat on a wooden bench with his back to the wall. Always he behaved as if he was being watched. This wasn't arrogance, merely self-consciousness. Even in private, he never lost this sense of being scrutinized. Or of being found wanting. In public, of course, it was far worse. Who could be watching him? He had no idea. Why would anyone bother? Again, that was a complete mystery to him. But still there was this sense of a wrinkled lip hovering somewhere above his head. A disappointed eye in the clouds.

Fortunately, no one seemed to have taken any notice of him tonight. Edmund took a sip of his beer. Although there was nothing complicated about the manoeuvre, still it had to be carefully done – arm, mouth and glass brought into proper alignment – in case he was undone by a sudden surge and upended his glass on his head or hurled it over his shoulder. He managed it fluently enough. But then something snagged at the corner of his eye.

He glanced up – and saw to his alarm that he was being watched. From a table no more than five feet away from where he was sitting. Two men and a girl, all staring in his direction. Lowering his head and concentrating very hard, Edmund took another drink of his beer. As he did so, he felt their eyes shift away, and allowed himself a moment of relief that the danger had passed.

But when he looked up again, he saw that he had been wrong – that he could hardly have been more wrong. The girl was no longer sitting down. She had stood up and was now coming towards him. At this, a major surge passed through Edmund's system. So intense that in other circumstances it might have forced him to his feet and made him dance a frenzied, unrhythmical jig. With a great effort of will he managed to stay where he was.

What had he done wrong? Plainly he had offended against the proprieties of the place in some way. Irredeemably conformist, he supposed. Objectionably drab. Fair enough – there could be no quarrel with that. He would leave quietly, of course. Anything to avoid a scene.

The girl was in striking distance now. She was heavily built and wore red dungarees. When she walked she slapped her feet down on the floor. As soon as she reached Edmund's table, she pulled out the chair opposite and dropped into it.

'Have we met before?' she asked.

Edmund shook his head – this resulting in a light, sideways wattle movement.

'But you work here?'

'That's right.'

'Mmm . . . I thought I'd seen you around.'

Several more moments of appraisal followed. The girl had a flattened nose and a tracery of small scars on her cheeks. Then she said, 'I'm Pippa,' and stuck out her hand.

'What?' said Edmund. 'Like the canary?'

'No. I'm not with you.'

'Nothing.'

Tentatively, Edmund extended his own hand. Pippa's grip was much stronger than he expected, with a keen competitive edge to it; their handshake being more like a bout of horizontal arm-wrestling than a traditional exchange of courtesies.

'Why don't you come over and join us?' she said.

'Join you? Whatever for?'

'Just to be friendly.'

Friendly . . . friendship . . . No other word had such an effect on Edmund as this. It made his heart flip over and smack against his ribcage while at the same time putting him on maximum alert. What was this Pippa up to? There appeared to be a lot of anger in her; inadequately suppressed too, by the look of it. She struck Edmund as one of those big bolshie girls, full of surface aggression, but with a deep well of sentimentality. Good with homesick children and injured animals, yet apt to turn nasty at any sign of resistance.

Perhaps she felt sorry for him? That was kind of her on the one hand, and not very nice at all on the other. How shaming it was to be such a focus for pity. Desperation must shine out of him like a beacon. To refuse to budge, though, was to risk causing offence. That was to be avoided.

When they reached the other table, Pippa said, 'This is . . . Hold on, you didn't tell me your name.'

People unused to social contact, Edmund had noticed – his theory being partly based on personal experience – often found it hard to pitch their voices correctly. They spoke either too loudly or not loudly enough. Either way, the happy medium eluded them.

'My name is Edmund Crowe!' he bellowed.

The bar fell silent. The two men at the table looked up in surprise. Come quickly death, thought Edmund in the ensuing silence. He half shut his eyes.

When everyone had recovered, introductions were made. There were grunts of greeting – nothing more. One of the men, called Steve, wore a shirt that was far too small for him. The sleeves stopped just below his elbows, and were so tight that he had difficulty moving his arms. His hair had been cut in a style resembling an Afghan hound's: shortish at the front, long everywhere else. He also had two large protruberant teeth, both edged with brown, which rested on two flat indentations on his lower lip.

The other man – Ronald – was black, with long dreadlocks. He was wearing a sweater which had a leaf pattern of some sort woven into the wool. Although Ronald wasn't especially large, his shoulders were wide and his chest impressively muscled. His finger-nails were long and buffed to a yellow sheen at the tips. The whites of his eyes had a similar yellowish tinge to them. Whenever he took a drink, he held his dreadlocks with one hand to stop them from falling into his glass.

Edmund stared at Ronald in fascination. He had only ever met two black people before in his life; both African students that his parents had invited to lunch some years ago. Both devout Christians and beneficiaries of a charitable scheme to give people from over-seas an opportunity to enjoy some traditional English hospitality.

The lunch, he remembered, had not been a success. There had been a brief discussion about possible links between mass baptisms and river blindness and then conversation had died out. No moves had been made to repeat the visit. Ronald, however, appeared different from the two Africans in every respect. He was less edgy, less distant; altogether less cowed.

After the introductions had been made, everyone started talking among themselves again. Edmund couldn't work out whether to be offended by this, or relieved. As so often, he felt large amounts of both emotions.

He hadn't been there long when a third man arrived at the table. All at once the atmosphere changed. This new arrival had tangled brown hair and walked in a slouching, loose-limbed manner. From behind this thicket of hair, his eyes appeared to be both dark and bright. He moved round the table touching people on the shoulder in a proprietorial way.

'Barney,' said Ronald flatly. 'Where you been then?'

'Me? I've been out in the car park looking at the sky,' said the new arrival – he appeared to have a faint Welsh accent.

'Yeah? What did you want to do that for?'

'The sky is very beautiful at this time of day, Ron.'

'It is?'

'Oh, very much so. Did you know, Ron, that there are more stars in the universe than there are grains of sand on all the beaches in the whole world?'

Ronald puckered his chin, nodded a couple of times and said, 'That's a shitload of stars.'

The other man grinned at him. 'There's just no poetry in you, is there, Ron?'

'I'm Head of Security,' protested Ronald. 'I've got no time to look at the sky. Besides,' he added, 'I have other talents.'

'You do? What would those be then?'

'Ron bangs good head,' said Steve after a brief pause.

'That's right,' said Ronald. 'I do. I bang 'em good.'

Apparently bored by this exchange, the new arrival's eyes turned towards Edmund.

'And who's this?' he asked.

'My name is Edmund Crowe,' said Edmund for the second time.

'I didn't catch that. You'll have to speak up.'

'Edmund Crowe!'

'Christ! Ease up there! What's his game, eh?' said the newcomer, addressing the others. He turned to Edmund. 'Well, I'm Barney. But you probably knew that.'

'No,' said Edmund. 'No, I didn't know that.'

'Oh . . . right. So, Edwin, what brings you here?'

'It's Edmund, actually.'

Barney appeared genuinely puzzled by this. 'Your name is Edmund Actually?'

'No,' said Edmund. 'Just Edmund.'

'OK, Just Edmund. Let's start again. What brings you here?'

'I work upstairs.'

'Uh-huh. And what do you do there?'

All his life Edmund wished that he'd been better at dissembling; at being evasive, even deceitful. Yet such concealment had always proved beyond him. Whenever he was confronted by a direct question, the truth always seemed to shoulder its way to the front of his mouth.

'I'm an accountant,' he said.

'An accountant?'

'Yes.'

'What the fuck do they need an accountant for?' asked Barney, his grin still in place.

'Just checking the books,' said Edmund. He tried to grin back, aware that this must be making him look like a dog about to vomit over a much-prized rug.

'Books? What books?'

'Interesting you should say that. There don't in fact appear to be very many.'

'But why are you checking them?' Barney wanted to know.

Edmund didn't know what to say. Anything but the whole truth – that was obvious enough. Yet still it rose unbidden: up his windpipe, into his throat, and out on to the back of his tongue. His hand stole towards his cheek, then sank back down again without making contact. There seemed every likelihood that he was about to have another surge. Behind his ears his blood had begun to roar.

'Well?' said Barney.

And then Edmund was saved. A fourth man had arrived. He was Indian in appearance and wore a suit with a double-breasted jacket and neatly pressed trousers.

'Sadim!' said Steve.

'Hey, Sadi,' said Ronald.

'Look who's here,' said Barney.

Edmund had heard Clive talking about this Sadim. He had first come to England accompanying his younger half-brother – an eleven-year-old 'divine child', believed to be blessed with great healing powers and spiritual insight. British people had quickly taken this young guru to their hearts, much moved by his message of purity and asceticism. For his part, the young guru had proved to be just as smitten with Western culture. Within months, he was being driven around in a gold Rolls-Royce by a liveried chauffeur and living on a diet comprising entirely of ice-cream. Soon he grew hugely fat, his weight soaring to over fourteen stone. Special gusseting panels had to be sewn into his robes to accommodate his ballooning bulk.

At first this chubbiness simply enhanced his air of benevolence. After a while, though, fears began to be expressed about his health. But still the young guru kept on eating: cornets, tubs, choc-ices, special industrial-sized catering buckets – he wasn't fussy. Before going to bed, handmaidens would rub his skin with special oils to ward off pangs of night starvation.

Then one day he collapsed – clutching his sides and shrieking in agony. An ambulance was called, the young guru was winched into the back and eventually a hospital was found that would admit him. There, a burst ulcer was diagnosed. After two weeks in intensive care, he flew back to India to recuperate at a health farm. Sadim had stayed on, living in a mansion block flat in Swiss Cottage. He was a good deal less concerned with spiritual matters than his brother.

After he had sat down he took a handkerchief from his breast pocket, blew his nose and folded up the handkerchief again.

'I don't think we've met,' he said to Edmund.

Before Edmund could speak, Steve said hurriedly, 'His name is Edmund Crowe. He's an accountant.'

'An accountant? Really? How interesting. The economy is in an appalling state, isn't it? Really appalling. All these strikes, one after the other. Makes me ashamed to be British.'

'You're not British, Sadi,' said Ronald.

'I'm as British as you are, Ron. But this country, it's going to the dogs.'

'You're right there,' Ronald agreed. 'I don't know how long I can stand it. Maybe I'll emigrate. In fact, I might even go to India.'

Sadim began to laugh. 'Ha! Ha! Ha! You'd be lucky.'

'What do you mean?'

'They don't want riff-raff like you there.'

'Riff-raff? What do you mean, riff-raff? They'd have me.'

'No they bloody wouldn't. Besides, they've got enough problems of their own.'

'What sort of problems?'

'Famine. Pestilence. Earthquakes . . .'

'Really?' said Ronald. 'Pestilence? I don't fancy the sound of that. Maybe I'd better stay here after all.'

'So how's your brother, Sadim?' asked Pippa.

'Much better. He's able to walk unaided again, so that's quite an improvement.'

Steve cleared his throat. 'Er . . . Sadim.'

'Yes, Steve. What is it?'

'I don't want to be critical or anything. But that last stuff you sold us . . .'

'What last stuff? The powder or the pills?'

'No, the pills – the pills were fine. The powder . . .'

'What about it?'

'It didn't do anything for me.'

'Nothing at all?' said Sadim.

'Not quite nothing. I mean, it made me go, all right. Couldn't stop actually. Not that I mind some baby laxative. Even quite like it sometimes if I'm a bit . . . blocked. But this, it just made me . . .'

'Spit it out then.'

'Raw,' said Steve.

'I'm sorry to hear that. I'll have to look into it,' said Sadim. 'But I think I can promise you something very special soon. Just as soon as the road hauliers can clear the backlog of eggs.'

'What kind of special?' Barney wanted to know.

'You won't be disappointed, Barney boy.'

'Go on then, tell me.'

Sadim put his face close to Barney's. In a loudish whisper he said, 'Elephant anaesthetic.'

'Jesus!'

'Exactly. I tell you, you won't get up from that in a hurry.'

'What's it supposed to do?'

'No idea.'

'Is it safe?'

'No, I wouldn't have thought so, not for a moment. But let's not jump the gun. Try to be patient.'

From his jacket, he took a silver hip flask and unscrewed the top. Ronald watched with dismay. 'You don't have to bring your own booze in here, you know, Sadi.'

'I'm fine, Ron. Besides, I don't think they'd serve this behind the bar.'

'They might do, you know. They've got a lot of different stuff here now. All kinds of malt whiskies and the like.'

'Even so,' said Sadim, 'I rather doubt it.'

'What is it then?'

Sadim tipped his head back, took a swig and swallowed. When he had finished he said, 'Urine.'

'Urine?'

'That's right.'

'What? You're drinking your own piss?'

'Mmm. On the whole I find it preferable to anyone else's.'

'But – but what do you want to do that for, Sadi?'

'It's all a matter of balance, Ron. Indulgence on the one hand, purgation on the other. Whenever I've been burning the candle at both ends, there's nothing like the occasional nip. People have been doing it for thousands of years, you know. It reinforces one's sense of self, as well as increasing potency and heightening creativity. There are all sorts of other uses too. For instance, a little dab between the toes does wonders for athlete's foot.'

Ronald's face was still furrowed with disbelief. 'What does it taste like?'

'Like a slightly tart Lucozade,' said Sadim. 'But without the bubbles, of course.' He held out the flask towards Ronald. 'Do try some if you want.'

Ronald shrank back. 'No fucking way.'

'You don't know what you're missing, Ron.'

'Just keep that thing away from me. I'm warning you.'

Meanwhile Barney had taken hold of Ronald's sweater. He was rubbing the wool between his fingers.

'Where did this come from, Ron?'

'My – my mum knitted it,' said Ronald. 'If you really want to know.'

'Did she now? Of course, you're lucky to have a mother, Ron. Especially one who cares so much about you. A lot of love has gone into this garment – anyone can see that. Now what are these leaves here?'

'Ganja,' said Ronald promptly.

'Are you sure? I thought they were mistletoe.'

'Mistletoe? No, no. They're definitely ganja.'

Barney gave an elaborate sort of shrug.

'Have it your own way, Ron.'

Soon afterwards Barney stood up and walked over to the other side of the table. There he crouched down and began to stroke the back of Pippa's neck. Immediately, she pulled away from him. Barney, however, took no notice of this at all. He continued running his long fingers along her shoulders, then back up into her hair – even rubbing her earlobes. Pippa made further efforts to swat him off. Still Barney ignored them.

Edmund watched with mingled embarrassment and envy. He'd never seen anyone behaving with such assurance before; such blindness to the possibility of rejection. No one else at the table took any notice – or else they pretended not to. Perhaps they'd seen it all before.

'Come outside with me,' murmured Barney, none too softly. 'Come on, baby. Don't be cruel.'

Pippa continued to squirm about, trying to shrug Barney off, showing every sign of being about to lose her temper. And still Barney kept stroking her.

Abruptly Pippa pushed her chair back and stood up.

'All right!' she said in an exasperated voice. 'All right. But I don't want to look at any sodding stars. It's far too cold for that.'

Barney raised his hands in a gesture of surrender. 'No stars then. I promise.'

Still appearing thoroughly fed up, Pippa hooked her bag over her shoulder. Then the two of them made their way out of the bar, Pippa first, Barney following. He had one arm lifted in farewell and the other one extended in front of him in case Pippa should veer off track.

When they had gone, Ronald lowered his head to his glass until his nose was on a level with the rim. Then he started chuckling to himself.

Sadim also started to laugh. 'That Barney. He's a one, isn't he? Oh yes, he's quite a one.'

'I'm Head of Security, remember,' said Ronald.

'Of course you are, Ron. No one is disputing that. But Barney – Barney is the King of the Roundhouse.'

★

Edmund's car was encircled by puddles. He sat inside it, not moving. From inside the Roundhouse came a long rumbling sound, like a lorry-load of wardrobes being tipped down a mountainside. At first Edmund assumed it must be thunder – heavy rain had been forecast for several days. Then he realized that the first drum solo of the evening was underway. He knew from experience this could go on indefinitely.

Before getting into his car, Edmund had tilted his head back and looked up at the sky. Nothing – except a thick wash of grey cloud and the usual disappointed eye hovering behind. According to Barney, something wonderful was going on up there; something magical and transforming. But whatever it was, Edmund couldn't see it. He too had no poetry in him. He knew that.

4

The Right are Taking Over

The next afternoon it began to rain again. The sky turned an angry grey colour and flashes of lightning crackled over Primrose Hill. When the rain fell it filled up the pot-holes in the car park. Streams of muddy water ran down the Chalk Farm Road towards Camden Market and the Grand Union Canal.

The rain fell on the strikers standing outside the fire stations, the hospitals and the bus depots, and extinguished their makeshift braziers. But still they stayed by their picket lines, huddled beneath sheets of polythene. The rain also fell on innocent pedestrians as they sought shelter from the downpour, flattening their perms into ill-fitting Balaclava helmets. And it fell straight through the remains of the Roundhouse roof and on to the auditorium floor below.

From there it drained down the stairs and into the open sewer in the basement. This in turn flooded and left a residue of dried filth over everything when the sewage finally subsided two days later. Buckets were put out to try to catch the rain, but these had little effect. There were far too few buckets to go round and those that could be found soon overflowed. Meanwhile the petrol pumps ran dry and the rubbish piled higher and the streets echoed to the footfalls of giant baby-eating vermin.

'Ir-re-deem-able?' said Mr MacConachie, drawing out the word to such a extent that narrow strings seemed to be strung between the syllables.

Through the window behind Mr MacConachie's chair Edmund could see a sheet of rain descending at a 45-degree angle on to the street below.

'That's right,' said Edmund. 'Quite irredeemable.' He found

himself speaking with unexpected passion. 'An absolute shambles,' he added with a twist of his head.

'I can't say I'm surprised. And what about the people?'

'Very much the same. Feckless, muddle-headed. Congenitally workshy. Often high on drugs.'

Now it was Mr MacConachie's turn to shake his head. He did so sadly with a far-away look in his eye. Edmund realized that he knew nothing about his employer apart from the fact that he liked to go birdwatching at weekends. Mr MacConachie had a pointed chin, long, delicate fingers and two pocket-sized books on ornithology between the brown-cardboard files on the shelf beside his desk.

'I can't say I'm surprised there either. I do feel for you, Edmund. I really do. But this is important work – you know that. Just as soon as you complete your audit, the place can be shut down and sold off. We've already had one inquiry from a company asking if it would make a suitable site for a carpet warehouse. But obviously we can't give any sort of answer until you've finished. How much longer will it take, do you think?'

'Shouldn't be more than ten days,' said Edmund. At most, he hoped, although it wouldn't do to rush – however strong the temptation. That way mistakes crept in.

'Good.'

Mr MacConachie picked up some pieces of paper and ran his long fingers over the pages, handling them like feathers. There was no reason for Edmund to prolong their conversation, but he suddenly found himself reluctant to leave. He looked around him fondly: at the neat rows of desks with their neat stacks of paper piled neatly on top of them. At his colleagues working quietly and diligently away. Now this, he thought – this was what an office was supposed to look like.

As if divining Edmund's reluctance, Mr MacConachie gave him a sympathetic smile. 'Off you go then, Edmund. The sooner you go back, then the sooner you'll be finished.'

The following afternoon Edmund went looking for the lead from the roof. Not that he had any real hope of finding it – he just couldn't stand listening to Clive twittering away for a moment longer. Besides, searching for the lead would give him an opportunity to explore the building. So far he'd only seen the office and the bar.

Clive, of course, took no notice when Edmund stood up to go. He had his mouth pressed up against the bars of Pippa's cage and was nibbling at a piece of cuttlefish. From its little wire trapeze, the bird stared back at him with a look of what Edmund chose to believe was cold detestation.

There was no concert that night and so the place was almost empty. Edmund pushed open the double doors that led into the auditorium, a huge round room with no seats, just an expanse of sticky black floor. Around half the circumference of the wall ran a balcony held up by thin metal legs. Through holes in the roof patches of daylight could be seen.

On the far side of the auditorium to the double doors was the stage. It was piled high with speaker cabinets and a jumble of electrical gear. There was a smell in the auditorium – not as bad as the smell in Edmund's lodgings, but still bad enough. A smell of stale beer and cigarettes and overloaded electrical circuits.

Edmund climbed up on stage. He turned and faced the empty auditorium. As he did so, he seemed to see a mass of upturned faces gazing at him, their mouths hanging open, waiting expectantly to be entertained. He shuddered and walked through into the backstage area. Narrow doors led off a corridor into a succession of tiny dressing rooms. These were very primitive, like monk's cells, with no basins, no lavatories and nowhere comfortable to sit – just broken chairs and mirrors and despairing slogans scrawled on the walls. In jagged letters above a mirror in one of the rooms someone had written, 'Woody has run off with all our money. Gone to Portsmouth.' Beneath it another – untidier – hand had added, 'He has abandoned us. The Bastard.'

In the corridor outside was a battered sofa with a greasy brown line running along the back of it where people had rested their heads. Next door, in the smallest room of all, normally screened off by a curtain from the corridor, was the dark mouldering bulk of the Sanilav.

Today, though, the curtain was drawn back and Barney was sitting on the Sanilav. He had a guitar in his hands. When he saw Edmund, he said, 'Hello, Edwin.'

'It's Edmund,' said Edmund.

'Suit yourself.'

Barney continued to move his hands over the guitar; not playing it as such, just forming the shapes of chords. Edmund was struck by how pale Barney's hands were as they moved over the guitar. They looked almost unused, like Clive's plimsolls.

'Are you practising?' he asked.

'In a way,' said Barney. 'A bit of practising. And a bit of composing too.'

'You write your own songs, do you?'

'I don't know if you would call them songs. They don't always conform to a conventional melodic structure.'

'In what way?'

'In what way what?'

'In what way don't they conform to a conventional melodic structure?'

'Well, they're different,' said Barney.

'I see. But you have a creative bent?'

Barney's hands stopped in mid-air. 'Come again?' he said sharply.

'An artistic temperament.'

Barney shrugged. 'I guess I must do.'

'That's quite a gift,' said Edmund.

'Yes, it is a gift,' Barney conceded. 'Although it can be a burden too.'

'Yes, I'm sure. What sort of subjects do you write about?'

'Mainly love,' said Barney.

'Love?'

'Mmm. You know how it is when something pierces your heart very deeply and you have to find a way of expressing it.'

'No,' said Edmund. 'I don't.'

Barney looked up, his dark eyes regarding Edmund through his tangle of brown hair. 'Then you haven't lived, have you?'

'No,' agreed Edmund. 'I haven't.'

'Love,' said Barney thickly. 'It makes the world go round.'

34

'Strictly speaking, that isn't true, of course –'

'I'm not speaking strictly.'

'No,' said Edmund. 'Right . . .'

'Do you play yourself?' asked Barney, indicating his guitar.

'Heavens, no.'

Edmund laughed at the absurdity of such an idea. Just as there was no poetry in him, so there was no music either. His place lay among dry things; among columns of figures, endless exactitude and the clatter of adding machines. He knew that. Again Edmund found himself struck by Barney's ease of manner, his poise, his natural authority, his rich inner life. His dark Byronic charm.

'Was there anything you wanted to talk to me about?' Barney asked.

'As a matter of fact there was. Yes . . . Staffing rotas.'

'Staffing rotas?' Barney looked amused in a private sort of way. 'All right then.'

'You see, I just don't understand how –'

'But not now,' Barney broke in.

'I'm sorry?'

'Not while I'm composing.'

'Ah. Some other time then.'

'Have to be, won't it?'

'Right . . . I'd better leave you to it then.'

As Edmund retraced his steps along the corridor, he kept expecting to hear the sound of Barney playing his guitar. But it never came. He must have put Barney off his stride.

With no desire to go back upstairs to the office, Edmund went around to the other side of the stage. Here, hidden behind another curtain, he found another door. Two steps led down to it. Edmund had to crouch so as not to bang his head on the lintel. The door wouldn't budge at first. It only opened when he pushed against it with his shoulder.

Ahead of him stretched another corridor, which was dimly lit by single bulbs hanging from the roof at irregular intervals. The smell had changed. Now it was a damper, more underground smell. The air too was colder here and there were puddles on the floor.

'Hello?' he called out. 'Is anyone there?'

There was no reply – nothing except for a lapping kind of echo. Edmund propped the door open with a piece of wood and began walking down the corridor. It sloped downwards, the gradient growing steeper the further on he went. At the bottom the corridor led into another large circular room, about the same size as the concert arena upstairs, but with a much lower ceiling. Unlike upstairs, it was divided up by a series of brick arches – three concentric rings of them.

In the middle of the inner ring of arches was a circular space about ten feet across. Props and pieces of scenery from old productions had been heaped there: a throne, a sundial, several wooden trees laden with chipped wooden fruit. Running across the floor on Edmund's right-hand side was a channel full of water, approximately two feet wide. Although the room was lit with the same tremulous, low-watted bulbs, both the walls and the ceiling gave off a strange blue glow, a phosphorescent gleam, like the dial on a luminous watch, that seemed to shimmer off the walls and fill the room.

There was no lead here – none that Edmund could see, anyway. He was about to go back when he heard a noise. A light rustling noise interspersed by a series of grunts. His first thought was that it might be a rat. Recently there had been some more disturbing news about rats. The latest information, broadcast on the news and printed on posters displayed outside public buildings, warned that these new mutant rats were more aggressive than their smaller relatives. Mothers with young babies had been advised to fit their prams with special protective mesh in order to prevent them from being carried away. Although the mesh couldn't guarantee a child's safety, it could at least hold up the giant rats until help arrived – thereby buying valuable time. However, a few unfortunate children had already been snatched. One of these incidents had been just down the road in Camden. Witnesses, several of them, claimed to have seen glossy beaver-like creatures cantering down the High Street with squirming prey held in their jaws.

Then a man emerged through one of the arches. He was doing

36

up his trousers. Behind him was another shape – female, as far as Edmund could tell. She was bending over, as if touching her toes.

Edmund began to back away.

As he did so, Ronald said, 'It's all right, we're done. At least I'm done.' Glancing over his shoulder, he said, 'How about you?'

'Yes, I'm definitely done,' came a voice.

Soon afterwards the other figure emerged. She was also fastening up her trousers.

It was Pippa.

'Hello, Edmund,' she said.

'Hello.'

From down by Edmund's feet came a gurgling sound. He looked down at the channel in the floor.

'Open sewer,' explained Ronald. 'Runs right underneath the building. You'd think it would stink, wouldn't you? Considering what's floating in there. But it's not too bad really.'

As they stood there, the phosphorescent gleam grew even stronger; it was like being surrounded by a very dim version of the Northern Lights. Edmund looked around, trying to work out what could be causing such an effect. Seeing his confusion, Ronald laughed. 'Pretty good, eh? They covered the walls with blue asbestos a few years ago as fireproofing.'

'But surely it's a health hazard?' said Edmund.

'Probably. Trouble is they can't afford to take it away. Well, I'm going back upstairs. You two coming?'

Together, the three of them made their way up the corridor and back into the auditorium. From there they walked across the reception area towards the bar. The only other person standing in the reception area was the ice-cream vendor. A cheery middle-aged man, he wore a striped jacket and had a tray hung round his neck. He greeted them warmly as they went past.

'There's something about that man that pisses me off,' said Pippa. 'But I can't put my finger on what it is. He definitely pisses me off, though.'

'A lot of people piss you off,' said Ronald. 'Practically the entire world.'

37

'That's true. But why do you think he has mirrors on his shoes?'

'Search me.'

They headed towards the bar. As they did so, the doors were pushed open from the other side and a tall woman with long red hair came out. She had a bony face and held her head very erect. In her hands was a pile of papers.

She walked across the reception area towards them. When they saw her Ronald and Pippa immediately started to run in the opposite direction.

'Where are you two going?' Edmund called after them.

'*Run!*' shouted Ronald over his shoulder, his dreadlocks flapping behind him.

After a moment's hesitation, Edmund followed. They ran back into the auditorium and hid in the shadows beneath the balcony. On a couple of occasions Edmund was about to speak, but each time Pippa shushed him. Several minutes went by. Then Ronald whispered, 'It must be safe by now.'

'I don't know,' said Pippa. 'Go and have a look.'

Soon afterwards Ronald came back to say that the coast was clear.

'That woman's face is very familiar,' said Edmund. 'Who is she?'

'Vanessa Redgrave,' said Pippa, even more bitterly than usual. 'She comes in here all the time, selling her Workers Revolutionary Party magazine. Telling us how downtrodden we are and how we should rise up against our oppressors. Don't get stuck with her, Edmund. Whatever you do. She can talk the hind legs off a donkey.'

'And the front ones,' said Ronald.

When they walked into the bar only one person was there. It was Steve. He looked even more stick-like than before. His trousers and shirt both appeared to have shrunk, exposing further shanks of arm and leg. He sat staring at his empty glass, his chin in his hand and his two protruding teeth resting on his lower lip.

'You all right?' Pippa asked him.

'No, I'm bloody not,' said Steve.

'Ah . . . Did she get you then?'

Steve gave a weary nod.

'I tried to run, but she was too fast for me. Then when she'd got me cornered, she never stopped. My guts were playing up again and I was desperate to, you know . . . go. But she wouldn't let me. Just kept banging on and on about the Right taking over.'

'Poor Steve.'

'Sometimes I wish the Right would take over,' said Ronald.

'You don't mean that,' said Pippa.

'Oh yes I do. I feel the need for firm leadership. Bang a few heads together – that's what's required. This country needs a saviour. A figure who will emerge from an obscure misty place and lead us back to glory.'

'My God, you talk crap sometimes, Ron.'

Soon afterwards Ronald stood up to go. Then Pippa decided that she also had to be off. She walked out, her arms flailing, her feet slapping down on the floor.

That left Edmund alone with Steve.

'Pippa can be a bit tricky at times,' said Steve – he sounded almost apologetic.

'Why's that?'

'Because she's in love with Barney. That's the main reason. But he doesn't want to know. Of course, he'll bang her whenever he feels like it. Trouble is, she adores him. She'll do anything he asks her to. If you ask me, I think it's sent her a bit mad. Not that it's stopped her having sex with other people. Quite the opposite, in fact.'

'How do you mean?'

'You know Pippa – she'll screw anybody.'

'Anybody?' said Edmund after a pause.

Steve scrunched up his face. 'Almost anybody. Although I know she turned one person down.'

'Who was that?'

'Me, as a matter of fact. She said it was because of my teeth. But women can be funny like that, can't they?'

'I believe they can.'

'Anyway, probably not your scene, Edmund,' said Steve.

'What?'

39

'Fooling around. Sex just for the hell of it.'

'No,' agreed Edmund, sounding more sincere than he would have believed possible. 'No, it isn't.'

Lying there that night, swaddled in his own secretions, Edmund found himself thinking about both love and sex. Just as he craved a physical outlet with the active, or at least partial, participation of a fellow primate, so he longed to have his heart opened up; its locks unpicked, its armour-plating removed. But at the same time he dreaded the exposure this would bring. He hadn't even taken his heart out of its box yet – but already it felt old and tarnished. Probably best to keep it under wraps, at least for the time being. Yes, that was probably the best thing.

At this point another memory stole unbidden into Edmund's mind, lodging there like a bone in his throat. He remembered how, when he was fifteen, a dance had been organized between his own direct-grant single-sex school and a convent in Rickmansworth. A special bus was laid on to take them there. By the time they arrived, the girls had already lined up along one wall of the gymnasium. The boys trooped in in single file and took up their positions against the opposite wall. For several minutes they each looked at one another with expressions of mingled scorn and interest. Someone, it seemed, must make the first move.

But no one did.

Then, as if on an unspoken signal, the boys turned round and went back outside. Again they stood in line, this time on the other side of the wall. Still, no one spoke. Then they all undid their fly buttons and proceeded to have a wanking competition. It was the interaction they'd been unable to face, the dry-mouthed attempts at conversations, their fear of failure. They were happier with their own kind.

The winner of the competition was the first one to ejaculate. There were no prizes as such – only the respect of one's peers. Although Edmund had not been the winner, he'd given a creditable account of himself.

As he thought about it now, it struck him that there had been something peculiarly British about this behaviour; at least it was hard to imagine any other country on Earth behaving in such a manner. No wonder our decline had been so calamitous if this was the state of the nation's youth. It was a miracle anyone managed to reproduce at all.

Mind you, this had all been a long time ago. The same competitive rules no longer applied. Quite the reverse. Even so, Edmund thought, as he lay listening to the groans of his neighbours rising and falling all round him . . . Even so, it was hardly an encouraging precedent.

5

Down in the Flood

Rain streaked the glass and ran down in cascades where the gutters had filled up, or rusted through and become detached from the brickwork. It fell on the railway tracks and made them glisten in the light. It fell on the strips of scrub on either side of the tracks and turned them to mud.

In the reception area Ronald and Barney were bent almost double, carrying the Sanilav out to the car park. More puddles of blue disinfectant slopped out on to the floor behind them. On his way up to the office, Edmund noticed that previous spillages appeared to have eaten through the linoleum to the hessian webbing beneath. Buckets were dotted about the floor to catch the leaks from the roof.

As Edmund watched, Ronald and Barney staggered on for a few more paces. Then Barney put his side of the drum down on the floor.

Ronald shouted with annoyance, 'Just lift the fucking thing! Come on, Barney!'

Barney merely said, 'Hi there, Edwin. Everything OK?'

'Good morning,' said Edmund, strongly suspecting that this show of interest was being staged solely to annoy Ronald. He stepped round the puddles and headed for the stairs.

In the office Clive was standing in his normal position, staring out of the window. The clouds were so low this morning they looked as if they'd become snagged on the chimneys opposite.

'How's the flooding?' Clive asked.

'Not as bad as might have been expected.'

'See? I told you everything would be all right. The weather has warmed up considerably. I'm wearing a lighter trouser than usual, as you've probably noticed.'

Edmund had not noticed Clive's trousers. He had, however, noticed that Clive often used a singular noun when a plural one was the norm – or vice versa. Hence 'trouser'. Also 'monies' – this being a particular favourite, and more than usually irritating.

'More rain is forecast tonight,' he said. 'Even heavier rain.'

'Is it really? Well, I daresay it won't be as bad as they say.'

This morning Edmund felt as if his head had been wrapped in some form of electrified turban. He was even more unsettled than usual. He too stood and stared out of the window – a different window – gazing out over the railway tracks and the sodden expanse of clinker below.

'Penny for them, Edmund?' said Clive after a while.

Used to being the most abstracted person in the room – any room – it must have come as a surprise to Clive to see anyone else sunk in thought. Possibly an element of competitiveness played its part in his question.

Edmund didn't reply, not immediately.

'What's on your mind?' Clive asked again.

'Pippa,' said Edmund dully.

Clive was delighted by this. 'Good for you, Edmund. What about Pippa?'

'Steve was talking about her yesterday.'

'Steve? Really? I didn't know he took an interest.'

'Only up to a point.'

'What does that mean?'

'She turned him down.'

'Turned him down?' said Clive, his voice rising slightly. 'What do you mean?'

'Well, she didn't want to have anything to do with him.'

'Why? What did he want to do to her?'

'What do you think?'

'I have no idea.'

'It's not hard to guess.'

'Isn't it?'

'She's famous for it, apparently.'

'Famous for what, exactly?'

'Everyone's had her.'

'Everyone?' A more dazed note had come into Clive's voice.

'Almost everyone,' said Edmund, correcting himself.

'I had no idea.'

'That's because there are no proper channels of communication between management and workforce.'

'But – but how?'

'Where there's a will, there's always a way.'

'For pity's sake, Edmund.'

'She's not even my type to be honest.'

'Oh, don't try to spare my feelings.'

Edmund took no notice. He continued staring out of the window as the rain lashed down outside. 'Still . . .' he said. 'If all you've got to do is ask.'

The phone rang.

Neither of them made a move to pick it up. Eventually Edmund did so. A voice at the other end said, 'Is Rhodri Rees there by any chance?'

'I don't think so. But hold on a moment, can you?' He turned to Clive. 'Does someone call Rhodri Rees work here?'

Clive did not react.

Edmund asked again – more loudly this time.

Now Clive turned towards him. His eyes looked glazed, as if they were covered with gummy film. 'What was that?'

'Rhodri Rees? Does he work here?'

Slowly, Clive shook his head. 'Never heard of him,' he said.

6

The Emperor of Ice-cream

Two days later Edmund came downstairs from the office to find
an argument taking place. A huddle of people was standing about
in the reception area. Barney was there, along with Ronald and
Steve. Voices were being raised. Barney had his hands spread out
and was making indeterminate shapes in the air.

'Come on, Ron,' he said. 'Just come on now. You're fucking me
here.'

'I'm not fucking you, Barney. I'm just giving you an order.'

'No, you're fucking me, all right,' said Barney. 'That's what it
feels like.'

'Remember, I'm Head of Security. This falls within my sphere.'

'Sphere?' said Barney scornfully, with further spreading of his
hands. 'Sphere?'

Their argument was to do with the ice-cream vendor. Earlier in
the day he had been arrested by the police. His shoes proved to
be his undoing – the pieces of mirrored glass in his toecaps
had apparently been angled so that he could look up little girls'
dresses. There had been a number of complaints – first to Clive,
who had naturally ignored them, and then to the police. It trans-
pired that the man had a stream of previous convictions; every
other concert venue in London had banned him from their prem-
ises. Only in the Roundhouse had he been given a warm welcome. All of which meant there was no one to sell ice-creams that
evening.

'You should never have let him work here in the first place,'
Barney was saying.

'How was I to know?' Ronald protested. 'He said he'd been
charged with minor offences. I didn't realize he meant offences

45

with minors. Anyway, someone's got to sell those ice-creams. Otherwise there could be a security problem.'

'Now you're shitting me, Ron. What are you on?'

'It's the hippies. They need sweet things for their blood sugar. Otherwise they can turn nasty.'

'How can they turn nasty? Most of them haven't even got any teeth.'

'They've gotta have their lollies,' insisted Ronald. 'It's medical.'

'Well, I'm not doing it.'

'But you've got to.'

'No.'

'It's the spirit of the place, Barney. You know, all for one and one for all.'

'I've got my reasons.'

'Such as?'

'The cold.'

'The cold?' said Ronald. 'How do you mean?'

'It numbs my hands, then I can't play my guitar properly.'

'If you don't sell the ice-cream, then I'm not helping you with the Sanilav again, Barney. However full it is.'

'No,' said Barney again, and crossed his arms.

'Jesus! Well, who's going to do it then?'

Barney's eyes moved slowly back and forth for a while. Then they settled. 'Edwin,' he said.

'Who? Now be sensible.'

'Why not?'

'He might put people off.'

'Not if they want their lollies badly enough,' said Barney reasonably.

Several moments' consideration followed.

'OK, OK,' said Ronald. 'I guess he'll have to do. Although I meant what I said about the Sanilav, Barney. Here's the uniform, Edmund.'

He held out his arm. There was a striped jacket hanging over it. In his other hand he held a hat, like a cross between a tam-o'-shanter and a kepi. The hat was stiff with choc-ice residue.

In theory, Edmund supposed he was a free agent; he still retained some element of choice. In practice, though . . . in practice, he knew he'd been stuffed.

He took the jacket from Ronald's arm. Now that a decision had been reached, Ronald was prepared to show a degree of flexibility. 'You don't have to wear the hat, OK, Edmund? I mean, not unless you want to.'

An hour later Edmund was standing in the foyer with the striped jacket on and the ice-cream tray strung round his neck. As he stood there, it struck him that he felt surprisingly good; a lot better than he might have expected anyway. Admittedly, the jacket was even more repulsive on than off. It bore a multitude of encrusted hand-prints of all sizes – from tiny mit to giant paw. Some of these handprints had the fingers fully extended, while others appeared to scramble more desperately at the cloth. The fabric itself was so stiff, so unyielding, that he could hardly move; it was like wearing a suit of armour.

Yet, for the first time, Edmund felt as if he fitted in; as if he had a role to play at the Roundhouse – one that didn't involve secrecy or pretence. There were other benefits too. Instead of worrying about appearing ridiculous, now he could relax in the knowledge that there was no longer any doubt about it.

Not that Edmund was a figure of fun to his clients – quite the reverse. They treated him with mumbled deference and gratitude, shuffling patiently forward, digging about in the pockets and leather pouches where they kept their belongings, undoing the drawstrings and then pulling out little talismans and pieces of fluff, as well as occasional coins.

'So they roped you in for this, did they?'

Edmund looked up to see Sadim standing before him. Sadim wore the same fawn suit as before and had the same neatly combed hair. He pointed down at the ice-creams and said, 'My brother would have made short work of that lot, I can tell you.'

'Surely not all of them?'

'Oh yes. Like elevenses to him. Tell me, have you seen Barney around?'

Edmund directed him towards the bar. At the interval of the evening's concert, the audience came back out, bought more ice-creams and then shuffled back inside. That signalled the end of Edmund's shift. But just as he was about to take off the tray, three more people came over to be served. A man and a woman – both middle-aged – and a younger woman. The man was short with glossy black hair. The woman was taller and had a dreamy look to her, as if there was a cushion of air between herself and the floor.

As for the younger woman, she was dark in a varnished, dimly lit sort of way. She had dark, straight hair down to her shoulders and a swelling in her cheeks that gave her a slightly hurt, but also slightly reproving, look. Her lips, Edmund noted in passing, were browny-pink and her lower one jutted out – not too far, although possibly further than he would have liked ideally. There was also something very erect, very poised, very careful about the way she stood. This too he noticed in passing.

She stood to one side as the man bought three choc-ices, then walked away when he did.

A few moments later the man came back.

'These ice-creams you sold me – they're soft.'

The man had an American accent. In his hand he held up the choc-ices. The wrappers were baggy, the contents starting to drip.

Edmund felt the remaining ice-creams in his tray. All of them had turned soft. He apologized, took the three ice-creams back and refunded the money. The man didn't move. Then he stuck out his hand in an overhand, dive-bombing kind of way.

'I'm Corky,' he announced. 'Corky Montcalm.'

With difficulty, Edmund extended his own hand – he had to go round the outside of the canvas strap first.

'Edmund Crowe,' he said, at a more-or-less normal volume.

'You're new here, right?'

Edmund explained that he was only standing in.

'What happened to the normal guy?'

Edmund explained this too.

After he had finished, the man said, 'So he liked little girls, did he?'

There was nothing disapproving about his tone of voice; he might have been describing a hobby, or an optional evening course at college. The man's features were oddly inverted; as if he'd once sucked so hard on a boiled sweet that his face had never regained its natural shape. When he spoke he stood a little too close. Even with the ice-cream tray between them, Edmund felt crowded, forced on to the back-foot.

Although this Corky was a small man, the effect was like having a swimmer surface unexpectedly in front of you – an impression heightened by his glossy, wetlook hair. He called to the two women to come over. The older one looked as if she was being pulled on castors – she hardly moved her legs as she walked.

The younger woman followed a few paces behind.

'Honey,' said Corky. 'This is Edmund. He works here. This is my wife, Tinker.'

Edmund shuffled round to face her. As much as his restricted movements permitted, he lifted his hand in greeting.

'Edmund here was telling me that he's just standing in for the normal guy, who was arrested this afternoon.'

'Arrested? What for?'

'Child molestation.'

'Oh, the poor man!'

She sounded genuinely grief-stricken; her voice having a sharp, honking note to it, as if her nostrils had been pinched together.

'And this,' he said, indicating the younger woman, 'is my daughter, Lia.'

'Hello,' said Edmund.

'Hi.'

Behind Lia's shoulder, Edmund saw Barney emerging from the bar. He started walking over to where the four of them were standing. But when he was only a few paces away, he stopped and stared. Then he turned abruptly and walked off in the opposite direction.

'Tell me about yourself, Edmund,' said Corky.

'What do you want to know?'

'Are you maybe here as the result of some industrial accident?'

'I – I don't understand.'

'Your posture, man.'

'But that's just the uniform,' Edmund explained. 'Normally I walk fully upright.'

'You do?' Corky sounded doubtful. 'OK. As for me, I sit on the board of governors here. See' – and he pointed at the wall of bricks signed by the Heroes of Counter Culture – 'there I am.'

For the next few minutes Corky spoke about the building – about its history, atmosphere and cultural importance. As he did so, Edmund was aware of the choc-ices melting in his tray. Several of them were now floating free of their wrappers; thin rafts of chocolate drifted about on milky-white puddles.

Corky meanwhile kept burbling on. Without meaning to, Edmund caught Lia's eye. The next thing he knew she had stepped forward and was saying, 'Come on, Dad. The poor guy's ice-creams have all disintegrated.' She also had an American accent, although less pronounced than her father's.

Corky made to hit himself on the forehead with the flat of his hand. 'Aww, that's terrible.' He gazed down at the melted slop running about in the tray. Then he took his wallet from his jacket pocket and began pulling out notes. 'Here,' he said. 'This should cover it.' He thrust the money at Edmund, taking no notice of his protests, stuffing the notes into the breast pocket of his jacket. 'No, go on. Take them. Maybe do something about that jacket too. Have you never heard of dry cleaning – they can do miracles these days. And look, why don't you take one of these as well.' He took out a business card and stuffed that in too. Then he held out his hand again. It came at Edmund on the same dive-bombing trajectory as before.

'Sorry about my father,' said the daughter. She was shaking her head in mock-exasperation and grinning at Edmund in a way that made her lower lip flatten out and look less protruberant than before.

'I get carried away, you see,' explained Corky. 'I don't mean to, but I can't help it. Do you know what that's like, Edmund? Getting carried away?'

Not directly, Edmund thought, although I have an inkling.

The girl now had hold of Corky's arm and was pulling him towards the door, tugging away. He was making playful efforts to resist her.

'My women are calling,' he said, 'And I must away. Anyway, it's been good talking to you. Goodbye then.'

'Bye.'

In the freezer room Edmund unslung the tray from his neck and was tipping the contents down the sink when Barney came in.

'How did you get on then?' he asked.

'All right, thank you,' Edmund replied, more primly than he might have wished.

'No, nothing to it, is there? Tell me, who was that man you were talking to earlier?'

'Someone called Corky Montcalm,' said Edmund. What a ridiculous name it was; it seemed to sit on his tongue like a lugworm.

'Corky Montcalm,' repeated Barney almost to himself. 'I thought it was him.'

'Who is he?'

'Who is Corky Montcalm?' said Barney in astonishment. 'Why, he's only the editor of *Quest*.'

'What's *Quest*?'

'Eh? You mean you don't know that either? *Quest* – it's a magazine exploring people's sexuality.' Barney spoke more stiffly than usual.

'What? A porno magazine?'

'No, no, no. Not a porno magazine. It's much more scientific than that. They have a team of internationally renowned sexologists to deal with readers' letters.'

'I see,' said Edmund. He didn't care to hear this, but although he couldn't manage to hide his disapproval completely, he managed to keep it down to a spinsterish minimum.

'Who were the two women with him?' Barney asked.

'His wife and his daughter.'

'His daughter? Yes . . . I thought I'd seen her before. She was on the cover of the February issue. Lying on a hay bale.'

'What was she doing on the hay bale?'

'She wasn't doing anything much. She was just lying there with a piece of straw sticking out of her mouth.'

'You mean he takes photographs of his own daughter for his porno magazine?'

'Look, I just told you. It's not a porno mag.'

Such distinctions, however, meant nothing to Edmund. He found himself thinking what a contrast this was to his own background. He'd had his ups and down with his parents, of course he had. But at least they'd never asked him to pose naked on a hay bale with a piece of straw in his mouth.

'Hold on,' said Barney. 'Just hang about here. What's all this?' He was looking at the bundle of notes poking out of Edmund's breast pocket. 'How many ice-creams did you sell, for Christ's sake?'

Edmund told Barney what had happened. When he had finished, Barney said, 'No kidding. And what are you planning to do with the money?'

'I don't know . . . Perhaps put it towards the cost of some new lead for the roof.'

Barney shook his head in a way that managed to convey pity and disbelief beyond any previously known limits of either. Then, reaching his hand out, he deftly transferred the money from Edmund's pocket to his own.

'What are you doing?'

'One for all and all for one,' said Barney. 'It's the spirit of the place.'

'But I thought you didn't believe in that.'

'What makes you think that? No, I believe in it, all right. Now what have we here?'

Barney had hold of the business card Corky had given Edmund. The card was green with raised brown letters that looked as if they were emerging from a swamp.

'It's Mr Montcalm's card.'

'So I see.'

Barney handled the card reverently, by its edges. Only after Edmund had asked for it twice did he hand it back – and then with obvious reluctance.

'You're lucky to have that, you know, Edwin. Very lucky.'

'It's not Edwin,' Edmund told him.

'What isn't?'

'My name.'

'No?'

'No. It's Edmund.'

Barney frowned. 'Are you sure?'

'Positive,' said Edmund, although he was beginning to have his doubts.

In bed that night, Edmund thought about Lia. He didn't like to think about her lying on a hay bale, with or without a piece of straw in her mouth. But this had plainly been her father's idea; the man must have forced her into it – what a disgusting creature he was. No, she couldn't be held responsible for that.

Instead, Edmund tried to remember just what Lia looked like. He remembered her browny-pink lips readily enough. Also the erect and careful way she stood. And the slight swelling in her cheeks. But there was something else too. Something not quite right.

He had to crane forward, peer into his mind's eye, to see what it was. His gaze raked back and forth, up and down her imaginary form. Was it something to do with her shoulders? No. Her neck? No. Her nose? No. Her hair then?

Yes, her hair – that was it. Something was not quite right with Lia's hair. It may have been straight and dark and falling to her shoulders, but it was no longer as shiny as it had appeared to be. Now it seemed oddly dull. And not just dull – worse than dull. But what could possibly be worse than dull? The realization hit Edmund with a stab of disappointment. Lank! That was it. Lank, lank, lank . . .

No, he thought, it would never do.

7

Country Roads

'Just a progress report, really,' said Mr MacConachie. 'To make sure everything is on schedule.'

'I think so,' said Edmund. 'Of course, the paperwork is a disgrace.'

There could be no doubt about this. It was easy enough working out what money came into the Roundhouse: the grant from Camden Council; the money from the sale of food and drink; plus one or two endowments from patrons who had either remained loyal to the place, or else wrote them off as tax losses. Nor was it that difficult working out the outgoings: the wages of the remaining staff, the sums paid out to the agency responsible for booking the bands, the circus acts and the cleaning contractors. And then there were standard running expenses such as heating and electricity.

The difficulties arose in trying to work out any correlation between the two. In theory, the figures should have balanced. In practice, this was nowhere near the case. The incoming sums only amounted to a tiny fraction of the outgoing amounts. There was no indication of how the deficit had arisen.

Edmund explained this to Mr MacConachie. He thought he'd made as succinct a job of it as possible. However, it seemed as if Mr MacConachie was slightly distracted today; his eyes kept veering outside. Edmund followed his line of sight, but could see nothing there worthy of his attention.

'And you, Edmund,' said Mr MacConachie, soon after Edmund had finished his explanation, 'how are you bearing up?'

'Oh, not too bad.'

'Good for you, that's the spirit.'

Edmund stood up to go. As he did so, he was aware that the office was looking a little more drab than usual – although he couldn't be sure how this could be, or what had caused it. Probably a trick of the light, he thought. Nothing more than that.

Barney was moving slowly across the reception area, dragging the Sanilav behind him. With no one to help him, he was plainly finding it hard work. Even more blue disinfectant than usual had slopped out. So much so, it seemed unlikely that much could be left inside.

'Be a pal and help us with this, will you Ed–, Eddie,' Barney called out.

Edmund stopped and retraced his steps. He picked up one side of the drum. It weighed far more than he had expected.

'Even heavier than usual today,' said Barney. 'I don't know what Sadim thinks he's up to.'

They staggered to the main door and out into the car park. There, they emptied the drum into one of the deeper pot-holes. All the others around were full to the brim with the same bright blue slop.

When they had finished, Barney said, 'We could have that talk some time if you like.'

'What talk?'

'Didn't you want to have a talk? Something about staffing rotas?'

Edmund looked at Barney to see if he was serious. There was nothing in his expression to suggest he wasn't being serious. On the other hand, that didn't mean anything. It could quite easily be a practical joke.

'Staffing rotas, yes . . .' Edmund began. 'I don't understand how –'

'But not here,' Barney broke in – just where Edmund expected him to.

'No?'

'You've got a car, haven't you? Why don't we go for a drink this evening?'

'A drink?'

If this was a joke, practical or otherwise, it was obviously far more elaborate than Edmund had anticipated.

'Yes. Why don't you meet me down here at six-thirty?'

All the reasons why Edmund should have refused this offer seemed to wrap themselves round his feet, effectively upending him and making him accept it instead.

'All right,' he said.

At six-thirty Edmund was waiting in the foyer. There was no sign of Barney. He turned up twenty minutes later offering no explanation as to where he'd been. Once inside the Allegro, Barney took an unexpected interest in the fittings, first looking in the glove compartment, then pulling out the ashtray. He slid it back and forth along its metal track a number of times, apparently marvelling at the mechanism.

Then he transferred his attention elsewhere.

'You've got a square steering wheel.'

'I know,' said Edmund.

'Did it come like that?'

Did Barney imagine he'd had it made specially?

'Yes. Yes, it did.'

On Barney's instructions they headed west – through Swiss Cottage, and then down to Shepherd's Bush. In a desperate effort to beat the fuel crisis, increasingly strange vehicles had taken to the roads: machines put together from old go-karts, handcarts, dinghies, prams and lawnmowers – powered by all sorts of different means. The little fuel that was available often tended to be diluted. It made engines seize up. Cars drove along with clouds of black smoke fountaining out the back.

Edmund's own fuel levels were causing him concern. His petrol gauge was just under half full and there were hardly any petrol stations left open. He had assumed they weren't going to drive too far. However, as they climbed the elevated section of the M4, he began to have his doubts.

'Where are we going?' he asked.

'Anything wrong?'

'Wrong? No, not in the least.'

'I thought we might have a drink in the country,' said Barney. 'Assuming that's all right with you.'

'Fine.'

The suburbs looked even more bleak than usual this evening, thought Edmund. Emptier too with fewer cars than usual about and everyone huddled behind their net curtains trying to keep warm.

After another twenty-five minutes the houses began to thin out, then to disappear altogether. By now they were on the fringes of Heathrow Airport. Still they carried on, eventually pulling up outside a pub just beyond the furthest outskirts of London.

Barney climbed out of the car and stretched himself. 'Beautiful here, isn't it?' he said.

Edmund looked around him. In every direction the land stretched away, flat and featureless. As far as he could tell, it was mainly made up of potato fields. There was a strong smell of aircraft fuel. The reason for this soon became clear. They were directly under the flight path. Planes roared overhead every few minutes – so low their bulk blotted out what little sun there was.

'Lovely,' he agreed.

Set off to one side of the car park was a low brick bunker. Inside, it was done out in a violent parody of a traditional inn, with low plastic beams and horse-brasses hanging from the walls on long rubberized straps. What few customers there were had a sickly, comatose look to them as if they'd been poisoned by a combination of alcohol and fumes.

'Why don't we sit outside in the beer garden?' suggested Barney.

'Are you sure that's wise?'

'I don't see why not.'

Barney went outside to find some seats while Edmund stayed at the bar waiting to be served. As the beer hissed and frothed from the tap, another aircraft passed overhead. The building shook, glasses rattled, tables shifted of their own accord. No one took any notice. When Edmund came out, Barney was sitting on a chair next to a galvanized metal trough. A wind – not cold exactly, but not warm either and not necessarily of natural extraction – blew a selection of Cellophane packages round their feet.

Barney, he saw, had folded his hands in his lap. He was looking expectantly at Edmund, like a guest on a chat show awaiting the next question. Edmund ran through a list of possible topics in his mind, dismissing each one in turn. There were the staffing rotas, of course – there were always the staffing rotas – but now that he was here he found himself strangely reluctant to discuss them.

Instead he asked, 'What part of Wales are you from?'

Barney straightened in his chair. 'Wales?'

'You are Welsh, aren't you? I thought I detected it in your voice.'

'Possibly,' Barney conceded. 'In part.'

'Do your parents still live there?'

For a long time – even longer than he had spent looking at the ashtray in his car – Barney didn't speak. Once again, Edmund felt the pressure was on him to apply some sort of conversational prod to get him going again. Then, just when he'd given up altogether, Barney said, 'As a matter of fact, my parents are . . .' His voice tailed off.

'Diseased? Did you say diseased?'

'Worse,' said Barney. 'Deceased.'

'I'm very sorry to hear that.'

'Oh, just one of those things, really.'

Lowering his voice to what he hoped was an appropriate level, Edmund asked, 'Was it recent?'

'Not recent, no . . . But still very fresh in my memory.'

Edmund didn't expect Barney to go on, but he did so – almost immediately. 'Motor accident, it was. Dumper truck ploughed into both of them. My mother, her chest was crushed. Well, it would have been – the dumper truck went straight over her. All four and a half tons of it. As for my father . . .'

He stopped again, and seemed to look at Edmund with an expectant expression.

'What?'

'Decapitated.'

'No!'

Barney nodded. At this point a plane passed overhead. Patiently, Barney waited for it to go by. 'They found his head several hundred yards down the road. Sliced off by the dumper truck, it had been – still stuck in the radiator grill. You know those mascots that people have on the front of their cars sometimes to bring them good luck?

Well, like that – but different, obviously. I had to identify them both at the morgue. Wasn't easy, I can tell you.'

Edmund wondered if drinking more beer might settle his stomach. Almost certainly not, he decided. 'Please don't feel you have to tell me any more,' he said.

But once again Barney went on, with scarcely a break. 'My mother, she was draped over this trolley. Like pastry flopped over the rim of a baking tray, you know? But her face looked quite untroubled. Flatter, of course, but at peace. That's the main thing, isn't it?'

'I – I suppose so.'

'They'd tried to stick my father back together, but I don't suppose they had the time. Made a bit of a mess of him to be honest. You don't get over a shock like that easily, I can tell you. Scars you for life, that does.'

'I'm sure.'

'Afterwards the social services tried to take me in and send me to an orphanage. But I wasn't having that. And so I ran away.'

'You ran away?'

Edmund wasn't sure if he had ever heard of anything so dramatic before. Not outside of Dickens, or *Black Beauty* at any rate. It made his own history seem entirely incident-free by comparison. He thought of his father, who worked as a floor manager in a department store in Watford, and of his mother, who didn't. Of his non-existent brothers and sisters. Of his uncle, who still wore a fob-watch at Christmas, and of his aunt, who knew about cabbages and train timetables yet little else. None of this could hold a candle to what Barney had been through.

'I couldn't let them confine me, see. So I set off to make my own way in the world. For a number of years I worked in travelling circuses. First I collected the takings from the machines. And finally I got to look after the animals. Mangy old things, they were, full of fleas.'

Edmund's head was still reeling.

'It was a flea circus?'

'No, obviously not,' said Barney sharply. 'A proper-sized circus with animals and everything. There was an old tiger. He was my favourite. We used to call him Stripey.'

'Stripey?' exclaimed Edmund – he could hear the mingled awe and astonishment in his voice.

'Aye, Stripey. Been there all his life, poor devil. Wouldn't let anyone else touch him but me. Sometimes we just used to snuggle up together and go to sleep. We'd both suffered, you see. And I think in some corner of his primitive mind he knew that. I won't deny it was hard, though. And I suppose it's affected me in a number of very deep ways. Commitment for one. It's not easy for me to give myself to any one person, if you know what I mean.'

'You're always worried that they might be taken away from you. Like your parents?'

'That sort of thing,' agreed Barney, and tailed off again.

Another plane went by. Then Barney said, 'Since we're here, in this beautiful spot, there was something I wanted to ask you, er, Eddie. I suppose you might call it a favour, although it's nothing really. Hardly anything at all.'

'Fire away,' said Edmund with a heartiness that didn't come easily to him.

'You know you met Corky Montcalm the other night? I was wondering if you could call him up and ask if I could look at his offices.'

'I suppose I could.'

'Good man. I knew you wouldn't let me down.'

'Did you?'

'I have an instinct for these things.'

Barney lifted his head and sniffed. As he did so, his face took on a more far-away expression. 'No,' he said softly, 'it won't be long now.'

'What won't?'

'Time to move on.'

'Where to?'

'Not sure really. I might head for South America. Go rolling down to Rio. There's a lot of opportunity there for someone like me. It's in my blood, see.'

'What blood is that?'

'Gypsy blood.'

After everything that had gone before, Edmund supposed that this shouldn't have come as a shock.

'You come from Romany stock, do you?'

Barney didn't answer him directly. Instead he said, 'We are a wandering people, Eddie . . . Always wandering . . .'

Again he lifted his head and sniffed, as if all kinds of messages and scents undetectable to others were being brought to him on the air. Edmund too sniffed, but could smell nothing – nothing but aircraft fuel.

'The open road,' Barney continued. 'No possessions. Just me and my guitar. Simple pleasures, I know. But these things are as precious to me as bright buckles and turquoise rings.'

'Right.'

As Barney had been speaking, Edmund noticed that he did something peculiar with his right hand, holding it first palm downwards and then rotating it from the wrist. He did it once, and then twice. On the third go, Edmund asked, 'What are you doing?'

'This?' said Barney in apparent surprise. 'Oh, I find myself doing it sometimes, without even being aware if it. I think it must be a leftover from my childhood. Gypsy sign-language if you must know. A silent language that can't be understood by outsiders. This gesture here, now that wouldn't mean anything to you. Obviously. But to a fellow traveller, there'd be no question what I meant.'

'So what does it mean?'

'Well, I shouldn't really tell you, Eddie. This sort of information is not really supposed to go beyond the brotherhood . . . But if you must know, it means, "Help, my encampment is in danger."'

'It does?'

'That's right.'

Edmund couldn't help but feel privileged that Barney had chosen to share this information with him. He felt he wanted to give something back in return.

'Perhaps it's a good thing that you're going to be leaving soon,' he said.

'How's that?'

'Well, the Roundhouse can't stay the same for ever, can it?'

'I don't see why not.'

'But the world is changing. Everything is becoming more harsh, more businesslike. Haven't you noticed?'

'Changing?' said Barney. He appeared oddly unsettled by this information. 'It seems fine to me. Just fine. The outside world may change, yes. But the Roundhouse, that stays the same.'

'I wouldn't be so sure about that if I were you.'

'What do you mean?'

Once again honesty had crept up on Edmund unawares. Now that it was here, there was nothing he could do about it. 'You know when we first met, you asked me what I was doing at the Roundhouse. Well, I never told you. Not everything . . .'

'Go on,' said Barney.

And so Edmund did go on, sparing no details. He definitely felt better after doing so, he decided. Keeping secrets only made him bilious. When he had finished Barney didn't say anything – not for some time. Then, when he did speak his voice sounded quite different from how it had done before.

'You mean, they are going to close the place down?'

'Yes, but you'll be all right,' said Edmund. 'Since you're already going away and everything. You won't tell anyone, though, will you? A gypsy's word is his bond, after all.'

'Is it?'

'I always thought so.'

Although Edmund couldn't be sure how, or why, the atmosphere had altered. In an effort to put their conversation back on the same footing as before, he suggested they have another drink.

'I don't think I will,' said Barney, glancing upwards. 'I must be getting back.'

Edmund too looked up. The sky, he saw, had turned black.

On the way back to London it began to rain. As they went on, the rain grew steadily more intense. It was drumming on the roof of the car. The wipers could hardly cope. No sooner had they shovelled one load of water out of the way than another lot streamed down in its place. Then it began to thunder. Soon afterwards, the sky lit up with forks of lightning.

Barney sat with his arms clasped tightly around his chest. 'How far away would you say that lightning was?' he asked.

'A few miles,' said Edmund.

'Are you sure?'

'What's the matter?'

Barney gave an uneasy laugh. 'I just don't want to be struck by lightning, that's all.'

'I wouldn't have thought that was very likely.' Edmund peered out of the windscreen, following the blurred lights of the car in front. 'The chances of being hit by lightning in a car must be negligible.'

'How would you know?'

'Well, I don't know for certain.'

'Exactly. You don't know.'

'But surely you get a lot of that on the road?'

'A lot of what?'

'Exposure to the elements.'

'You always take shelter behind a rock,' said Barney after a pause. 'That's one of the first rules of outdoor life.'

Edmund found his concentration on the road ahead wavering briefly. '"Always take shelter behind a rock" is one of the first rules of outdoor life?' he asked.

'That's right.'

'But what happens if there isn't a rock around?'

'Then you have to find the nearest equivalent. That's another thing you learn. Anyway, you wouldn't understand. People need to feel earthed.'

'How do you mean?'

But Barney wouldn't elaborate. He just wrapped his arms more tightly round his chest. As they drove on, the rain began to die out and the thunder to fade away. All the way back, Edmund drove with one eye on the petrol gauge, watching the needle as it sank down towards the red. Much of Hounslow, Chiswick and parts of

Maida Vale were blacked out – due either to the storm, or to another power cut. There were no street lamps or lights in the houses. Only the flicker of candle flames and torch beams swinging about in the darkness.

But by the time they had reached Swiss Cottage, the rain had stopped and the streets were quite dry. They were approaching the bottom of St John's Wood Road, not far from the Tube station, when Barney said, 'Stop here, will you?'

'Where exactly?'

'*Here!*'

Edmund pulled in by the entrance to an all-night garage. In the garage forecourt a mannequin dressed up as mechanic faced the traffic. The mannequin had an electric arm that swung back and forth in a loose, jerky way, beckoning in passing drivers.

'Where are you going?'

'Me? Nowhere in particular,' said Barney.

He slammed the door behind him. Edmund could see him in the wing-mirror, walking off back up the road, disappearing into the darkness. Once he had gone, Edmund turned the car into the forecourt by the motorized mechanic, hoping to fill it up with petrol. But the forecourt was in darkness and the pumps weren't working. Only the motorized mechanic had been left switched on. The expression on his plastic face stayed quite blank as his arm kept beckoning away.

'Did you say Camden?'

'Are you deaf? Not Camden – Croydon.'

Behind the toughened glass, the man shook his head.

'No trains going that far tonight.'

'Why not?'

'Flooding. Southern suburbs all flooded out, all the way down to Godalming.'

'But what am I supposed to do?'

An elaborate and possibly much-practised shrug resulted. 'Nothing to do with me, pal.'

'No. Nothing ever is.'

'How's that?'

'No one taking responsibility for his actions. That's . . .'

'That's what?'

'That's what's wrong with this blasted country!' cried Barney, wheeling away from the ticket window.

8

Two Favours

Excerpt from statement issued by the Ministry of Health.

Members of the public are warned to be on their guard against a number of animals and birds. Like the mutant rats, these animals have also shown sudden spurts in growth. Several have also exhibited uncharacteristic predatory tendencies. In addition, they are believed to be carriers of diseases – diseases that might well prove untreatable in the present crisis. The following creatures should be approached with particular caution: goats, bobcats, badgers, jackdaws, toads, tortoises, pinemartins, voles, ferrets, bats, ocelots, parrots, adders, jiggers, pigeons and squirrels.

'You all right in there, Edmund?'

Steve had poked his head through the curtain that screened off the Sanilav from the dressing-room corridor. His teeth hung there like old tusks in the semi-darkness.

'Yes, thank you.'

'What's going on?'

This was Barney's voice – coming from the other side of the curtain.

'It's Edmund,' said Steve.

'Eddie? What's he doing there?'

'He's just . . . What are you doing in there, Edmund?'

Edmund didn't say anything.

'I dunno,' said Steve. 'He's just sitting there.'

'Is he having a dump?'

'I don't think so.'

'What makes you so sure?'

'He's still got his trousers on.'

'Oh. Well, is he –?'

'No, I don't think so. Like I said, he's just sitting there. What are you doing, Edmund?'

'Just thinking.'

'Funny place to do it. What are you thinking about?'

'. . . Things.'

'What did he say?' Barney asked.

'He said he was just thinking.'

'Yeah? Funny place to do it. Well, he can't stay there all day. We've got to empty the drum. And Eddie, you promised to do me a favour, remember? Calling Corky?'

'I remember.'

'Perhaps the drum's not full,' said Steve. 'Edmund, could you maybe look down and see if it's full?'

'Of course it's full,' said Barney.

'How can you tell?'

'Because it's always bloody full.'

Edmund picked up the telephone and dialled the number on Corky Montcalm's business card.

'May I speak to Mr Montcalm, please? My name is Edmund Crowe. Mr Montcalm? Hello. We met the other night at the Roundhouse. I sold you some melted ice-creams. Hunchback? Ah! Yes, that's right. No, no – no offence at all. There was something I wanted to ask you, Mr Montcalm. It's just I have a friend who's a great fan of your magazine. A real devotee –'

'Tell him I've got every issue ever published,' whispered Barney.

'He's got every issue ever published. That's right. Every single one. The thing is, he was wondering if it might be possible to visit the magazine's offices. To have a look round . . . It would? That's fantastic. Well, anytime that would be convenient really. A conference in Stockholm? I see . . . But back on Thursday? I'm sure Friday evening would be fine. About seven? Perfect. Thank you very much, Mr Montcalm.'

Edmund replaced the receiver.

Barney took hold of him by the shoulder again and shook him.

'I knew you wouldn't let me down, Eddie.'

'Actually . . .' said Edmund.

'Mmm?'

'I was wondering if you would do me a favour. In return.'

'In return?' said Barney. 'I don't know about that. What sort of favour?'

'It's quite difficult to explain.'

'You'll have to tell me. Unless you want me to try and guess.'

'I rather doubt if you'll be able to do that,' said Edmund.

While he told Barney what it was, he kept his eyes fixed on the telephone receiver, sitting in its cradle. Barney, however, started to laugh some time before he had finished speaking. And he continued laughing for some time afterwards.

'You sly old dog, Eddie,' said Barney when he had finally stopped laughing. 'I never would have thought it – not of you.'

It was true that Edmund would never normally have contemplated such a thing. He wasn't sure what had come over him now.

'But will you try?' he asked.

'Well, that's quite a favour you're asking there.'

'I know.'

'. . . All right,' said Barney. 'Yeah, why the hell not.'

'I really am very grateful.'

'So you bloody should be.'

9
The Nightrunner

To begin with, everything had gone so well that Edmund wondered why he had been so nervous. Indeed, the whole exercise had an eerily preordained quality to it. When he left the office he saw Pippa outside the bar – in exactly the spot where he had hoped to find her.

She was standing on tiptoe and peering about. He saw that she was wearing a clean pair of dungarees and the tracery of scars on her cheeks was covered with make-up.

'Are you waiting for someone?'

'What? Oh, hello, Edmund . . . What did you say?'

'I wondered if you would like to come for a drink.'

'A what?'

'A drink.'

'Who with?'

'With me.'

'With you?'

'Correct.'

Admittedly, there was a lumbering, under-rehearsed quality to these exchanges. You wouldn't want to pay to hear people talk like this. None the less, it served its purpose.

Pippa looked around for one last time. 'All right,' she said. 'If you want.'

'I thought we might go down the road.'

'OK.'

At the pub down the road they talked for a while about nothing in particular, although with an acceptable degree of fluency. As Edmund had suspected when they first met, Pippa was a peculiar mix of sentimentality and aggression. It was as if they both operated in tandem, with each one bringing out unforeseen aspects of the other. He did what he possibly could to keep her as close to sentimentality as possible. But as they talked, he found that a fog of longing had descended upon him. It seemed to slow down his speech and make his entire body feel as if it was leaking sweat. Or rather, as if something akin to sweat but with the adhesive properties of Araldite was being squeezed out through his pores by very small men using even smaller sets of bellows.

He made himself concentrate on the television above the bar where two wrestlers in leotards were grappling with one another. One of the wrestlers was lying on his back and drumming the soles of his feet on the canvas. The other man was sprawled on top of him.

'Are you all right, Edmund?' Pippa asked.

'Why do you ask?'

'You haven't said anything for a while.'

'How long?'

'I don't know how long, obviously. I haven't been timing you.'

'I'm fine.'

'I just wondered if you were bored.'

'Bored! Absolutely not.'

'What is it then?'

The fog grew even thicker. He must proceed with caution, like a traveller on a foggy night, walking down a narrow path and holding a lantern.

'I need an outlet,' he said carefully.

'A what?'

'An outlet,' he repeated.

Pippa was looking at him in consternation. 'What sort of outlet?'

Edmund was aware that the path now dropped away on both sides. No, not drops – slopes would do it.

'A physical outlet.'

'You'll really have to speak up, Edmund. I can't make out what you're saying.'

'I need a physical outlet!'

'Sshh. Not so loud, for God's sake! What are you saying? Do you want the toilet?'

'No, no . . .'

'What then?'

Christ. He'd never anticipated such difficulties. Not at this stage. On the screen one of the wrestlers was swinging the other one round and round by his ponytail; it looked as if they were engaged in some incredibly primitive form of folk-dancing.

Edmund had to expel a good deal of surplus air from his mouth before he could speak. 'Will you go to bed with me?' he asked.

'Go to bed with you?'

'Yes.'

Pippa was looking with an expression of disbelief. 'I had you marked down as the shy type.'

'I am the shy type,' explained Edmund. 'But I have these surges.'

'Surges? You mean, like an epileptic?'

'Something like that. Without the foam, though,' he added hurriedly.

A period of silence followed.

'So why choose me?' Pippa asked.

'Because – because I like you.'

'You've never shown any sign of it before.'

'Too repressed,' said Edmund, feeling fairly satisfied with himself.

'Are you repressed, Edmund?'

Aware that he had reached a relatively safe section of the path, he nodded violently.

'Why's that?' Pippa asked.

'Just the way I am, I suppose.'

'But why do you like me?'

He hadn't expected Pippa to be so inquisitive.

'I just do.'

'There must be more to it than that?'

'Oh. Must there?'

Pippa picked up her glass and drained it. Then she said, 'What the hell,' in an over-hearty way.

'You mean you will?'

'All right. But I want another drink first.'

Edmund realized he was supposed to buy this too. Well, that seemed fair enough, he reckoned. All things considered. He went back to the bar. On the television, the wrestling match was over. Both men now looked very groggy. The winner ran round the ring with his arms raised while the loser sucked on a sponge. Edmund wondered what was on the sponge. Vinegar, probably.

When they left the pub, Pippa took hold of Edmund's hand and pulled it towards her, hooking his thumb through one of her belt loops. He drove to her home, a squat not far away from the Roundhouse. It was a flat-fronted Victorian house belonging to the Church Commissioners, which had been extensively gutted by its present occupants, who had removed most of the doors and bannisters, along with a number of load-bearing walls.

'There's something I think I should tell you,' said Edmund when they reached Pippa's room – a small attic done out with strips of velvet and thickly brocaded lampshades.

She stood facing him, her feet planted some way apart. 'Have you got the clap?'

'No, no . . . Hardly. It's just that I've never done this before.'

'What? You mean you're a virgin?'

'Yes,' said Edmund, 'I am a virgin.'

'Blimey. You have led a sheltered life, haven't you?'

If he nodded any harder, Edmund thought, there was a very real risk that his head might fly off.

'Still, I suppose you've got to start somewhere, haven't you?' said Pippa – this in the manner of one contemplating an enormous pile of dirty dishes.

'That's what I thought.'

'How do you mean?'

'Nothing.'

Then they undressed, with no preamble or fussing about. Nothing was said either, which came as a considerable relief to Edmund. Pippa half turned towards the wall as she took her clothes off, letting her dungarees drop to the floor in a heap and hurling her shoes against the skirting-board. She was somehow bigger without her clothes on. Bigger and broader; with wider hips and narrow ankles, and yet smaller, more pointed breasts. These breasts made her look unusually young.

She lay down on the bed and said, 'Come over here, Edmund.'

He did as he was told.

'Now, lie on top of me.'

He did this too.

'How does that feel?'

It wasn't particularly comfortable – that was the truth. On the other hand, he supposed it wasn't meant to be comfortable. Tentatively, he reached out a hand and touched Pippa on one of her pointed breasts. The moment he did so, with no warning whatsoever, he had an orgasm. It was as if his testicles had just doubled up and sneezed. Afterwards, he rolled off her and lay on the bed gazing up at the ceiling. He'd seen people in French films doing this, looking sleepy and satiated and thoroughly pleased with themselves. But they didn't have a disappointed eye in the clouds staring back at them.

'Is that it?'

'Sorry,' he said.

'Well . . . Never mind. There's always next time. Why don't you put a record on? They're over there, in the crate.'

Edmund scuttled over to the record player. He picked the first record he found – the names meant nothing to him – and dropped the needle into the groove. A quavering voice began to sing. 'O'er Crispin's lake, my love flew low.'

'Thorazine *bach*? Oh, all right. If you must,' said Pippa when he was back beside her. 'You still haven't said why you picked me, Edmund. After all, there are plenty of other girls in the Roundhouse.'

'Not like you,' he said truthfully.

'In what way?'

'You know . . .'

'No,' she said, 'I don't think I do know. Tell me.'

Edmund felt the blood beginning to roar in his head. As hard as he could, he tried to redirect it towards his groin.

73

'Barney . . .'

'Barney?'

'Yes. Of course.'

'What about Barney?'

'You know.'

He heard his voice flap about a little irritably.

'Don't keep saying that. If I knew, I wouldn't be asking you, would I?'

'Because – because he talked to you.'

'About what?' asked Pippa.

Something dark and cold and very hungry began to take large bites out of Edmund's flesh.

'Barney did talk to you, didn't he?' he said.

'What about?'

'About me.'

'About you, Edmund? I don't think so.'

Edmund reached up and felt his throat. His Adam's apple certainly seemed to be still there, although not in its normal place. Now it was set off to one side and much heavier than usual.

'Are you saying he didn't talk to you?' he asked.

Pippa had popped herself up on one elbow.

'Just answer the question. What was Barney supposed to have talked to me about?'

Despite his fear, Edmund once again found he was powerless to dissemble.

'Well, he said that he'd ask you to sleep with me . . . As a favour.'

'A favour to who.'

'To him. He said . . .'

'Go on.'

'He said that you'd do anything he asked you to.'

Pippa fell back on to the sheets, twisting round as she did so and pushing her head into the pillow. When she next spoke her voice was muffled. 'You're telling me that Barney farms me out to friends of his who can't get fucked anywhere else?'

'I wouldn't put it like that.'

'No? How would you bloody put it then?'

Admittedly, it was hard to think of any other way to put it. Edmund reached out and touched Pippa's shoulder.

She jerked away.

He lay there for a little longer, then said, 'Would you like me to go?'

Still Pippa said nothing.

'I'll . . . I'll take that as a yes then.'

Edmund got out of bed. He put his clothes back on. When he was dressed, he said, 'I'm going to go now. Goodbye then.'

There was no reply.

Outside, he sat in his car. A sense of inadequacy washed over him. He felt unmanly, ashamed of himself. Technically, he supposed, he was no longer a virgin, although he wouldn't want to have to swear to it – in court, or anywhere else. And even if he wasn't a virgin, somehow it didn't seem so important any more.

When he tried to start his car nothing happened. He tried again. The engine turned over, but wouldn't catch.

For a third time he tried.

Nothing.

He looked at the petrol gauge. It was empty. While he'd been in Pippa's house, someone must have sucked the remaining petrol out of his tank.

10

Waikiki Wassail

'Oh no, not again,' said Barney.

He had pulled the curtain across and was looking at Edmund sitting on the Sanilav. 'You're spending a lot of time on that bog, Eddie. Really, a lot of time. What's going on?'

'Nothing,' said Edmund, and pulled the curtain back to shield himself.

'You can't just stay there all day, you know.'

'Why not?'

'I've got to empty it for a start. And besides, you've got to drive me to Corky Montcalm's office. Don't tell me you've forgotten?'

'I'm not coming,' said Edmund.

'What do you mean you're not coming?'

'Because – because you didn't keep your side of the bargain. That's why.'

'What the fuck are you talking about?'

'You promised to talk to Pippa for me.'

'So?'

'Well, you didn't, did you?'

There was a pause from the other side of the curtain.

Then Barney said, 'Yes, I did.'

'No,' said Edmund. 'No, you didn't.'

'Are you calling me a liar?'

'That's exactly what I'm calling you,' said Edmund.

'I'm not having that. Anyway, what are you so het up about?'

'Because I thought you'd talked to Pippa, didn't I?'

'. . . So?'

'So I approached her on that understanding.'

'What, you thought I'd –? And you –? Ooh . . .' said Barney. 'What happened then?'

'Never mind what happened then.'

'Go on, tell me. I'm curious.'

'*Never mind what happened then!*'

'All right, have it your own way. Anyway, I don't suppose any damage has been done.'

'How the hell would you know?'

'Either way, it's no reason not to drive me to Corky Montcalm's office. I thought we were friends – you and me.'

'You thought wrong, didn't you?'

When Barney next spoke a wheedling tone had entered his voice. 'Come on, Eddie. Be a mate.'

'No.'

'Why not?'

A huge number of reasons suggested themselves. Edmund took the first to hand. 'Even if I wanted to, I couldn't. I'm clean out of petrol.'

'Oh,' said Barney. 'Is that all? No need to worry there, Eddie. I'll have a word with Sadim. He can sort it out. Now, are you moving, or not?'

'Not a hold-up then?' said Mr MacConachie.

'No, no,' said Edmund, reassuring him. 'Not a hold-up – nothing like that. It's just that correlating the information is taking a little bit longer than I had anticipated.'

'I'm relieved there's not a hold-up, Edmund. For your sake as much as mine. I can see what sort of effect that place is having on you.'

'Can you?'

'Very much so. You look tired. Not yourself.'

'It is pretty hard work,' Edmund said.

'I'm sure. Don't worry, though. I have complete faith in you.'

'That's good to hear.'

'Complete faith,' Mr MacConachie repeated.

Edmund looked over Mr MacConachie's shoulder, and saw that the view out of his window was almost completely obscured. He wondered what could have caused such an effect. Soot, he supposed. Soot, and general muck in the air. There was a lot of muck in the air. Muck everywhere, come to that. He glanced down. To his surprise, he noticed that some sort of partitioning had been erected – or was in the process of being erected – around Mr MacConachie's desk. It looked like a small garden fence, designed to separate one flower-bed from another.

Edmund was about to ask what this was, when Mr MacConachie spoke again. 'You just carry on. As long as we have the audit all done and dusted by the middle of next week. That shouldn't be a problem for you, should it, Edmund?'

'No problem at all.'

'Splendid.'

He might have asked about the fencing now, but the moment seemed to have passed. He said nothing. However, on his way out Edmund noticed that several – perhaps all – of the other desks in the office also had this same low partitioning around them. In each case the fence was made of the same type of wire. Chicken-wire by the look of it. Some of these fences were higher – at a more advanced stage of construction – than others.

Barney was already waiting in the reception area when Edmund arrived. He was wearing a baggy cap made up of different triangular sections of denim. In his hand he held a jerry-can. Together they walked out of the main entrance and across the pitted tarmac to Edmund's car.

Barney emptied the contents of the jerry-can into the tank. When Edmund turned the key in the ignition, the car shuddered, almost stalled, then leaped forward with a blast of indignation. Barney showed no sign of being remotely abashed by what had happened with Pippa; he was preoccupied with their visit to the *Quest* offices.

'I've got every issue of the magazine ever published, Eddie. Did I tell you that?'

'I thought you said you didn't have any possessions.'

78

'I didn't say "any". I said "not many". There's a big difference. They even published one of my letters once. It was about something that happened to me on a late night train with a party of student nurses from King's Lynn.'

As Barney went on to explain just what his letter had been about, Edmund found himself thinking what a boon it would be if human beings were able to close their ears and shut out whatever was being said. Nature was clearly deficient here, having provided large flaps on either side of one's head intended for folding forward as well as backward, yet omitting to include hinges allowing them to do so. No doubt the mistake would be rectified at some later stage of evolution. Too late for him, though – much too late.

Afterwards, Barney went into a more general explanation of what the magazine was about. Much of it, he said, consisted of letters from readers in which they outlined their sexual experiences in unstinting detail. These letters, said Barney, had shaped him and taught him that sexual opportunities were out there waiting at every turn. It was, he said, hardly a matter of making an effort – although a lot depended on having the right temperament, and on not being prone to nervous seizures, or having tiny men pumping Araldite out through your pores.

Alongside this litany of depravities, Corky Montcalm also wrote a column entitled 'Pan's Big Pipe'. In it he detailed his own sexual exploits. Apparently he and his wife Tinker had an open marriage and would often host parties at their club – the Nutkin Club – established specifically for the use of readers. There was one other service the magazine offered its readers: a 'Sex Lab' where couples could have their techniques of lovemaking filmed and then analysed by a panel of straight-faced professionals.

Within the last few days, Edmund had developed very fixed ideas about sexual behaviour and its place within the bonds of marriage. He couldn't help thinking that he'd be lucky if he ever found one woman to love. To think that it might happen more than once . . . plainly, that was going too far.

They drove around Marble Arch and headed down Park Lane. Broken-down vehicles had been abandoned by the sides of the roads and were being systematically stripped by gangs of children. At Speakers' Corner the mound of rubbish bags covered an area the size of a football pitch.

The entrance to Corky Montcalm's office was a large door on one of the roads leading into Shepherd Market. When Barney rang the bell there was an answering buzz from within. The door opened into a hallway with bare brick walls and a metal staircase.

From upstairs a voice called down, 'Come on up, boys. It's on the third floor.'

They climbed the staircase, their feet clanking on the metal steps. There were framed magazine covers on the walls. To begin with these featured cars or World War Two tank battles. But between the second and the third floors these gave way to photos of partially clad girls. Barney pointed at one of them. It was a photograph of Corky's daughter, Lia. As Barney had described, she was lying on a hay bale with a piece of straw sticking out of her mouth. Edmund felt disapproval swelling rapidly inside him. He didn't linger, but carried on up the stairs.

Corky Montcalm was waiting on the next landing. He was just as eager, as full of vitality, as he'd been when they first met – possibly even more so. When Edmund introduced Barney, Corky took hold of his elbow as well as his hand, presumably for added purchase. But Barney had no intention of being outdone here. He pulled Corky into an embrace, then thumped him several times on the back.

When Corky emerged – shaken, but soon rallying – he cried, 'Isn't this great? We're like old friends already!'

They were ushered into a small office with a desk and three chairs. Corky sat down behind the desk. The only picture in the room was a lifesize self-portrait that hung on the wall behind his chair. This portrait had clearly been painted several years earlier. The effect was disconcerting – two Corky Montcalms instead of one; both equally proportioned and dressed in almost identical clothes. The younger Corky gazed over the older Corky's shoulder with a wolfish gleam.

Barney looked around, savouring the atmosphere. 'So where do the team meet?' he asked.

Corky hesitated momentarily. 'What team is that then, Barney?'

'Why, the team of international sexologists, of course.'

Corky grinned back at him, harder than ever. 'We tend to do a lot of our business over the phone these days,' he said. 'The sexologists all have very busy schedules. On account of their international renown.'

If Barney was disappointed by this, he didn't show it. 'What about the Sex Lab then?'

'Ah,' said Corky, 'the Sex Lab . . .' His grin remained fixed in place. 'Sadly, the Sex Lab is out of action at the moment. We had a flood down there – a burst water main. We managed to drain the water without too many problems. However, there appears to have been this organism that found its way into the upholstery. Then it burrowed into the skin of the volunteers.' He shook his head sadly. 'Poor devils came up in these terrible welts. Rubbed themselves till their skin bled.'

'You mean they couldn't have sex?'

'Barney, have a heart. They had to be strapped down and sedated.'

'Oh . . . How about the mail rooms where the readers' letters are sorted?'

'The readers' letters are sorted in the basement. By our specially trained mail-sorters.'

'Yes, I know all about that. I'd very much like to see them at work.'

'Unfortunately, they've already gone home.'

'What? All of them?'

'I'm afraid so.'

Barney seemed unsure what to do next. He looked around, to make sure he hadn't missed anything. Then he said, 'So this is it then?'

'This is it,' said Corky. 'Why, isn't it what you were expecting?'

'No,' said Barney firmly. 'No, it isn't. I thought it would be bigger – much bigger. And more –'

'More what?'

'Alive.'

Corky jumped up from his chair. 'I tell you what, boys. Why don't I take you round the corner for a drink? A cocktail maybe. Then we can relax and have a proper talk.'

Barney shrugged. 'All right,' he said quietly.

They went back downstairs. Corky strode ahead. Within a few minutes they had reached the Hilton Hotel. Corky strode past the brocaded flunky standing outside, and on to another, smaller, door a few yards beyond him. Inside was a staircase leading into the basement. The stair carpet was so thick and springy it was like being on a mattress. They bounced down, one after the other. Standing at the foot of the stairs was a woman wearing a grass skirt and with a red flower tucked behind one ear.

'Good evening, Tohotaua,' said Corky. 'I've brought along two young friends of mine.'

Another woman – also in a grass skirt – stepped forward and draped floral garlands around each of their necks. Barney lifted his garland to his nose and sniffed it suspiciously. Then they were led into a large room. Hawaiian music played over the speakers, one note sliding into another in a soapy, twangless drone. In the corner was a rock-pool with tropical greenery and a mini-cascade. Rush matting had been hung from the ceiling to form the roofs of little open-sided huts. Inside these huts people sat around low tables on small teak stools – silvery men accompanied by glassy-looking women many aeons their junior. Several of these silvery lechers, Edmund noticed, had the same shaped faces as Corky's – the same sucked-in features and eager, probing looks.

The woman escorted them to a hut at the far end of the room. A waitress came to take their orders. Corky reeled off the name of a favourite cocktail, adding a few South Sea pleasantries of his own.

Then she turned to Edmund.

He pointed at the first name on the list.

'The Waikiki Wassail?'

'Make that two,' said Barney.

When the cocktails arrived, they were in plastic pineapples the size of ice-buckets. Corky took a long suck at his straw.

'Isn't that nectar, boys?'

'I wish I'd been able to see that mail room,' said Barney.

'Some other time maybe.'

'I suppose those mail-sorters must get pretty tired, though.'

Corky blew a large bubble into the depths of his pineapple at this.

'How do you figure that one out, Barney?'

'You know. Carrying all those sacks of mail around.'

'Oh . . . sure.'

Corky took another suck at his straw. When he resurfaced, he said, 'Look, I'm going to level with you boys. How many letters do you think we receive a week?'

'About three hundred?' said Barney.

'Try again.'

'Four hundred then.'

'More like twelve,' said Corky.

Barney whistled. 'That many?'

'No, not twelve hundred, Barney. Twelve. That's two more than ten. And most of them are written by people who can barely spell their own names. Some of them, they just make these kind of . . . marks. Anyway, never mind that. The truth is that there are no correspondents – not any more.'

Barney took some time to adjust to this. 'But who writes the readers' letters then?'

'We make them up. I still do quite a few myself, but more and more I prefer to paint. I do copies of the Old Masters, you know. Anatomically correct in every detail. My wife comes in to help with the letters sometimes. However, it's my daughter, Lia, who is the real inspiration. Her imagination is so fertile.'

'And the team of internationally renowned sexologists?' asked Barney – his voice more hollow than Edmund had heard it sound before.

'Barney, there is no team of internationally renowned sexologists. We did have a couple of guys in Copenhagen, but they ran foul of the local livestock commission. Just look outside. You can't run a sexual revolution in conditions like this. People can't even keep warm.'

There was something in what Corky was saying, thought Edmund. It was true that people weren't geared up to enjoying themselves any longer. They were tense, neutered, expecting the worst. In this sense, maybe he was a figure of the times, after all . . .

While he was still thinking about this, Corky's wife and daughter arrived. Corky greeted them – Tinker first.

'You remember Edmund, honey? From the other night?'

'Oh yes,' she said in her pinched-nostril way. 'The child molester.'

'Edmund was only standing in for the child molester, honey. I think you'll find that he has no actual convictions of his own. Do you Edmund?'

Edmund found that his flushing was accompanied by quite severe vocal constriction.

'And this is his friend, Barney,' said Corky.

'Hello, Bunny,' said Tinker.

'Hello, Edmund,' said Lia, and sat down next to Barney.

Corky called for more drinks. Edmund noted that Lia's hair was not as lank as he remembered. Not lank at all, in fact. Not that it mattered, of course. Having made up his mind that he didn't like her, that it would be fruitless paying her any attention, Edmund made himself concentrate on Tinker instead. She appeared to be some years older than Corky, but perhaps this was a result of all the partying they went in for. She was bigger too – taller and bigger-boned, although she had opted for a frail, wraith-like look, with her frizzy grey hair and her face covered in pale powder.

It wasn't simply because Lia had made him ill at ease that Edmund had decided that he didn't like her. She appeared to be both chirpy and self-possessed – an especially infuriating combination in his book. There was something phoney about her too, he decided. For a start, she appeared to have only two expressions. The first of these was a silent gasp of disbelief. She'd listen to whatever was being said with great attentiveness, with her head reared back and her mouth open, as if she'd just heard news so extraordinary that she could hardly take it in.

By any normal standards, this seemed ridiculously contrived. The second expression, however, was even worse. It involved her

84

furrowing her brow with great intensity, while at the same time clutching on to whoever she happened to be talking to. She looked as if she needed to bring herself back down to earth, from whichever frivolous cloud she had climbed on to.

Edmund looked about for something else to concentrate on. While he was doing so, Lia – to his surprise – began talking to him.

'Did you enjoy looking round the offices?' she asked.

There was a slight trill to her voice that he hadn't noticed before. He added it to the debit list.

'Very much so.'

'There isn't really much to see, though, is there?'

'Maybe not, no. But what there was was extremely interesting.'

Lia was looking at him with a glimmer of amusement in her eyes.

At this point Barney butted in. 'Your dad, your old man was saying you write a lot of the letters yourself.'

'He told you that, did he?'

'That's right. You must have some imagination on you.'

'I just try to visualize what people like to read. Are you a fan of the magazine?'

'Very much so.'

'And what about you Edmund?' Lia asked. 'Do you read it?'

'No,' he said. 'No, I don't.'

'Not your scene?'

Before he could speak, Barney butted in for the second time. 'You musn't mind Edmund. He's a bit, you know . . .'

'A bit what?'

'Straight,' said Barney after an unnecessarily long pause.

'There are worse things to be than straight.'

'Of course. Of course there are,' Barney said. 'What sort of things, just as a matter of interest?'

'Arrogance. Boorishness. Lack of consideration towards others.'

'Those are exactly the same things I was thinking of.'

Amid his flushing and his vocal constriction, it struck Edmund that Corky hadn't been that wide of the mark when he'd posed Lia on a hay bale. Despite being pampered and perfumed and chock-full of contrivance, some spirit of the farmyard still clung to her. At any rate she was rather more down-to-earth than he had expected.

She turned back to him. 'But are you happy being straight, Edmund? Surely that's the important thing.'

Edmund found himself thinking about this carefully. 'Most of the time,' he said.

'But not always?'

'No. Not always.'

'Perhaps you pay too much heed to your fears.'

'It's possible,' he conceded.

'Why do you think you do that?'

He found himself thinking about this too. 'It's just that you build everything up in your mind,' he said. 'And half the time these fears are unfounded. But the other half of the time they're not. They're quite real. The trouble is you never know which half is which.'

Edmund wondered if he was drunk. He had drunk two Waikiki Wassails and so he supposed he must be fairly drunk. But he didn't feel drunk. If anything, he felt abnormally clear-headed. But he'd been taken aback by his own fluency; forthrightness too. This was the longest speech about himself that he had given in years, outside of a job interview, or a doctor's surgery.

'I know what you mean,' said Lia.

'I very much doubt that.'

'Even so,' she said, 'I do.'

Edmund was aware of Barney staring at the two of them in turn, his face scrunched up in confusion. Corky meanwhile had paid the bill. The Montcalms were going to the theatre that night and had to leave.

Outside, the wind caught Tinker's frizzy grey hair and sent it swirling round her face. She stood still, waiting patiently until her hair had been returned to its original position.

'Sorry we've got to rush off,' said Corky.

Then he pretended to slap himself on the forehead again. 'Hold on, I've had an idea.'

'Oh God,' said Lia, and looked to Edmund for sympathy. At least that was how it appeared to him.

86

'No, wait. This is a good one. Why don't you guys come to our party?'

'Party? What party is that?' said Barney.

'On Saturday. At the Nutkin Club. We're having one of our get-togethers. To be honest they're not what they were. In fact, this could be the last party of all – we may even have to close down. But we still have a pretty good time, as long as enough people make an effort. Lia will be there, won't you, honey?'

Lia said she would.

'And Tinker – Tinker just adores a party.'

Tinker confirmed this with one of her wannest smiles.

'Great. That's settled then.' Corky held up his clenched fist and shook it at them in farewell. 'Till next Saturday, boys.'

'Bye then,' said Lia.

'Goodbye,' said Edmund.

To begin with, they drove in silence. Both were still wearing their floral garlands. Barney drummed his fingers on the dashboard. Then he said, 'Well, you certainly didn't hold back in there.'

'How do you mean?'

'All that bollocks with Lia. Telling her about your innermost fears. Jesus!'

'She didn't seem to mind.'

'She could hardly tell you to shut up, could she?'

They drove on.

Edmund found himself troubled by questions. By one question in particular that he was unable to stop himself from asking. He kept it in for as long as he could, which wasn't as long as he would have wished, then said, 'What did you think of her?'

'Think of who?'

'Of Lia.'

'Stuck-up,' said Barney promptly.

'Really?'

'Very la-di-da. I've seen loads of girls like her.'

'Have you?'

'Loads and loads. Why, what did you think?'

'Oh . . . not much.'

Barney had twisted round in his seat. 'What was it you particularly disliked about her?'

'It was more general than that,' said Edmund.

'I know what you mean. And she seemed a bit of a know-all, didn't she?'

'Did she? I suppose she did.'

'Mmm. I can't stand that.'

They drove on.

'Are you off soon?' Edmund asked.

'What do you mean, off?'

'You said you were going to take to the open road.'

'Oh that,' said Barney. 'I haven't decided when exactly.'

'Not much point hanging about, I wouldn't have thought.'

'It's just a matter of picking the right moment. Anyway, you don't have to keep going on about it, Eddie. Anyone would think you wanted to me to go.'

They drove on.

'So, are you going to the party then?' Edmund asked.

'What party is that?'

'At the Nutkin Club.'

'Oh, that. To be honest, I hadn't given it a thought. I suppose I might – if I haven't got anything better to do. What about you?'

'I thought I might.'

'Really?' said Barney. 'I wouldn't have thought it was your scene at all.'

'No, well maybe you don't know what my scene is,' said Edmund.

They drove on.

II

Closer to the Edge

In addition to the power cuts, the food shortages, the lack of waste disposal and widespread strikes, the Irish Republican Army announced that it was stepping up its bombing campaign on the British mainland. In London a plan to bring the city to a complete standstill was averted only by chance. Bombs were placed at two adjoining reservoirs in East London. The plan was that when the bombs exploded, the reservoir walls would be breached. Whereupon a tidal wave of water – estimates varied from between twenty to fifty feet high – would flow downhill towards the west, funnelled between the buildings, gathering momentum as it went.

Right in its path was the entrance to Bethnal Green Tube station. The water would sweep into the station – by this stage it would be moving at more than 20 mph – down the escalators and on to the District Line. Once there it would continue to move west, on to Liverpool Street. Upon reaching Liverpool Street, it would then wrap itself around the Circle Line.

The whole of the Tube network would be crippled. There would be massive shortings-out. Trains would be derailed by the force of the water. Thousands of people would be drowned or electrocuted. Within an hour the whole of the Circle Line would be flooded. Once these tunnels were full, the water would continue to flow out towards low-lying western areas such as Fulham and Putney, continuing to cause havoc, eventually dispersing around the various termini. The damage would take months, possibly years, to repair. In addition, much of East London would be without water for several weeks.

The plan was ingenious, and was foiled only when an animal gnawed through the fuse-wire, thereby setting off the detonator, but not the actual bomb. The animal was destroyed in the explosion and could not be identified. At first it was thought to have been a dog. However, it was estimated that only a creature with unusually strong jaws could have bitten through the casing that contained the bomb. A dog would never have been able to manage it. There could be no doubt about it: everyone had had a very lucky escape.

Sadim sat on the bench and took a swig from his hip flask. 'Top of the morning to you,' he said.

'I wish you wouldn't drink that stuff, Sadi,' said Ronald. 'Not in here.'

'You don't know what you're missing. Where's Pippa?'

'She hasn't been in for several days.'

'Perhaps she's sick.'

'Could be.'

'Women's problems . . .'

'I daresay.'

Edmund tried to shut this out. He didn't want to think about Pippa.

'Are you coming to the concert then, Sadim?' asked Steve.

'What concert is that?'

'Thorazine *bach*.'

'Thorazine who?'

'*bach*. They're like a Welsh version of the Grateful Dead.'

'Ye Gods! What an appalling thought.'

'They're playing with the Gwalian Male Voice Choir. Performing a new work called "Arthur's Seat". It represents a big change of direction for them; apparently it's got a theme and everything.'

'What's the theme then?'

'Something Arthurian.'

Sadim raised his eyebrows. 'I might have guessed.'

'Legend has it that at time of national crisis King Arthur will rise from his bed of clay and lead Britain back to its former glory.'

'I wish he'd get a bloody move-on then.'

'I've even got a photograph,' said Steve. He took out a newspaper photograph from his breast pocket, smoothed it out on the table and showed it around. 'That's Reggie Deakin, their instrumental genius,' he said, pointing at one of the musicians, a small man all but buried beneath an enormous perm.

'Ugly little buggers, aren't they?'

'I wouldn't say that.'

'No, Steve,' said Sadim. 'You wouldn't.'

'It's in two weeks' time,' said Ronald. 'Biggest concert we've had in years. Almost like old times. Obviously we don't want anything to go wrong.'

Steve put the photograph back in his pocket. 'Have you noticed there's a funny smell downstairs?'

'What sort of smell?'

'Just a really bad smell. I first noticed it yesterday. But it's stronger today.'

'There's an open sewer down there, so it's hardly surprising.'

'Yeah, but this is even worse than usual.'

'Probably just this rain we've been having,' said Ronald. 'It'll go away. Everything goes away in the end.'

Barney walked into the bar. Ambling, assured, half lifting a hand in greeting.

Sadim offered him the hip flask. 'Very good for you, Barney. Restores lost zip.'

'Nothing wrong with my zip.'

'Of course not,' said Sadim. 'I've got some good news for you, Barney. That elephant anaesthetic – it's here.'

'About time too. What's it like then?'

'How should I know? You don't think I'm touching that stuff. Now, Barney, what you have to remember is that it needs to be kept cold. That's very important. I've got it in a Thermos outside. But if I were you, I'd keep it in a fridge.'

'Fine.'

'What's it cut with this time?' Steve asked.

'Cut? It's not cut with anything,' said Sadim angrily.

Barney sat down. 'So, Eddie. Made your mind up about Saturday?'

'What's happening on Saturday?' Ronald asked.

Taking his time, Barney stretched himself, extending both arms over his head.

'Oh, nothing much. Just that we've been invited to a party at the Nutkin Club.'

'Never!' exclaimed Sadim. 'The Nutkin Club – my God, that's some place by all accounts. Orgies and what have you. Do the waitresses still dress up as squirrels?'

'Wouldn't be the Nutkin Club if they didn't, would it?'

'How did you wangle that then?'

'Personal guests of Corky Montcalm.'

Whatever disappointment Barney had felt about the visit to the *Quest* offices had now disappeared. Meanwhile Sadim was shaking his head admiringly at him. 'What a man of parts you are.'

'I guess I am,' Barney agreed, grinning.

'Telephone call!' shouted the man behind the bar.

No one took any notice.

'Telephone call for Rhodri Rees!'

Again there was no reaction, apart from some slight stiffening from Barney.

'Rhodri Rees?' said Ronald lifting his head. 'Who the fuck's Rhodri Rees?'

'Apparently he works here!' shouted the barman.

'Could have fooled me.' Ronald looked around. 'Anyone else heard of him?'

No one had.

The smell that Steve had mentioned grew steadily worse over the next few days. A strange, pervasive and peculiarly dank smell – apparently coming from the basement. Various attempts were made to find what was causing it. They all proved unsuccessful.

12

Squirrels at Play

Extract from a report jointly published by the Ministry of Health and the Institute of Trichology.

Incidences of baldness have increased dramatically over the last year. Much of the blame is being put on the current fashion for 'bubble perms', which entail treating the hair with chemicals that render it brittle as well as weakening the roots. Normally, baldness tends to be a gradual process, but in several cases reported recently, it has been almost instantaneous, with both women and men being affected. 'Obviously, this has proved very upsetting for those concerned,' said a spokesman. People feel naked without their hair. Women regard their hair as an integral part of their femininity, while in men baldness has traditionally been associated with loss of potency. The only cure in this case is prevention. People are warned not to have their hair permed without seeking medical advice beforehand. Despite the advocacy of a number of different folk remedies, there is, it seems, little that can be done for those who have already started to lose their hair. Earlier reports that the consumption of small amounts of urine can aid hair retention have been dismissed as mischief-making.

The entrance to the Nutkin Club was on the other side of Shepherd Market from Corky's office. There was a small brass plaque by the side of the door – nothing more. The door was answered by a woman dressed as a squirrel. She had on a large brown nylon tail that was stuck to the back of her leotard on a piece of Velcro. Once, this tail must have been bushy and would have stuck up proudly in the air. But now it had lost a good deal of its bounce and trailed along limply behind her. On her feet were special squirrel shoes with long plastic claws that jutted out the front and clattered on the floor as she walked.

The woman handed Edmund and Barney glasses of white wine. As she was doing so, Corky appeared in a long cream cardigan.

'There you are, boys! Are you ready to party then? I certainly am.' Corky put his hand up to shield his eyes. 'Hey! That's some outfit you're wearing there, Edmund.'

This was the first reference anyone had made to the shirt Edmund had bought specially for the party. It was unlike any garment that Edmund had ever worn before – although it demonstrated some degree of taste, he hoped.

They were shown through into a large room. Two of the walls were covered from floor to ceiling in books; yard upon yard of identical leather bindings. The other two walls were hung with paintings. Most were nudes. All looked vaguely familiar. Edmund remembered about Corky's Old Master copies. As far as he could tell, the brushwork appeared skilful enough, the proportions just about right. None the less, the paintings looked far more like centrefolds than the original artists could ever have intended.

In the centre of the room was a pit the size of a small swimming pool, with steps leading down into it and cushions scattered about inside. Around the pit were a number of sofas covered with rubber sheets. There were only about twenty people in the room. Most were middle-aged. There was an atmosphere of nervous expectation, of brittle civility. Hardly anyone was talking.

Several other squirrels were handing out drinks or circulating among the guests. These squirrels appeared to be in a similarly bedraggled state to the woman who had answered the door. They were a good deal older than Edmund had expected. All had the same sagging – and, in a number of cases, matted – tails stuck to their bottoms. Some were having difficulty walking in their squirrel shoes and moved slowly round the room, fearful of tripping over their claws. This made them look even more infirm than they really were.

'This is fantastic, isn't it?' said Barney.

'You think so?'

'Definitely.'

At this point Corky climbed on to a chair. When he clapped his hands everyone fell silent.

'My fellow Nutkins,' he began, 'welcome. May I say first of all how delighted I am – we are – that you were able to make it here tonight. A number of you have had to come a considerable distance – some from as far away as Sidcup and Rickmansworth. One or two new faces have been able to join us and I trust you will show them a traditional Nutkin welcome.'

A low chuckle ran through the room.

'Before we begin, I must apologize for the additional levy I had to impose on top of the original ticket price. This is to cover unforeseen expenses, such as breakages and cleaning expenses, from our last evening together. May I also take this opportunity to thank those Nutkins who generously contributed to Squirrel Veronica's cataract operation.'

Here one of the squirrels lifted her arm and waved gaily at the guests.

'As you can see it's been a huge success and with luck should mean that our breakages are kept to a minimum this time. Now to more serious matters. A number of people have asked me how much longer the Nutkin Club can keep going. They wonder if, in this ever-changing world of ours, there's still a place for traditional Nutkin ideals of good fellowship and irregular union. What I say is this: as long as there are Nutkins to live and breathe, so those ideals will never die. However hard we are finding life at the moment, our time will come again. Somewhere out beyond the dark clouds of social unrest and the garbage mountains there is a bright new dawn of sexual opportunity. So, fellow Nutkins, be bold, be confident, and be of good cheer.'

There was a burst of applause. Corky climbed down from the chair. Barney wandered off to look at the pit. Edmund decided to stay where he was.

A hand brushed his sleeve. He stared at it, then up at its owner.

'Hello,' he said.

'And hello to you, Edmund,' said Tinker. 'What an extraordinary shirt! I've never seen anything quite like it. Are those little frogmen or beetles?'

'There are several of each,' he told her formally.

Tinker's hair was pinned up, but she was wearing more or less the same clothes as she had done when they first met – the same starched skirt and pressed front. She had the same dry skin, dry hair and watery eyes too. For some reason Edmund found this woebegone air more disturbing than anything else. Again he wondered if she was genuinely put-upon, or just adept at dishing out punishment from behind a veil of drabness. She struck him as one of those people who thrived on discomfort. Nothing brought her so much pleasure as to be the cause of it in others; the more acute the better.

'Where's Lia?' he asked.

'Oh, around somewhere.'

Tinker had no interest in her daughter's whereabouts.

'Have you ever been to a party like this before?' she asked.

'Never!'

'Just try to relax, Edmund. That's the main thing. We're all good friends here. All with the same attitudes. What are your particular interests? Your hobbies. As for myself, I pot, you know.' Tinker smiled in confident anticipation of the lowering of spirits this news was bound to produce. 'Recently, I bought a wheel,' she went on. 'Pedal-powered, of course – not electric. Look, there are some examples of my work.'

She was pointing at the nearest wall. Along with Corky's finely worked centrefolds, Edmund saw a number of ashtrays, jugs and nobbled beakers he hadn't noticed before. All in the same mottled green colour; all looking as if they had been designed principally for hurling, with any decorative function a minor afterthought.

'This one I call "Nowhere to Turn",' she said.

Tinker picked up a lump of clay and passed it to him. At first Edmund thought it was nothing more than an unusually ham-fisted attempt at making a sphere roughly the size of a tennis ball. As he looked more closely, though, he saw that there was a face in there – contorted and twisted, but a face all the same, with bent sides and squashed mouth. There were limbs too, wrapped around the head in what might have been a protective sort of way. Except that they didn't appear in the least protective. Instead, the limbs were knotted round one another in such a way that any movement was sure to cause further constriction.

'See the little chap,' said Tinker, pointing at the agonized face. 'He's all stuck, isn't he? He's got "Nowhere to Turn".'

To distract himself, Edmund tried to recall a few European capital cities. Norway? That was easy enough: Oslo. Sweden? Stockholm. What about Denmark? Surely that would be Copenhagen, with its world-famous Little Mermaid statue. Finland? Now, what was the capital of Finland . . . ?

Then he saw Lia. She was on the other side of the pit, partially concealed. She had hold of someone's wrist – Edmund couldn't see who it belonged to – and was talking and smiling away. Every so often Lia would rear back in mock-horror, and then close in again.

Edmund found that he had become very keen on the idea that beneath Lia's chirpy exterior there must be a large reservoir of pain, with all this bright surface stuff nothing but a valiant front. However, he knew that he had absolutely no evidence to back up this theory.

He tried to crane round, to see who she was talking to, but a sizeable brute of a swinger was blocking his view. Slowly, cumbersomely, the view-blocker shifted himself.

Lia, Edmund saw, was talking to Barney.

'Helsinki,' he snarled.

'I beg your pardon, Edmund?' said Tinker.

'Nothing. Can I use your toilet?'

'Toi-let?'

'That's right.'

'Toi-let. Toi-let . . .'

Tinker gargled with the word in the back of her throat for a while until it became the stupidest word that Edmund had ever heard. Then, reluctantly, she told him where it was. Several people were now sitting in the pit. But they seemed unsure how to behave. Two or three of them were embracing; a few were kissing. Others were simply stroking one another. Not with any great enthusiasm, though; more as if they were dabbing at stains on their clothing. So far, thought Edmund with relief, it seemed to be a very English sort of orgy.

Meanwhile the squirrels moved around the guests with trays of food, trying not to kick people with their plastic claws. Those guests who weren't stroking one another were doing their best to eat off paper plates – the plates buckling whenever any pressure was put on them and depositing the food in their laps. Corky was standing in the middle of the pit, next to a tall, thin woman. His head was almost resting on the woman's chest, his beaming face upturned like a seal's, as if at any moment she might drop a fish into his mouth.

There was a man outside the toilet. He wore a wig and a black satin zip-up jacket – one shoulder of which had ridden up to his neck, while the other shoulder had slipped down to his elbow. It made him look as if unsuccessful efforts had been made to straighten him up. He was staring at one of Corky's paintings. It showed a naked woman lying on a divan. Edmund saw that the naked woman was Lia. This time there was no piece of straw in her mouth.

'They've got some lovely things here,' said the man. 'Really lovely things. That little number's quite an eyeful, isn't she?'

When Edmund had finished in the toilet, he stood by the entrance to the room. The lighting had dimmed. A few couples were dancing, shuffling round the little dance floor.

There was a clatter of plastic claws on the floor beside him.

Lia had appeared on his left-hand side. As well as her tail and claws, she was wearing a pale blue cotton dress. Her surface sparkle – by no means under wraps when she'd been talking to Barney earlier – was now more evident than ever. She was practically bubbling over. It confirmed all his worst suspicions about her frivolous nature.

'Hello, Edmund. Where have you been?'

'Just wandering about.'

'Would you like to meet anyone?'

He wondered if he could ask her to drop this chirpy façade and let her fundamental gravitas show through – however painful that might be. But now was probably not the best time, he decided.

'No, I wouldn't.'

'Happier on your own?'

'Not entirely.'

'I've been talking to Barney.'

'I know. I saw you.'

'I like Barney,' she said.

'Do you?'

'Of course. Why, don't you?'

'He's my friend,' said Edmund, and wondered if this was true.

'You're very different, though. I'm surprised you hit it off so well.'

Edmund cast about for a form of words that would give some flavour of the relationship between Barney and himself. Certain kung fu films that he'd seen caught it more accurately than anything else. The wise master, still in outstanding physical shape and also possessed of remarkable mental powers, passing on gobbets of information to his eager but unworldly pupil: an ignorant, goofy type from a far-flung mountain village. A slow learner, practically a simpleton, yet keen – desperately keen – to learn.

'Maybe he's everything I'm not,' he said.

'Maybe you're everything he's not.'

Edmund laughed at the absurdity of this. 'Barney's got hidden depths.'

'Are you quite sure about that?'

'I certainly am. He writes his own music.'

'That's not everything, you know.'

'It's quite a lot,' retorted Edmund sincerely.

'I love these parties,' said Lia. 'I remember my parents would bring me here as a child. Going to sleep on one of the sofas. Then waking up with the noise and seeing everyone laughing and embracing each other.'

'Didn't it bother you?'

'You mean the sex?'

'Yes,' said Edmund. 'The sex.'

'The sex doesn't mean a thing,' said Lia.

'It must mean something.'

'I don't see why. It's harmless. An opportunity for people to lose themselves – to forget everything. Just try to lighten up, Edmund. Be a bit less grumpy.'

Did she have any idea what she was asking? Contradictory forces were at work here. Part of him didn't care to be called grumpy, although it was obviously a lot better than being called sunny, or bonhomous, or full of goodwill – seasonal, or otherwise. Another part of him, however, couldn't help feeling grateful that she had noticed. As Edmund knew from previous experience there was nothing worse than making a special effort to appear grumpy, then realizing that no one was paying any attention.

At the same time he felt consumed with curiosity about Lia; eager to find out everything about her that could possibly be known. But he also dreaded finding out too much – in case the connections between her and her parents became too apparent. It appalled him that she should have anything to do with such a ghastly pair: the priapic monkey of a father – Corky had just surfaced from a mass of bodies in the pit and was brandishing a bra above his head – and the dry stick of a mother. What a horror she was.

'It's all very well for you,' he began angrily.

'What do you mean?'

'You've got it all wrong, don't you see? This is like your version of innocence. Because of your ghast– because of your upbringing. But it's not innocent. No, it's nothing of the kind; it's just squalid and rather pathetic. If you ask me.'

'How would you know, Edmund?' said Lia. 'You haven't even tried it, have you?'

'No,' he said breathlessly. 'No, I haven't.'

'Exactly. You don't know what you're talking about.'

Edmund found Lia's triumphal air of certainty especially aggravating. Her conviction that she knew the answers to everything. Granted, she must know more answers than him; but then he barely knew any of the questions, so it was hardly fair to put him in the same category. It annoyed him too – not quite as much, but very nearly as much – that there should be something absurdly innocent about her on the one hand, and utterly unshockable on the other. In fact, she appeared to be shocked only by cynicism, which Edmund suspected could well turn out to be quite a speciality of his.

He shook his head to try and clear it; shook it with awful scrotal delinquency. What was he thinking of? Coming to such a place? He didn't belong here – or anywhere, for that matter. 'I'm leaving,' he announced.

'But, Edmund, you've only just arrived.'

'I don't care. I can't stay here.'

'Hold on. Just wait a moment.'

He did wait, but miserably, heavily, like someone in a serge suit caught in a downpour.

'What's the matter with you?' Lia asked.

'Nothing,' he said. 'Go and talk to your smart friends.'

'You can talk to me, you know, Edmund.'

'Talk? Talk? What about?'

'Anything you want.'

He wished he could have stamped his feet on the floor and fastened his teeth around some metal object. A crowbar, or a javelin, or even a tin-opener; that might have helped. Not talking, definitely not talking. Talking, he decided, was a complete waste of time.

'What's on your mind?' Lia asked.

'Don't ask.'

'Please, Edmund. I want to know.'

There was something almost beseeching about Lia's expression; as if she needed to soak up other people's difficulties.

He was aware that something inside him was gathering force. A wave, a convulsion, an avalanche. He clenched his fists until there could no longer be any doubt about it. He was in surge.

'I like you,' he said.

'I'm sorry?'

Again he clenched his fists. 'I like you . . .' he repeated, as if addressing someone whose rudimentary command of English was exacerbated by their almost total deafness. 'A lot.'

'That's nice.'

He lifted his chin and roared, 'Nice! Nice!'

'Steady on, Edmund. Get a grip. So what are you saying? That you like me?'

Lia's head was on one side. Her expression had changed to one of almost scientific curiosity. But quite coquettish too, although presumably this was accidental.

'Yes.'

'But you don't even know me.'

'I know you enough.'

'Enough for what?'

'Enough to want to kiss you,' he said.

What's happening to me? Edmund wondered. What is going on? I am not as I was.

'You want to kiss me, Edmund?'

'Yes, I do. Very much.'

Her head stayed on one side – more weighing up appeared to be going on. Along with a possible glimmer of a smile.

I have no time for this, he thought. No further appetite for humiliation. Away! Away!

'All right then,' she said.

Edmund came to with difficulty, as if troubled by hearing difficulties of his own.

'Did you say all right?'

'If you want.'

He put his arm round Lia's tail, drew her towards him and kissed her. Although she did kiss him back, it wasn't quite what he had been hoping for. It was more like a courtesy kiss, or even a consumer test; as if she was trying out a brand of mouthwash with some new radical ingredient like pineapple instead of peppermint. But then, after a moment's hesitation, she did kiss him properly. He felt her tongue inside his mouth and tried to visualize her pinky-brown lips against his.

When they had finished she pulled back and said, 'Now I have to go off and circulate. I'm one of the hosts, remember.'

'But when will I see you again?' Edmund asked.

'That depends.'

'Depends on what?'

Lia walked away without replying. Edmund watched as one of the other squirrels walked towards him. She was carrying a tray of glasses. Following behind her at a loping run was the man Edmund had seen earlier outside the toilet. Now, though, the man looked different. In order to take his mind off the absence of Lia, he tried to work out what was different about him. He realized that the man's wig was missing – he was now quite bald.

At this moment, the squirrel passed Edmund. He saw that her tail looked bushier than the others. It still trailed along the floor, but was fuller, fluffier, less mangy. There appeared to be several clumps of hair fixed to it. He thought at first that these had been added to give it more body. Then he saw they were toupees. They must have become detached from guests' heads and were now stuck to the squirrel's tail by static electricity.

The bald man caught up with the squirrel, plucked a toupee off her tail and tried it on. Realizing he had taken the wrong one, he reached forward for another, replacing the original toupee where he had found it. He put his own toupee back on his head and wandered off.

'What a night eh, Eddie?' Barney was now standing beside him. He was so excited he could barely talk. 'This woman, she put her hand on my parts, Eddie. Without a by-your-leave. Right on top of them. My *parts*. Unbelievable. So, what have you been doing?'

'Talking.'

'Talking? Typical. Who to?'

'To Lia.'

'Lia?' said Barney. 'What were you talking to Lia about?'

'This and that – and other stuff.'

'What sort of other stuff?'

'I kissed her.'

'You kissed Lia?' said Barney.

'That's right.'

'Did she kiss you back?'

'Yes,' said Edmund. 'She did.'

'Doesn't mean much, though,' said Barney. 'Not in a place like this.'

'Doesn't it?'

'Did she put her hand on your parts?'

'No – no, she didn't.'

'Probably just being friendly then. I wouldn't read too much into it, Eddie.'

Silently, stealthily, Tinker had appeared alongside.

'Will you dance, Edmund?' she asked.

'I never dance,' he told her with uncharacteristic firmness. 'But Barney might like to,' he added.

Tinker shifted her gaze.

'Dance?' said Barney, and gave a horrible laugh. 'What, with you?'

Tinker continued to stare at him.

'Why not?' he said eventually. 'I'm up for anything.'

'I'm very glad to hear it,' said Tinker.

When they had gone Edmund went to try to find Lia. The pit now reminded him of a full-scale re-creation of an air/sea rescue, with various naked or semi-naked bodies lungeing upwards, or trying to extricate themselves from the heap of heaving swingers. Lia was sitting on the side, her claws swinging over the edge, her tail tucked behind her.

Edmund knelt down next to her and said, 'Will you come away with me?'

She gave one of her phoney gasps of disbelief – although possibly not so phoney in this case. 'Where to?'

'Anywhere you like. We could even go back to my lodgings, although frankly I wouldn't recommend it. It's just that I've decided that it might help me to talk to you, after all.'

'Have you, Edmund?'

'Yes, I have.'

Lia stared at him. Then she gave a nonchalant-looking shrug, as if something weightless had just landed on her shoulder.

In the background Barney and Tinker completed their second

circuit of the dance floor, with the hem of Tinker's dress banging against Barney's knees.

'All right,' said Lia in the same nonchalant way. 'I don't see what harm it can do.'

13

Squirrels at Rest

Afterwards, when he replayed the scene in his mind, Edmund realized he had no recollection of how he got back to Lia's house. He must have driven, presumably, but he couldn't remember being in his car. Nor could he remember Lia sitting beside him, or parking his car outside the large house in Hampstead where she lived with her parents. He couldn't remember anything until he was upstairs in Lia's bedroom.

'Here we are then,' she said.

Having run out of European capitals, Edmund needed something else to stop his mind from shooting into outer space. There was a quiz show on television that he'd often watched in which items of dubious desirability passed by on a conveyor belt. Once the belt had stopped contestants had to remember as many of these items as they could. To calm himself, he went round the room itemizing pieces of furniture: sofa – wicker – with in-built magazine rack; standard lamp . . .

Lia was slightly more tense than Edmund might have expected, sitting on the bed with her legs jutting out in front of her.

'Now what was it you wanted to talk about, Edmund?'

'I have these problems,' he said.

'What sort of problems?'

Oval table with orange coverlet . . . beige carpet . . . chest of drawers with some sort of mirror attachment . . .

'Sexual problems.'

'Oh.'

'And it's not very easy for me to talk about them.'

'No, of course.'

Yet the extraordinary thing was that it wasn't anything like as difficult as Edmund had anticipated. It was partly because there seemed to be a pane of glass between him and Lia. In other circumstances, he might have been annoyed about this pane of glass. Right now, though, he was grateful for it. Somehow it enabled him to say what he wanted to say, to pause where he wanted to pause, and to behave in a much more deliberate manner than he would otherwise have been able to do.

'I've only slept with one woman,' he said. 'And then only once. It – it didn't go as well as I had hoped.'

'Tell me what went wrong.' Lia spoke in her understanding voice; lower than usual, with no hint of a trill.

'I became carried away,' said Edmund.

'Carried away?'

'Yes.'

'Do you mean you had a premature ejaculation?'

Two small chairs . . . clock with an unnecessarily large face . . . pair of antique fire tongs . . . or forceps . . . or gargantuan tweezers . . .

'Quicker than you could say knife,' Edmund admitted.

'Probably just nerves.'

'I know. I know . . . But I worry.'

'About what?'

'About it happening again. And,' he said, trying to sound as normal as possible, 'I worry about not being normal.'

'But what is normal, Edmund?'

He felt they were in danger of drifting off the point here.

'I want to have a proper sexual experience,' he said.

'What form do you think that experience might take?'

'Well, two people for a start. After that I hadn't really thought.'

'And how do you think I could help?'

'I just thought you might be able to.'

The glass was becoming thinner – that was bad. But at least it was still there. Lia had that slightly doctorish air about her, as if trying to calculate which remedy might be best, and how it should best be administered.

'Would you like to kiss me again?' she asked.

'Yes, I would,' he said.

She raised a thin brown arm and held it out towards him. Edmund was pleased to see there was a look of deep – possibly even protective – concern on her face. As he moved towards her, he was suddenly aware of how good it felt to abdicate all responsibility for your actions, yet still retain some illusion that you were in control. That was a really first-rate feeling; in fact, there was nothing to beat it.

Lia, meanwhile, was still looking concerned, moving her pinky-brown lips, but not saying anything. He wanted to reassure her that he wasn't really in such a wretched state; that he was putting quite a bit of it on for effect; that he was being uncharacteristically – or perhaps characteristically – sly. He wasn't sure which.

But he didn't say anything. The nearer he got, the less point there seemed. When he kissed Lia her lips kept moving, as if she was conscientiously completing whatever sentence she'd begun inside her head. At the same time, though – and the physics of this were way beyond him – he felt that the pane of glass was still in place, and that this was a thoroughly good thing for both of them. It allowed Edmund to feel that he was reassuringly separated from his own actions, and Lia to behave as if she was dealing with a medical emergency.

'How was that?'

'It was good,' said Edmund truthfully. 'And now I'd like to have full sexual intercourse with you.'

'All right, Edmund. Steady on. Why don't you just lie back? Head the other way, otherwise you'll fall off. Now, I want you to think of something relaxing.'

'What sort of something?' Edmund couldn't recall ever being relaxed. Not once in his entire life.

'Anything you like. For instance, when I want to feel calm and happy I always think of a meadow,' said Lia. 'With a carpet of wild flowers I can lie down on.'

'Boats,' said Edmund after a while.

'What sort of boats?'

'Sailing boats. Yachts.'

'And what are they doing, these yachts?'

'They're not really doing anything much. Just floating in a harbour.'

'If you close your eyes, can you see them?'

'I don't want to close my eyes,' he said.

'Just try, Edmund.'

'They're in a big horseshoe bay. With a quayside in the distance.'

'Are there people on the quayside?'

'A few. Holiday-makers – men in sandals. Ugh!'

'What's the matter?'

'Men in sandals – disgusting.'

'Just think them away.'

'I'll try.'

'Have they gone?'

'They fell in the water and drowned. Every single one. That was excellent.'

'Now, I want you to do this,' said Lia. 'Move your hand here. See. And I'll put my hand there –'

'Boats!' cried Edmund in sudden panic. 'Boats! Boats!'

'Sshh, it's all right . . . They're still there. All rocking away, in the harbour.'

This was true. They were still there. And after a while he found himself growing fed up with this harbour and these rocking boats. It was like being back in the Sea Scouts. Still – it had served its purpose, he had to concede that.

'Whew. I almost –'

'But you didn't, did you, Edmund? You saved yourself. That's what you did. Now I'm going to take your clothes off.'

Edmund felt that if she wanted to, she could have removed his skin as well and stripped him down to the bone. He realized that he had never felt less self-conscious about his nakedness before. While he didn't feel proud of it exactly, he didn't feel ashamed either – and that was a very unusual state of affairs for him. His erection, too, he noticed in passing – or not quite in passing – was a triumph.

Then he helped Lia remove her clothes. She was more beautiful naked than he had dared imagine; even more beautiful than in the portrait he'd seen earlier. She was glossy in the places where glossiness was appropriate, and matt in the places where matt belonged. And warmer – much warmer than anyone he had ever touched before.

What he had dared hope would happen next and what did actually happen next then coincided in certain key areas. But with the latter surpassing all expectations of the former by a very wide margin. He felt himself being guided inside her, hearing Lia's grunt as he did so. That, however, was only the start. He then fell into a bottomless swoon where time and space and everything else dissolved into one another.

It was some time before he emerged. Afterwards Edmund lay against the headboard and looked out over the room with its beige carpet, its glass-topped coffee table with twisted bamboo frame, its chest of drawers with complicated mirror attachment . . .

He'd won the lot; every blasted thing on the whole blasted conveyor belt. The whole damn room was his. What had just happened to him – what was still happening to him – was like a moment of pure happiness that he'd already nailed up on a wall inside his head.

The only problem with this, he reflected briefly, was that it made the rest of the wall look awfully blank. But no doubt there would be other moments of pure happiness to join it very soon.

Edmund woke in the night to find Lia gone. A dim light shone through the cracks in the door from the corridor outside. Edmund wrapped a blanket round himself. The bathroom was directly opposite. The bathroom door was open – not wide open, but not completely shut either. At least there was a door; in some households Edmund had read about – purportedly enlightened, open-minded places – there was no bathroom door at all. That was so vile as to be barely credible.

'Lia?' he called.

'. . . Yes.'

'Are you all right in there?'

He waited outside. Through the crack he could see Lia's back view. She was sitting on a chair in the middle of the bathroom, facing the window.

'Can I come in?'

'If you want to.'

He walked inside. Lia's feet were up on the seat of the chair, her feet tucked beneath the hem of her nightdress.

'What are you doing?' he asked.

'Just thinking. I often come in here to think.'

'What? Like your wild-flower meadow?'

'I . . . I suppose so.'

'What were you thinking about?'

'Nothing much.'

'Were you thinking about us?'

Lia didn't answer.

'There's something I want to tell you,' Edmund said.

'No – don't.'

But he carried on, regardless. He couldn't help himself.

'I love you,' he said.

'Please don't talk like that, Edmund!'

'But I do. I've decided, you see. And once I've decided something, that's it.'

'But I don't want that. Not from you, or anyone else. What happened between us, don't you see, it was just fun.'

'Fun?' echoed Edmund. 'Fun? But I meant it,' he said. 'About loving you.'

'Just leave me alone.'

'What's the matter?'

'Nothing is the matter, Edmund.'

'Are you sure?'

'Quite sure.'

'You're absolutely positive nothing is the matter?'

'Yes!'

'Right,' he said. 'I'll go then.'

Edmund went back out into the corridor. He heard the door shutting behind him. It was followed a few moments later by the sound of a key turning in the lock.

When Edmund walked into the kitchen the next morning, his first thought was how normal everything appeared to be. There was a table in the middle of the room. At one end of this table was a high-chair with a large child sitting in it. The child barely fitted in the high-chair – he bulged over the bars that were supposed to keep him seated safely inside. Indeed, the whole high-chair looked as if it might burst apart at any moment and collapse in a pile of kindling.

Corky was cooking breakfast at the stove. He wore a white chef's hat.

'Hi there. Eggs, Edmund?'

'No, thank you.'

'Not a morning person, eh? What about you, honey?' he said to Lia, who had just appeared in the doorway.

'Not for me, Dad.'

Edmund's eyes were drawn to something on the wall about two feet above Corky's head. To begin with, he thought it was a painting – possibly one of Corky's Old Master copies, although more abstract and degenerate than usual. As he looked more closely, he saw that this painting appeared to be moving very slowly down the wall. Then he realized that it wasn't a painting at all, but a plate of scrambled eggs. It must have stuck to the wall and started to slide, leaving an eggy trail down the paintwork.

'This is our son, Omar,' said Corky.

The boy glowered at Edmund. The high-chair creaked and swayed as he shifted his weight about.

'He was an afterthought,' Corky added.

Soon afterwards Tinker came in. She was wearing what looked like a kind of house-coat upon which the faded remains of a floral pattern could still be detected. Her dry eyes gazed impassively at Edmund like a conjuror trying to gauge an audience's suitability for a particularly inventive new trick. Then she moved aside with an easy, theatrical sidestep.

Behind her stood Barney. His hair was even more of a mess than usual, his clothes even more rumpled. He sat down.

'Eggs for you, Barney?'

'No.'

'Toast?'

'Nothing.'

'Bunny's not hungry,' said Tinker. 'He's eaten already.'

At this Barney emitted a low private groan and sat with his head bowed, glaring at the tabletop.

Omar smashed the handle of his spoon down on the tray of his high-chair several times.

'When's his karate?' asked Tinker.

'Ten o'clock.'

Corky ladled more eggs on to the child's plate.

'You spoil that boy,' said Tinker.

'Maybe I do. I can't help myself, though. He's only four, you know, Edmund, but already he's wearing clothes to fit a seven-year-old. He's a boisterous kid too. The headmistress of his nursery school complained that he was bullying the other children. Told me that when he went to his new school he would get beaten up by the older boys. She even wanted us to send him to a child psychologist. I said to hell with that, I've got a much better idea. We'll send him to self-defence lessons instead. That way he can beat the crap out of anyone who tries to mess with him.'

The boy sat with his spoon still gripped in his hand, fixing each of them in turn with a look of distilled malice.

'See his little face puckering up?' said Corky. 'He always does that when he's happy.'

Then Omar smashed the spoon down one more time and began to declaim in a harsh, snarling voice:

> I, that am curtailed of this fair proportion,
> Cheated of feature by dissembling nature,
> Deformed, unfinished, sent before my time
> Into this breathing world, scarce half made up,
> And that so lamely and unfashionable,

That dogs bark at me, as I halt by them; –
Why I, in this weak piping time of peace,
Have no delight to pass away the time;
Unless to spy my shadow in the sun,
And descant on my own deformity;
And therefore – since I cannot prove a lover,
To entertain these fair, well-spoken days –
I am determined to prove a villain!

This last line was spat out with great venom. When he had finished, Corky said proudly, *'Richard III.* He knows all the king's speeches – every one.'

After breakfast was over Edmund tried to talk to Lia on her own. It wasn't easy. She went back upstairs and only came down again as he was preparing to leave. Something of her mother's dreaminess had come over her. Not as bad as Tinker, obviously, but still not what he'd been hoping for.

'Can I see you again?' he asked.

'If you like.'

'When?'

'I hadn't thought.'

'Tonight?'

'No,' she said, firmly enough. 'Not tonight.'

'Friday then? There's a big concert at the Roundhouse. Thorazine *bach* are performing a new work entitled "Arthur's Seat". It's a reinterpretation of the King Arthur legend for our troubled times.'

This at least made an impression.

'Are you being serious?'

'Absolutely. Go on, say you'll come.'

'. . . All right.'

'Great. Until Friday then.'

He leant forward to kiss her. As he did so, Lia moved her face to one side so that his lips caught her more of a glancing blow than he might have wished.

Edmund and Barney walked out to Edmund's car. Barney didn't

speak until they'd been driving for several minutes; he didn't even show any interest in the ashtray.

Then he began muttering to himself, 'Oh God . . . Oh God . . .'

'What's the matter?'

He shuddered and gave another groan. 'I thought I was going to die in there. I did. I thought I was going to fucking die.'

'What happened?'

'You don't think I'm going to tell you that, do you? Dreadful things, though. Dreadful things.' Barney clutched his chest with his arms and hunched forward in his seat until his chest was parallel with his thighs. Once there, he rocked back and forth.

'And I don't want you telling anyone at the Roundhouse what happened,' he said. 'If you do, then I'll . . .'

'Then you'll what?'

'I don't know what exactly. I haven't decided yet. But it won't be nice, believe me. And I don't want to hear about what happened to you either. Understand? No, I don't want to hear that at all.' He sat up and tried to wind down the window, wrestling with the handle – first turning it one way, then the other. 'What's the matter with this bloody thing?' Barney cried. 'I need fresh air. I can't breathe in here!'

14
Mistaken Identities

However much of a strain it was for Edmund to keep his happiness under wraps, he was determined to do so. It felt as if he'd finally cast off all the things about himself that he didn't like. Previously he had thought that he would need at least an army of volunteers to take all these away. But since he'd slept with Lia they just seemed to have vanished from his shoulders. Any doubts or fears that scratched away at his contentment had now safely been banished. Naturally, he wished to crow about this; to dance a specially adapted jig of delight which showed him off to best advantage and didn't make his extremities vibrate too much. But he didn't; he stayed quiet. He wished to be dignified. Or if not dignified, then at least mature. As mature as Lia – which plainly was very mature indeed. Above all, he wanted to be worthy of her.

Over the next few days preparations continued for the Thorazine *bach* concert on Friday night. Wooden rostra were brought in for the Gwalian Male Voice Choir to stand on. In addition, another small stage was constructed next to the main one, to accommodate the timpani and the temple bells that were also to accompany the band.

The Roundhouse was unusually busy. Advance ticket sales were encouraging and morale was high. The only worry was that the smell from downstairs continued to grow worse. Air-fresheners were used, but without success. Although the outside doors were left open during the day, this too had little effect. The smell got so bad that Ronald asked Edmund and Steve if they would come down to the basement with him – to make one last effort to find out where it was coming from.

Before they did so, Steve said, 'Hold on. I've had an idea.'

He headed off towards the stairs.

'Where are you going?' called Ronald.

'Wait a moment.'

When he came back down Steve was carrying Pippa's cage. Ronald looked at it in surprise. 'What are you doing with that bloody bird?'

'This is what they do in mines, Ron. I've read about it. When they're checking for gas they take a canary down. They're super-sensitive to smell, you know.'

'They are? That thing doesn't look very supersensitive to me.'

'Trust me.'

'I don't have a trusting nature,' said Ronald.

Together they made their way through the auditorium and down the passageway into the basement. The smell was worse here than anywhere else. It had a dark, almost primeval quality to it. At the end of the corridor they stopped. The blue light from the asbestos shimmered before them, a soft eerie glow. There was a broomstick leaning against the wall. Steve put down Pippa's cage, picked up the broomstick and took some string from his pocket. He tied the cage on to the end of the stick. As if challenged, the canary emitted several shrill cheeps.

'See?' said Steve. 'She's all fired up now. Good girl.'

He held the broomstick out in front of him. Slowly they advanced into the basement, with Steve swinging the cage from left to right and then back again. When they reached the open sewer they stopped once again. The smell here was certainly bad, but no worse than elsewhere.

Ronald went wandering off to one of the arches. He hadn't been there long when he called out, 'Hey! I've found something.'

'What is it?'

'I think they might be droppings.'

Steve put down the cage and went over to where Ronald was standing. Edmund followed him.

Ronald pointed downwards. 'Now what the fuck done that?' he asked.

'It looks – it looks almost human to me,' said Edmund.

'I never,' said Steve immediately. 'Never.'

'I never said you did, Steve.'

'No human being done that,' said Ronald. 'Must have been an animal.'

'What sort of animal?'

'A bloody big bastard animal by the look of it. Hold on, just wait a minute – these look like tracks.'

'I don't like this,' whispered Steve. 'Not one little bit.'

'Follow me, men,' said Ronald.

Leading away from the droppings were a set of footprints. They were large and splayed, yet with thin, tapering toes. Edmund was reminded of the squirrel shoes that the waitresses had worn at the Nutkin Club.

Steve went back and picked up Pippa's cage. Half-crouched now, and holding the broomstick at its furthest possible extreme, he followed the trail of footprints. Edmund came next, then Ronald. They hadn't gone far when Edmund caught Steve by the arm.

'*Jesus!*' said Steve. 'What is it now?'

'I don't think that's going to work any more, Steve.'

'Eh? Why not?'

'Just look in the cage.'

'What do you mean? Oh shit,' said Steve.

'What's the matter?' asked Ronald.

'It's bad news, Ron.'

'How bad?'

'Pretty bad, I'm afraid. The canary's just gone and died.'

'It can't have done.'

'See for yourself, Ron. I'm no expert, but it looks fucking dead to me.'

Ronald came over. He peered inside the cage.

'See how its feet are sticking up in the air,' said Steve. 'And its beak has turned black. That can't be good, can it? What do you think it means, Ron?'

'How should I know?'

'What are we going to do?'

Ronald took only a moment to make up his mind. 'We're going to get the hell out of here,' he said.

'Black, you say?'

'Completely black. Right the way down to the tip.'

It was an hour later. Ronald, Steve, Edmund and Barney were sitting in the bar. The mood around their table was sombre. Only Barney seemed in high spirits.

'It's only a little bird, for Christ's sake. I wouldn't worry.'

Ronald, however, wasn't convinced. 'There are public health implications,' he said grimly.

Barney waved his hand dismissively. Not for the first time, Edmund was struck by how graceful his movements were. Shapes – indeterminate yet elegant – were effortlessly carved in the air whenever he moved his arms.

'If we'd ever worried about public health implications this place would have been closed down years ago,' Barney said.

'He's got a point there you know, Ron,' said Steve.

Edmund listened without speaking. He didn't care what, if anything, was in the basement, just as long as it didn't endanger his meeting with Lia. Everything else was an irrelevance.

'You two don't know what you're on about,' said Ronald. 'As per usual.' Then he glanced up. 'Hey! Guess who's back.'

Edmund turned round and saw Pippa bearing down on them. Immediately, he grew very tense. Everything else was not an irrelevance – far from it. He had forgotten all about Pippa. Or rather, he had wiped her from his memory. However, the sight of her brought it all back. She looked thinner than he remembered – thinner and more drawn.

As she came closer, slapping her feet down on the floor, Edmund felt a distinct sense of dread. He didn't know what was about to happen, but he had a strong feeling that it would be something bad – and quite possibly worse than that. He thought of running away, but there was no time. Instead, he closed his eyes.

When she reached their table, Pippa didn't waste any time. 'I don't know what you're looking so pleased about,' she said. 'Acting like you're God Almighty's cousin Charlie. What makes you think you can get away with it?'

She sounded even more annoyed than usual.

Behind his closed eyes, Edmund said nothing. He didn't know how he could possibly be looking pleased with himself. He hoped if he didn't react then Pippa would shut up. But she didn't shut up. She just carried on.

'I mean, it's not as if you've really got anything to be proud about, have you? Certainly not in the bed department anyway.'

What's left for me now, wondered Edmund. Missionary work? Deep-space exploration? Head transplant? Nothing, nothing . . .

'In fact,' Pippa continued, a more thoughtful note coming into her voice, 'all things considered, you're just about the worst fuck I've ever had in my life.'

There is a movement that people do in films when they've been shot, or are having a heart attack. A reeling, clutching movement, with one hand thrown out to the side and the other holding their chest. Edmund found himself doing it now, even though he was still sitting down.

A hush had descended.

Pippa, however, hadn't finished yet. With an almost triumphal note, she added, 'Even worse than Edmund.'

Edmund opened his eyes.

Pippa's gaze was focused on a point above his head.

He twisted round, following her eyeline.

Barney was standing behind him. He had turned very pale.

Still no one spoke.

Barney stayed there motionless for a moment. His lips were pinched together and he quivered slightly. Then he turned and walked out of the bar. Everyone parted before him.

After he'd gone, the silence had a booming emptiness to it, like the aftermath of a gong-beat.

Then Ronald lowered his head to his glass and began to laugh. 'Heh, heh, heh, heh.'

*

When Edmund went back upstairs to the office, he heard the sound of crying. Clive was sitting at his desk with his back to Edmund. As Edmund came closer, he saw that Pippa's body was laid out on a blotter in front of him. The bird's body was in the same position as it had been in the cage – she was lying on her back, with her legs sticking up in the air.

Clive looked up. His white hair had fallen forward and his cheeks were wet with tears. 'My darling Pip is dead,' he said. 'What can have happened to her?'

'Perhaps – perhaps she was just old.'

'She wasn't old. She was in the prime of life. And why has her beak turned black?'

Edmund didn't know what to say.

'What are you still doing here?' Clive asked suspiciously. 'Is this anything to do with you?'

'Me?' said Edmund. 'No, nothing at all.'

'Hmm. You're all finished here, are you? Finally done?'

'Finally done,' he confirmed.

'You know what this is, don't you, Edmund?' said Clive. 'It's an omen.'

'What is?'

'Pippa dying. It's a warning that terrible things are about to happen. Dark forces will be unleashed.'

'Don't you think that's going a bit far?'

Clive gazed down at the little body lying on the blotter. 'Oh no,' he said. 'I have no doubt about it.'

15

Shadows are Falling

Something shocking had happened to Mr MacConachie. The partitioning that Edmund had noticed on his previous visit was now complete. Each of the desks in the office was now surrounded by a high fence of chickenwire. The spaces had, in effect, been turned into individual cages. Everyone was working away as diligently as before.

'Finished at last, eh, Edmund?' said Mr MacConachie from inside his enclosure. 'Well done. That must be a big relief for you.'

'Oh, it is,' Edmund agreed.

'So that's the completed audit, is it?'

Edmund was holding the file to his chest. 'This is it, yes.'

'Just put it there, will you?'

'Are you sure you'll be able to reach it?'

'Absolutely,' said Mr MacConachie. 'I can slip my hand through the wire with no trouble at all. Perhaps you'd like to come out for a drink, Edmund? To celebrate? I can't do tonight, I'm afraid. But most evenings they let us out soon after six o'clock. How about tomorrow – Friday?'

'That's very kind. But not tomorrow, if you don't mind.'

'Got something on, have you?'

'As a matter of fact, I have.'

'Some other time then.'

'Some other time,' Edmund confirmed.

Later that afternoon Edmund went to the Sanilav to collect his thoughts. But when he got there he found it was already occupied.

'What are you doing here, Barney?'

Barney didn't answer, not directly. He merely grunted.

'Are you all right?'

'Why shouldn't I be all right?'

'It's just, you look a bit . . .'

'A bit what?'

'Green. And I thought I heard someone being sick.'

'Nothing wrong with me,' said Barney. 'Nothing at all.'

'Are you looking forward to the concert tomorrow?'

'Oh that . . . I hadn't really thought about it.'

'Lia's coming, you know.'

'Oh,' said Barney heavily. 'Her.'

'I'm taking her to the concert. As my date.'

'Why are you telling me this? Why should I care who you're taking to the stupid concert?'

'No reason really. Do you want a hand emptying the Sanilav?'

'What Sanilav?'

'The one you're sitting on.'

Barney shook his head. 'I've done it already,' he said.

'On your own?'

'That's right. I don't need any help from anyone else.'

'Are you sure you're all right, Barney? Is it the smell from the basement?'

'What smell?'

'That's made you sick.'

'I'm not sick, I tell you,' said Barney. 'I'm right as rain. Anyway, I can't sit round here talking to you all day.'

He stood up and began to walk away.

'I think you've left something behind,' said Edmund.

He bent down and picked up a glass beaker from the floor beside the Sanilav. Then he held it out towards Barney. The beaker was about a third full of straw-coloured liquid.

Barney had stopped. He stared at the beaker. 'What's that?' he asked.

'I thought it was yours.'

'Nothing to do with me,' said Barney.

'No?'

'Certainly not. In fact, I've never seen that before in my life.'

123

'My mistake then.'

'Must be.'

After Barney had gone, Edmund held the beaker up to his nose and sniffed. Immediately, he recoiled in surprise and jerked his head away. Then he set the beaker back down on the floor.

Towards the end of the following afternoon Edmund found Ronald in the auditorium. He was pacing about looking concerned. Edmund was about to ask if he needed any help when the auditorium doors swung open and six men walked in. All had massive perms – far bigger than any Edmund had ever seen before. They were like mobile shrubberies on top of their heads. Five of them carried long black cases covered with stickers. They walked down the steps of the auditorium towards the stage.

'You can't come in,' Ronald called out. 'Not yet.'

The men took no notice. They walked down the steps, moving as if through thickened gravity, their hair wobbling from side to side.

'I said you can't come in here!' shouted Ronald.

Still they took no notice. Ronald was in no mood to mess about. 'Look, bugger off! I've already told you twice.'

The leading man had now stopped. He had a beard that was pulled tight into a little clump at his chin and held in place by a rubber band.

'We are *bach*,' he said simply.

'Come again?'

'We are *bach*,' repeated the man without changing his intonation in any way.

'You – you lot are Thorazine *bach*?'

Now that they were nearer, Edmund recognized them from the photograph Steve had shown him. Standing towards the back of the group was a figure with even bigger hair than everyone else. This must be Reggie Deakin, the instrumental genius. He appeared to be a good foot taller than he'd seemed in the photograph. Edmund looked down and saw that the soles of Deakin's boots were as thick as a good-sized encyclopaedia, with the heels being several volumes higher.

'I'd better show you to your dressing room then,' said Ronald.

When he moved off, the musicians dropped into Indian file behind him. Prompted as much by curiosity as anything else, Edmund joined them. When they reached the dressing room, the six men looked around at the cracked mirrors, the broken chairs and the despairing graffiti scrawled on the walls.

'Not bad at all,' said one.

'Are there any toilet facilities?' asked another.

'Very much so,' said Ronald, and with some ceremony drew aside the curtain shielding the Sanilav.

They peered in. There was a general murmur of approval.

'Do we have to empty it ourselves?'

'No, no,' said Ronald, 'that's all taken care of.' He leaned towards Edmund and whispered, 'Where's Barney gone? He was supposed to sort out the dressing-room facilities.'

'I haven't seen him all day.'

'Bloody typical. Could you help me out, Edmund?'

'I'd like to, Ron. But unfortunately I have to go.'

'Where you off to then?'

'I have to collect a friend. I mustn't be late.'

Ronald rolled his yellow eyes in exasperation.

'Then I suppose I'll just have to do it myself.'

Edmund left him in the dressing room and walked out to the car park. Before getting into his car, he turned round and looked at the Roundhouse. The building looked even bigger than usual tonight; even more monumental.

He turned away.

He wished he didn't feel such a nagging partiality for a place he was helping to destroy.

Tinker answered the door. Her skin was a peculiar beige colour this evening, as if she'd dusted her face with sand instead of flour in the interests of variety.

'I've come to collect Lia,' Edmund announced.

She looked at him for a moment, then gave the faintest vestige of a smile.

'But she's not here,' she said.

'Not here?'

'No. She went off some time ago.'

Behind her, Corky and Omar were coming down the stairs. Both were dressed in karate suits. As soon as they reached floor level, Omar started hacking away at Corky's legs with his bare feet.

'Oww!' said Corky. 'Now steady on, little fella.'

'Edmund's come to collect Lia,' Tinker told him.

'Lia? But she's already gone.'

'That's what I told him. But I don't think he believed me.'

'*Enough*! That's dirty, kicking someone there. However much you love them.'

Now the child began to pace about, snarling bitterly, 'I shall despair, There is no creature loves me. And if I die, no soul will pity me.'

'No, you've missed them, I'm afraid, Edmund,' said Corky. 'About six o'clock they went off.'

'They? Who else was here?'

'Why,' said Corky, giving a little chuckle, 'Barney, of course.'

'But – but what was Barney doing here?'

Tinker and Corky exchanged a glance.

'Well, he spent the day here, didn't he?' said Corky.

'. . . And the night,' added Tinker.

'Barney spent the night here?' said Edmund. He looked at Tinker. 'With you?'

'Oh no, Edmund. Not with me.'

There was a pause – not long, but long enough for Edmund to keep a flicker of hope alive.

'With Lia,' she said.

His hope blew out.

'I see . . . Do you know where they've gone?' Edmund heard himself asking. His voice sounded surprisingly level.

'Let me think, I believe I heard Barney say something about a concert tonight. Yes, that's right . . .'

Edmund walked back to his car. He sat behind the steering wheel

126

for some time. Then he started the engine and made his way back through the gathering dusk. Outside the Roundhouse, people were queuing on the front steps and all the way down the Chalk Farm Road.

16

Edmund's Two Ideas

Edmund ran inside. There were people milling about the reception area – so many that he had to push his way through. As well as the audience there was also the Gwalian Male Voice Choir – all fifty-eight members of them, all dressed in dinner jackets.

First, he looked for Barney and Lia in the bar, then in the auditorium, then in the office upstairs. There was no sign of them. The only place he hadn't checked was backstage. And so for the second time that day, he walked through the auditorium and down the narrow corridor to the dressing rooms.

At first he thought the dressing rooms were deserted. Then he saw that all six members of Thorazine *bach* were asleep. And not comfortably stretched out either, but just lying crumpled on the floor. He tried to wake one of them, without success. Then another. A third was equally unresponsive. Edmund knelt down, put his ear to their chests and listened. After a while he could hear a very distant thump, like a mattress being beaten with a ruler in some far-off universe.

In the bar he found Ronald – he was standing with his arms crossed over his chest gazing at the crowd as they shambled in.

'Quick,' said Edmund, 'you have to come with me.'

'What's the matter?'

'It's the band.'

'Are they all right?'

'No, Ron, I wouldn't say they were. Very far from it.'

'What's the matter with them?'

'I think they might be dead.'

They ran back to the dressing room. Thorazine *bach* were all lying where Edmund had found them. None of them had moved. Ronald also tried to rouse them – again without success.

'What can have happened?' Edmund asked.

'How should I know?'

Then, in a quiet voice, Ronald said, 'Oh no.'

'What is it?'

Ronald was pointing. Edmund turned round. The fridge door, he saw, was open. Ronald looked inside. From where he was standing, Edmund could see nothing apart from a single silver Thermos flask. Ronald picked it up and shook it. The Thermos was empty.

'You remember that elephant anaesthetic that Sadi got for Barney?' he said. 'Do you happen to know where he stored it?'

'No idea.'

'Didn't Sadi tell him it had to be kept somewhere cold?'

'I seem to remember he did. What? You mean . . .'

'Sweet Jesus,' said Ronald, putting his hand to his forehead. 'They've drunk the fucking elephant anaesthetic. They must have thought it was part of the refreshments. This is all Barney's fault. He was supposed to stock up the fridge.'

'How many doses were in there?'

'Enough to knock out a whole herd, so Sadi said. What are we going to do, Edmund?'

'Is there an antidote?'

'Not as far as I know. How long have we got?'

Edmund looked at his watch. It was ten past eight. 'Twenty minutes. Should we call an ambulance?'

'No point – they're on a go-slow, remember. Quick,' said Ronald, 'fetch coffee.'

'Right. Do you take sugar?'

'Not for me, you fool. For the band.'

Edmund ran back to the bar. By the time he came back, Ronald had propped up all six band members against the wall. All were still insensible. Efforts to pour coffee down their throats met with only limited success. Most of it dribbled out and slopped down their shirt-fronts.

Edmund and Ronald went round each in turn, trying to force as much coffee down them as possible. When they had finished, Ronald lifted up one of the men, trying to make him stand. It was hopeless. The man doubled over Ronald's arm – his legs sagging, his mouth hanging open. With his arms clasped round the man's chest, Ronald kicked at the backs of his ankles. The first few times this happened there was no response. Then, very slowly – as if fearful of being kicked again – the man slid one of his feet forward. When Ronald kicked at his other foot, the man gave a whimper. Then his other foot slid forward.

'You carry on, Edmund. I'll try another one.'

Edmund half twisted the man against the wall and managed to hold him upright – pushing him along while jabbing away at his ankles. By this time the man had started to groan quite regularly. While he wasn't capable of standing upright, he didn't fall over immediately either – he just sank back down to the floor.

'How long now?' Ronald called out.

As if in answer to this, the sound of slow hand-clapping came from the auditorium.

'It's time.'

'Let's just keep trying.'

For the ten minutes they worked away at trying to restore the six members of Thorazine *bach* to consciousness. By the time they had finished five of them were able to stand upright – not for long, but it was a big improvement on what they'd been like before. Walking, however, was more of a problem. Their motor functions were impaired. Some were able to walk unaided, but in nothing resembling a straight line. Instead, they blundered about, bumping into walls and tripping over their own feet.

The sixth man didn't respond to any amount of shaking. He was out cold. This was Reggie Deakin – the instrumental genius. Whenever Ronald raised him up on his stack heels, he keeled right back over again. Periodically, he would go into spasm – his limbs shuddering, his teeth chattering, tremors running in ripples across his skin.

'This one's no good,' said Ronald. 'He's a goner.'

'Just keep him there for a moment.'

'Hey! Where do you think you're off to, Edmund?'

Without answering, Edmund picked up a spoon from the counter and ran back out of the dressing room. He was away for five minutes – no more. When he returned he was carrying the spoon held out in front of him. He knelt down and held it under Reggie Deakin's nostrils.

To begin with there was no reaction. If anything he seemed to grow even weaker – his breaths were so shallow now they were barely detectable.

'Come on, Edmund,' said Ronald unhappily. 'This is no time to fuck about.'

Edmund kept the spoon where it was. Still there was no reaction. He was about to take the spoon away, when Deakin came to life with a wild start. Coughing and gagging, he scuttled across the floor on all fours and cowered in a corner.

When Edmund moved towards him with the spoon, he shrank back against the wall.

'My God, how did you do that?' said Ronald. 'What's on the spoon?'

'Creature droppings from the basement.'

'Now that – that shows real initiative, Edmund. Something that's in very short supply round here.'

Once more, they went round each of the band in turn – holding the spoon under their noses until they came gagging back to life, then trying to induce them to drink more coffee. As they were doing so, a man in a dinner jacket came in. He introduced himself as the leader of the Gwalian Male Voice Choir. He had an eager manner and thin fair hair brushed horizontally across his forehead. 'I just wanted to say good luck. We're all raring to go. Every man jack of us. I say, are those chaps all right?'

Two members of Thorazine *bach* were propped against the wall, their heads slumped forward, their tongues lolling out – Ronald had secured one of them to a radiator by a leather belt.

'They're fine. Just fine . . .'

'But that one there . . .' The man craned forward for a closer look. 'I don't want to be alarmist, but he looks as if he might have had, you know, an attack or something. Don't you think you should fetch a doctor?'

'All in hand.'

'If you say so.'

Ronald managed to guide the man out.

The sound of slow hand-clapping had now been joined by catcalls.

'It's no good, is it, Eddie? If only we had another half-hour. But that lot are never going to wait that long. No, it's no good, I'm afraid. We're just going to have to call the whole thing off.'

Edmund felt very tired. He leaned against a vacant patch of wall to stop himself from sinking to the floor. As he did so, he heard a familiar voice.

'Everything all right then?'

He looked up.

Barney had come into the dressing room.

'Does it bloody look all right?' said Ronald. 'Does it? Go on, make an educated guess.'

'No need to be like that, Ron. Just having a look round. Doing my job.'

'If you'd done your job in the first place, we wouldn't be in this shit.'

'No, I'm not with you, Ron.'

Ronald told Barney what had happened.

'That's not my fault,' Barney said automatically.

'Oh yes it is.'

'You always blame me for everything,' he said, changing tack a little.

'You were supposed to make sure the fridge was properly stocked up,' said Ronald. 'Instead, there was only elephant anaesthetic in there. They must have thought it was a cooling drink. And now look at them.'

'I've got an idea,' said Edmund.

'Don't you start,' said Barney.

'Actually, Edmund has been having some good ideas lately,' said Ronald.

'Really?' Barney shrugged. 'If you say so.'

'You remember you said that half an hour might make all the difference?' said Edmund.

'If only –'

'Well, why doesn't Barney go on for half an hour? As a support act. He could play some of his songs – his unconventional arrangements.'

'Hey,' said Ronald, 'that's not bad. Not bad at all. I think you've done it again, Edmund.'

'Now hold on –' Barney began.

'Just for a while. Until the band can stand upright.'

'No,' said Barney. 'No, definitely not. No way.'

'You spend half your life playing that fucking guitar,' said Ronald. 'This is your big moment. Besides, in the circumstances it's the least you can do.'

Barney began to shake his head – more of a rotation than a shaking, as if he was trying to unscrew it from his body. 'No,' he said again.

Ronald simply took a guitar from one of the cases and hung it round Barney's neck. His legs seemed to buckle under the weight.

'Now you listen to me, Ron –'

'No, you listen to me. You're going onstage, whether you like it or not. Understand? Play any old crap. It'll be better than nothing.'

Ronald started to push Barney up the corridor. Twice, Barney tried to come to a halt, bracing his hands against the walls. Each time Ronald shoved him forward.

They stopped on the other side of the velvet curtain separating the stage from the corridor. The sound of slow hand-clapping was much louder out here. The catcalls too had grown in both number and volume.

'OK, Barney,' said Ronald. 'Now give 'em hell.'

Edmund pulled the curtain back – and then Ronald shoved Barney through the gap.

17

Exits and Entrances

As soon as the audience saw Barney, the slow hand-clapping and the catcalls stopped. Both were succeeded by a puzzled hum. Clearly, this wasn't Thorazine *bach* – so who was it? The situation wasn't helped by Barney, who made no effort to explain anything to the audience. He just stood by the microphone with the guitar slung round his neck. This went on for some time.

Barney didn't move.

Once again, the audience grew restless.

'Get on with it then!' someone shouted.

Slowly Barney raised his hands. Then, just as Edmund has seen him do when he'd interrupted his practice in the Sanilav, he began to move them over the guitar strings. Back and forth they went – not playing a note, just describing these graceful shapes in the air.

'What the fuck's he playing at?' Ronald muttered.

Edmund looked out into the audience, searching for Lia among the ranks of upturned, perplexed faces. He couldn't see her anywhere. The only person he recognized was Sadim, dressed in his usual fawn suit, standing near the front of the audience.

Barney meanwhile was still moving his hands over the guitar strings, not touching them.

'I can't hear you!' came another shout from the audience.

There was a burst of laughter.

And then Barney walked off stage.

Ronald grabbed hold of him. 'Stop pissing about,' he said. 'What's the matter with you?'

Barney said something inaudible.

'What was that? Speak up.'

'I can't,' he said.

'What do you mean, you can't?'

Barney stood facing the wall. 'I can't,' he said again, his voice no more than a whisper.

'What's going on?' Ronald asked. He looked from Edmund to Barney, and back again.

In the auditorium, the slow hand-clapping had started up again. Barney stayed facing the wall.

'Am I missing something here?' said Ronald.

'He means he can't play,' said Edmund.

'Can't play? Why not? Is there something wrong with his hands?'

'Not exactly, no . . . I don't think he knows how to.'

'Can't play? But I've heard him,' said Ronald. 'Seen him anyway. What? Are you saying that he . . .'

Edmund nodded. 'He just pretends,' he said.

'Leave me alone!' cried Barney.

He unslung the guitar from round his neck, dropped it to the floor, then walked away.

'Jesus, this is turning into a whole week of surprises,' said Ronald. 'Right then, Edmund. You and me – we've got work to do.'

In the dressing room, they found a distinct improvement in the band's condition. Everyone could stand unaided and several were now able to talk.

'We can't wait any longer,' said Ronald. 'They'll just have to go on like this. Give them their instruments, Edmund. They'll never notice which is which.'

The band members took the guitars and tilted them about, staring enraptured as the shiny surfaces caught the light. Ronald and Edmund shepherded everyone into the corridor.

'Dim the house lights!' Ronald shouted. 'We're in business.'

The house lights started to dim.

There was a burst of applause. Then from the far side of the stage the Gwalian Male Voice Choir made their entrance. They walked on three abreast, all carrying folders of sheet music; a long line of them making their way on to the rostra. They stood in three tiers – each tier a head-height above the other. Next came the percussionists and temple-bell players; several of them in long robes, almost certainly of their own making. They too marched on and took up their positions.

And then came the entrance of Thorazine *bach*.

This was greeted with a chorus of whoops and cheers. None of the band members reacted in any way. They just stood bent over their instruments.

The cheers died away. Everyone was quiet. Then Reggie Deakin brushed his hand against the strings of his guitar. A deep thrum filled the auditorium. Off to one side of the stage, a temple bell began to toll.

'Arthur's Seat' was under way.

For the next fifteen minutes, everything went well – far better than Edmund could have anticipated. The Gwalian Male Voice Choir burst into song. The temple-bell players and percussionists banged furiously away. Jogged out of their stupor, the band joined in with a remarkable degree of unanimity.

Everything continued to go well – right up to the point when the cannon effects detonated. Even here, there was nothing wrong with the timing; only that these cannon effects proved to be far louder than expected. Initially, Edmund assumed that a bomb had gone off. The whole building shook. The music ground to a halt.

A cloud of smoke drifted across the stage and settled above the audience's heads. As the smoke cleared, Edmund saw Lia. She was with Barney. They were standing towards the back, pressed together by the crush.

'Don't leave me here, Eddie,' called Ronald. 'Not like this.'

Edmund made his way from the side of the stage into the auditorium. It was difficult for him to move. He kept looking up, trying to catch another glimpse of Lia. Then he carried on, shouldering more people aside. He didn't know what he was going to say when he reached her – remonstrations, pleas, demands for an explanation . . . He had no idea, but still he kept going.

Bravely, the choir had now resumed, followed by several members of the band. Edmund meanwhile continued pushing his way through the crowd. He was only about fifteen feet away by now.

He raised his arm and shouted, 'Lia!'

She turned towards him. Her mouth seemed to drop open, but at that moment the auditorium was plunged into darkness. The sound too cut out. In the confusion, people surged this way and that. Glasses were thrown at the stage. Fists lashed out. There were cries of pain and alarm.

Then, all at once, the chanting and the shoving ceased. Edmund was now facing away from the stage. He became aware that the auditorium seemed suddenly lighter. The lights, however, hadn't come back on; somehow it was a different sort of illumination. A shimmering blue light that seemed to lap out from the stage and over the heads of the audience.

'What's that?' came a man's voice from beside him.

'Back projection,' said his companion confidently.

'Very lifelike. But what's it supposed to be?'

'The Hound of Niflheim,' explained his companion, no less confidently than before.

'Hound of what?'

'Niflheim. The underworld of eternal cold and darkness.'

'Yes, yes. Of course.'

Edmund turned around. He saw that the whole of the stage area was now flooded with blue light. In the middle of this blue light was a silhouette. A large four-legged creature was standing on one of the speaker cabinets. Its head was raised, its jaws wide open. The light shimmered from its body – rippling out in waves. The creature tossed its head and turned to gaze out at the auditorium.

A shudder of excitement ran through the audience.

'Very lifelike indeed,' said the man beside him admiringly.

The creature stayed motionless while the blue light continued to pulse away. Then, lowering its shoulders, it began to scratch at the top of the speaker cabinet. After this, it took several steps backwards, and then disappeared. There was a groan of disappointment, followed by a burst of chanting.

'Arthur! Arthur!' the cry went up. 'Come back and save us.'

The chanting swelled. Everyone joined in – shouting and banging their feet on the floor. Just when it seemed as if the chanting couldn't grow any louder, the creature reappeared. Now it was no longer motionless. Now it was moving at a gallop, hurtling forward.

From the top of the speaker cabinet, the creature took a flying leap into the Gwalian Male Voice Choir. And from there – with another kick of its hind legs – launched itself into the auditorium.

18

Over the Hills and Far Away

It seemed to Edmund that the creature hung in the air for a long time – with legs splayed and tail outstretched – looking down almost disdainfully on the faces below. When it landed, there were screams of fright. The crowd began to rear back and sway.

Edmund looked back to where Lia had been standing, and saw that she had disappeared. So had Barney. As Edmund was trying to work out what to do next, the crowd surged again. He was carried along for several yards, then set down. People trampled over one another, desperately trying to reach the exit.

The creature appeared to have moved away towards the other side of the stage. Further screaming confirmed this. At this point, the lights came back on. Yet this did nothing to lessen the panic. Everyone continued to rush around. It took Edmund several minutes to push his way out of the auditorium. For the first time he smelled burning.

Still looking for Lia, he headed towards the bar. There was no sign of her. However, Ronald and Steve were there. Most of the furniture in the bar had been smashed. Someone had tried to set some of it alight, although only a few of the piles of wood had actually caught fire. Bottles had been looted from behind the bar. Even the food had been stolen, for use as projectiles.

'See?' said Ronald shaking his head. 'I always said those old hippies would turn nasty if they didn't have their ice-creams.'

'Where's the creature gone?' asked Edmund.

'Must be round here somewhere.'

'Horrible thing, isn't it?' said Steve. 'Horrible. Must have escaped from a laboratory somewhere, I suppose.'

Ronald continued shaking his head. 'This is all Barney's fault,' he said.

From floor level behind them came a voice.

'I wish you'd stop saying that, Ron.'

Barney and Lia had appeared from behind the bar. Lia appeared less sure of herself than Edmund remembered. Altogether more hesitant and ill at ease. She wouldn't meet his eye.

'How can it all be my fault?' Barney repeated.

'All right then, Barney,' said Ronald. 'Let me explain. First you left the elephant anaesthetic in the band's fridge. And then you didn't provide them with drinks and nibbles, like you're supposed to. That's why they drank the Thermos.'

'How was I supposed to know they'd do that?'

'And there's something else,' said Ronald. 'Tell me, Barney, where have you been emptying the Sanilav?'

There was a slight hesitation.

'What's that got to do with it?' Barney asked.

'Just tell me.'

Barney's eyes swung about.

'Usual place.'

'Yeah? So how come I haven't seen any puddles of disinfectant on the foyer floor? Besides, it needs two people to lift that thing and you don't have anyone to help you. Not any more. Come on, tell me.'

'If it's so important to you, Ron,' said Barney. 'If you really need to know – in the basement.'

'Did you empty it into the open sewer?'

'So what if I did?'

'You see what you've done, don't you? There must have been a rat down there, living off the raw sewage. Then you come along and empty cocaine slops into its food tray. Not just cocaine. Whatever else people have dumped into the Sanilav – uppers, downers. Acid too, I shouldn't wonder. No wonder it's gone crazy. Living down there alone in the dark, growing bigger all the time. It must have started licking the blue asbestos. That's what made it glow.'

'Not my fault,' said Barney.

Ronald sighed. 'Then whose fault is it?'

This time there was no hesitation. 'Edmund's,' said Barney.

'Edmund's? How do you work that one out?'

'Just ask him what he's doing here.'

'We already know what he's doing here.'

'Go on. Just ask.'

Ronald sighed again; he was trying to be reasonable. 'What are you doing here, Edmund?'

Although he normally found it impossible to dissemble, on this occasion Edmund did manage to stay silent.

'All right then, I'll tell them,' said Barney. 'He's not just an accountant. He's an auditor. He's been doing a financial analysis of the Roundhouse for the local council. Afterwards they're going to kick everyone out and close the place down. You understand what that means, don't you?'

'No,' said Steve. 'What does it mean?'

'It means it's all over. Finished.'

'All over?'

Steve turned to Edmund. His teeth had settled back into their two indentations on his bottom lip. Then they lifted up again. 'But you were our friend,' he said. 'We treated you like a person.'

'Is this true Edmund?' Ronald asked.

Still Edmund didn't say anything.

'He betrayed you, didn't he?' said Barney. 'All of us – he went behind our backs.'

From the foyer came the sound of breaking glass, followed by people shouting. Not just shouting – almost baying now.

'Ron, I don't want to be even more of a downer here,' said Steve, 'but I think they've started dismantling the box office.'

Ronald extended a finger towards Edmund. 'Don't you go anywhere. Understand? You've got some explaining to do.'

Together Ronald and Steve ran towards the foyer. The doors banged shut behind them. That left Edmund, Lia and Barney alone in the bar. None of them said anything for a while.

Then Edmund turned to Lia. 'I just want to know why,' he said.

Lia looked at him.

Although it hardly mattered any more, Edmund realized he had been right about her trilling manner concealing something else. All her know-it-all behaviour, all her outward mannerisms – they were just duckboards laid over the swirling mess below.

He was still trying to work this out when Lia started talking. 'Why, Edmund? Because you were so keen, if you must know. Because you started going on about love, and I couldn't handle that. And because Barney wanted to so much. He was really putting everything into it. And because I felt like it. Isn't that enough?'

'But I meant it,' said Edmund. 'I do love you.'

Tears had begun to roll down Lia's cheeks. She raised her hand towards her face but made no move to brush them away.

'Are you saying sleeping with Barney was just a way of putting sex back on to a more recreational plane?' Edmund asked – this sentence came out more awkwardly than any sentence he could ever remember speaking before. Still, at least it came out; that was something.

'If you like.'

'Hold on,' said Barney. 'What do you mean?'

'It's true, Barney,' said Lia.

'What's true?'

'I didn't not want to be with Edmund because I wanted to be with you. If that makes any sense.'

'No, it doesn't make any sense. You must want to be with me.'

She shook her head. 'I'm sorry, Barney.'

Lia was crying freely now. She dabbed at her cheeks with a paper handkerchief, but this just seemed to spread the tears around. Now that her frivolity had vanished, Edmund found himself wishing that some of it would come back, however briefly.

'Why does everything have to be so complicated?' she cried.

'Feelings are complicated,' said Edmund solemnly. Where had he got this from? he wondered. Not *Quest*, that was for sure.

'I'm going,' said Lia.

'I'll come with you,' said Barney.

'No, Barney. No. I just – I just want to go home. I don't want either of you to come with me.'

Lia walked towards the door. As she did so, Edmund looked in vain for further signs of distress: some breakdown in co-ordination; sudden lurching to left or right. But there was nothing. Nothing at all. She might have been going anywhere.

When she had gone Barney said, 'She'll regret that. Definitely she will.'

Edmund too started to walk away.

'There's no point following her, you know.'

'I'm not following her.'

'Where are you going then?' said Barney. 'Ron hasn't finished with you yet.'

'Too late for that.'

'What's too late?'

'It's too late for everything,' said Edmund.

He walked out of the bar.

There were only a few rioters left in the foyer, pulling at the remaining fixtures. The shouts had all died away; perhaps everyone had moved elsewhere, or gone home. Edmund badly wanted to go home too – except he didn't have a real home to go to.

But then, coming from some way away by the sound of it, he heard what he thought was thunder. A low, rumbling sound. The noise grew steadily in volume. People began to run towards him. They appeared even more panic-stricken than before.

'What is it?' Edmund called out as they ran past. 'The creature?'

Only one man answered him, and then with a single word. '*Worse!*'

Edmund stopped. He wasn't sure what to do. He looked down at the floor. There were footprints in the dust – the same big clawed feet as he had seen in the basement, with four long toes and a clearly defined heel. The footprints, however, were pointing in the opposite direction. He stood there, expecting at any moment a blue shimmering light to come towards him. But it never came.

Instead he heard a single set of footsteps approaching. Not running – just walking at a brisk, businesslike clip.

He waited.

The footsteps came closer.

Rounding the curve of the corridor, carrying an armful of leaflets, appeared a tall red-haired woman. As soon as she saw Edmund, she held up her leaflets and started shaking them about.

'The Right are taking over!' she shouted.

Now it was Edmund's turn to flee. When he looked back he saw that Vanessa Redgrave had started running after him. Her red hair was streaming out behind her. However, he had a twenty-yard start – even with her long legs that gave him quite an advantage.

On his left was a doorway into the auditorium. Edmund pushed open the door, then held it shut behind him. From the other side of the door came several shoves. And then the footsteps went away. The auditorium had been torn apart. There was broken glass lying on the floor; the balcony was sagging on its metal legs.

The only two people there were a middle-aged man and woman who were picking their way through the wreckage. The man wore a jacket comprising equal parts suede and crocheted nylon. When he saw Edmund he called out, 'I wonder if you can help us. Do you work here?' The man had a Welsh accent.

'In – in a manner of speaking,' Edmund said.

'We're looking for our son. Rhodri Rees. I believe he's on the staff here.'

'Sorry, but the name doesn't mean anything to me.'

'Oh dear. You see, he wrote a few months ago saying he had a job here, but we haven't heard anything since. When we heard about the concert we thought we'd come up and try to find him. We didn't want to be fussy parents, you see, but it's been several weeks now without a word and my wife, in particular, well, she hasn't been sleeping too well. Besides, he's due to start at Technical College in the autumn and he needs to sort out his grant application. We had hoped to see him beforehand, but we were held up in traffic. Fog at Swindon. I thought I caught a glimpse of him during the concert. But then that big blue rat came on and spoiled everything.'

'Can't help you, I'm afraid.'

'I thought I saw the top of his head,' continued the man, unstoppable now. 'He's got this mop of hair, see. A terrible mess actually. Cries out to be cut, or to have a comb run through it, but he won't listen. He was with this girl – rather attractive she was, in a slightly dark-skinned sort of way.'

A great deal of emphasis, simultaneously libidinous and disapproving, was laid on the word 'dark'.

'Rhodri, you say?' said Edmund.

'That's right. Rhodri Rees.'

'Does your Rhodri have any gypsy blood in him, Mr Rees?'

The man's attitude changed instantly. 'There are no gypsies in our family, young man. I can assure you of that.'

Edmund extended his right hand. He held it palm downwards, then rotated it slowly from the wrist.

The man looked on in surprise.

'What are you doing that for?'

'It's a secret hand-signal. I believe it means, "Help, my encampment is in danger."'

The man laughed. 'I don't think so.'

'I thought you said you didn't have any gypsy blood in you.'

'But that's nothing to do with gypsies. No, no, no. That's from the Highway Code. It means, "You are now safe to overtake, although always remember to do so with caution." I'm a driving instructor, you see. That's how I know.'

'Does your Rhodri have very pale hands by any chance, Mr Rees?'

'The hands of an angel,' said the man. 'Of an angel. Why, you'd think he'd never done a day's work in his life.'

'So you and your wife have never been run over by a dumper truck then?'

'I beg your pardon?'

'Nothing.'

Edmund pointed to the door he'd come through and told them how to reach the bar.

'I think you'll find him in there,' he said.

After they had gone Edmund sat on the floor. The world had changed; his world anyway. The world outside was changing too, but his world had altered for ever. It had moved from light into darkness. A new rage had come over him, deeper and darker than anything that had gone before. In future, this rage would sustain him. It would have to – there was nothing else left. He had laid his heart down and seen it trampled and squashed; he wouldn't make that mistake again. He'd looked to others to round him off, to plug his gaps. He wouldn't do that again either – not any more.

Outside in the car park, Edmund looked at the sky. Just the same flat grey heavens with the same disapproving eye squinting away. Then he looked back at the Roundhouse. Through the open doors, a few small fires could still be seen. Clouds of smoke blew across the railway tracks towards Primrose Hill. From down near Camden Lock came distant sounds of rioting.

Edmund climbed into his car and turned the key in the ignition. The engine coughed – once, twice – then caught. He put the car in gear, took hold of the square steering wheel and pulled away.

PART TWO
Lia

UK Press Gazette. *March 1977.*

CURTAINS FOR *QUEST*

Monthly magazine *Quest* – 'the laboratory of human sexual response' – is to close this month following steadily declining sales figures.

At its height in the late 60s and early 70s, the magazine sold almost 90,000 copies a month. But latterly circulation has fallen to a fraction of that amount. The format of readers' letters giving exhaustive accounts of their sexual experiences, alongside comments from a team of international sexologists, was innovative and daring in its day, but has begun to look increasingly stale, with other far more explicit magazines poaching its readership.

American Corky Montcalm, who founded *Quest*, and contributed a monthly column, 'Pan's Big Pipe', to the magazine, said that the decision had been taken with great reluctance. 'This is a sad day for England and for all pioneers of free love,' he commented.

Montcalm also ran the Nutkin Club, an offshoot of the magazine, in London's Shepherd Market. The club closed down earlier this year after several female employees – or 'Squirrels', as they were known – took him to court alleging contravention of employment laws and demanding full pension rights.

'It's been an extremely upsetting time for me,' Montcalm said. 'My family and I are moving back to the States. My wife is keen to research Amer-Indian potting techniques, while my daughter hopes to pursue a career in broadcasting. As for myself, I intend to devote myself to painting my increasingly popular Old Master copies. These are correct in every anatomical detail, although with additional humorous touches of my own.'

★

'Mr Crowe. Take a seat, do.'

Edmund sat down.

'I have studied your business proposal, Mr Crowe, and I'd be grateful if you could explain in a little more detail just what you want one of our new "Mini Mogul" start-up loans for.'

Edmund settled himself. 'What I am proposing is this,' he said. 'To manufacture and market a piece of rubber in the shape of a small tail, approximately five inches long, which one would attach to the back bumper of one's car.' He was aware that his voice sounded very dry; somehow this dryness seemed to have crept in everywhere.

After a pause the man behind the desk said, 'I see. At least I think I do. Go on, please.'

'This piece of rubber would come into contact with the road and would thereby earth the vehicle. As well as making the car safer in the event, say, of a lightning strike, it would also help alleviate the symptoms of car sickness by cutting down on the accumulation of static electricity.'

Edmund stopped. The man behind the desk was looking at him with his mouth open, as if his tooth had just become snagged on a piece of thread.

'And – and that's it?'

'I never claimed it was a complicated idea,' said Edmund. 'Its virtue lies in its simplicity.'

'But, Mr Crowe . . . forgive me. What makes you think that anyone would actually buy one of these things? The tyres of a car are also made of rubber, are they not? So the question of contact with the road surface surely doesn't arise. Not only that – if these rubber tails were hung from the back bumper of a car, wouldn't they simply flap about when the car started moving and lose contact with the tarmac? Besides, I've never seen any evidence that there are dangers attached to static electricity. Not in the sort of quantities we're talking about here.'

'People need to feel earthed,' said Edmund.

'I beg your pardon?'

'People need to feel earthed,' he repeated.

'Why is that?'

'They'll do anything to feel more secure.'

'It's certainly true that the last few years have been very tough. Very tough indeed in some cases. But, Mr Crowe, this is 1978, after all. I mean, just how gullible do you think people are?'

★

'Take me to Dulwich, will you, driver?'

'Which part of Dulwich?'

'What? Just drive me in the direction of Dulwich by any reasonable route and I'll tell you when we get nearer. I don't normally like catching mini-cabs. At least with a black cab you know that you're getting a reasonable degree of expertise. Can never find one at this time of night. Forced to take second-best. But a lot of you people don't really have a clue. I've had mini-cab drivers before who don't even know where Buckingham Palace is. You know where Buckingham Palace is, don't you, driver? Big house in the Mall, where the Queen lives. Marvellous woman. Marvellous children too. A lesson there for all of us. Oh, you're going this way, are you? Well, never mind. I daresay we'll get there in the end.'

The car stopped at traffic lights. There wasn't much traffic about – not at this hour of the morning. In the back seat the passenger sat with his arms extended on either side of him, braced against the windows. The back seat was not as securely fastened to the chassis as it might have been.

The lights turned to green.

The car didn't move.

Several more seconds went by.

Then the passenger leaned towards him and said, 'Snap to it, driver. We're free to go now.'

Just as he did so, the car leaped forward. The passenger was flung back into his seat, crying out in alarm. The seat in turn tipped over, sending the passenger's feet flying into the air and his head banging against the floor.

In the mirror, Barney watched this with satisfaction. It was little moments like these that made his life endurable.

★

'KPFW New York is delighted to announce the appointment of Lia Montcalm as its new radio therapist. Ms Montcalm is a graduate of the Human Sexuality Teaching program at Cornell Medical Center. Her father, artist Corky Montcalm, was the founder of *Quest* magazine, the legendary "laboratory of human sexual response".

'Lia says, "I hope that listeners will feel free to call me about any of their problems – however unusual or explicit. I am here to help, to give advice and to dispense practical solutions. It is paradoxical that, given the mass of sexually explicit material with which people are bombarded every day, a person with a real problem or question about sex may be hard pressed to find objective or trustworthy answers."'

★

Notice to be placed in all branches of Halfords motor accessory shops. March 1981.

DUE TO UNPRECEDENTED DEMAND, WE REGRET THAT WE HAVE TEMPORARILY RUN OUT OF RUBBER BUMPER TAILS. WE HOPE THAT NEW SUPPLIES WILL BE IN BY THE END OF NEXT WEEK. IN THE MEANTIME, CUSTOMERS WORRIED ABOUT THE BUILD-UP OF STATIC ELECTRICITY IN THEIR BODIES OVER THE COURSE OF A LONG CAR JOURNEY SHOULD CONSULT A DOCTOR BEFORE EMBARKING.

★

'Is there anything you feel you have an aptitude for, Mr Rees? Something that would suit your particular capabilities?'

Barney swung one leg over the other and gazed out of the window. The choice of insolent gestures open to him was limited.

For a start his chair had been bolted to the floor – either to stop thefts, or assaults. Assaults presumably; no one in their right mind would want to steal a chair like this.

'Let's have a look what's available, shall we? How about hod-carrying? Lots of fresh air, plenty of exercise . . .'

Increasingly, Barney felt as if a mistake had been made at a very fundamental level; some inadvertent mix-up which had led to him being given the wrong person's life. A person of low standing too, with very limited prospects.

'Now here's a very promising one. Ever worked with chickens, Mr Rees?'

What could he do to rectify this blunder? Barney wondered. Presumably someone would be along before too long – to sort it out, to apologize profusely and offer generous compensation. No doubt that would happen very soon. But in the meantime, it seemed, all he could do was wait.

*

'Hello, Lia. I'm Pete.'

'Hi there, Pete. How can I help?'

'I have a complicated problem.'

'Well, let's hear it then.'

'Lia – I think my wife is having an affair.'

'You do? What makes you think that, Pete?'

'When I have sex with her it's not the same as it used to be.'

'Are you saying she doesn't respond to you in the same way, Pete?'

'That's right! Normally when I go to bed and we, er, you know . . .'

'You make love.'

'Yuh. There's like this little thing that we do together. She gets stimulated and I, well, I make these noises.'

'What sort of noises, Pete?'

'Farmyard noises, Lia. I go, *Humph! Humph! Humph!*'

'You do? And then what happens?'

'Well, then she has an orgasm.'

'What, every time?'

153

'Sure. Why not?'

'You're a very lucky man, Pete. Do you know that?'

'But the thing is, it doesn't happen any more. That's why I think she must be having an affair.'

'Maybe she's just bored.'

'Bored? I don't understand you, Lia. How do you mean, bored?'

'Maybe she'd like a change, Pete. Have you thought of making any other noises?'

'Other noises? Jeez . . . That sounds a bit weird, frankly. Besides, I don't know any other noises.'

'Flexible thinking. That's the key here. Why don't you try watching some nature programmes on TV?'

'Oh, I really love those programmes. I watch them already.'

'Then why not listen to the mating calls the creatures make and try to imitate those?'

'You think that might work?'

'It might. You know what I always say, Pete, don't you?'

'Just remind me again, Lia.'

'If it feels right, then do it.'

'You really believe that, do you?'

'I really do, Pete. So good luck – and thanks for calling.'

*

Daily Mail. Financial Pages. October 1986.

TAILS OF THE UNEXPECTED

It all began in a bedsit in Finsbury Park. Bachelor Edmund Crowe, now 31, started selling his rubber car tails from his bedroom after everyone he approached refused to stock them. But after a slow start, demand has continued to grow and grow. In the last two years Crowe has made an estimated £1.5 million from the sales of tails alone. 'I've been very lucky,' he says. 'But fortunately this country is becoming more receptive to young entrepreneurs such as myself. Men and women with vision and determination,

154

who aren't hidebound by dogma and outdated business practices.'

Initially Crowe faced scepticism – even scorn – when he sought backing for his venture. Eventually he secured a £10,000 loan, enough to pay for the first consignment of tails. Finding anyone to stock them also proved an uphill struggle. But then came a series of newspaper reports claiming that build-up of static electricity in people's bodies over the course of a long journey could cause sickness – and in extreme cases death.

According to Crowe these reports were nothing more than 'a lucky concidence'. None the less, demand soon began to grow. 'I knew I had a product that could really catch on,' he says. 'It was just a matter of persuading people that they would have a safer and more relaxed motoring experience with a rubber tail fixed to the back of their vehicle.'

*

Police Gazette. *Announcement Section. February 1987.*

Congratulations to Desmond 'Des' Parnell and his wife Judy on the engagement of their daughter, Denise, to Mr Rhodri 'Barney' Rees. Des will be familiar to many of you: a respected dog-handler for many years, he was recently made Senior Animal Instructor at Hendon Police College. It's been said of Des that he's far more ferocious than any dog he's ever had to train! A fitness fanatic and total abstainer, Des is also a keen radio ham.

*

'Hi, Lia. Rick here.'

'Hi, Rick. What's your complicated problem?'

'I'm becoming increasingly attracted to my sister-in-law, Lia. And, you know, I think she is attracted to me too. But I'm finding it very difficult to keep it under control. Every weekend she comes over for dinner with me and my wife. And every weekend I find myself getting this, this big . . .'

'An erection, Rick?'

'Yeah, that's right. This massive boner. At the dinner table too. And it won't go away. I can't get up at the end of the meal for fear that everyone will see this kink in my pants. So I stay there for at least fifteen minutes. But then people ask me what I'm doing at the table by myself, so I've started eating very, very slowly. Like really timing my mouthfuls. But my wife – she's started to get suspicious. Not suspicious about me being horny for her sister. No, she's worried I might have like, you know, a, er, blockage.'

'How long have you been married, Rick?'

'Almost fourteen years now.'

'And your sister-in-law, is she married too?'

'She was married. Her husband was a longshoreman. Then he became a Moonie. But he lost his faith in the winter of 86 and now he sells novelty items.'

'You say you think she is attracted to you too?'

'I do, Lia. I really do.'

'OK, Rick. Now listen to me. You have to be very careful about this, where family is concerned. Talk to your wife. Explain the situation and ask for her advice. Be open with her. Be frank. And maybe she'll be cool about it. After all, you've been married for fourteen years, no wonder you want some variety. Where's the harm in a little variety? Remember what Blake said, "Sooner murder an infant in its cradle than nurse unacted desires."'

'Blake Carrington said that? Star of *Dynasty*?'

'No, Rick. William Blake, the poet.'

'I don't remember him.'

'Let me put it another way, Rick: if it feels right, then do it.'

'Oh . . . OK, Lia, thanks. That's really sorted my head out.'

'Goodbye, Rick. And good luck.'

★

Melody Maker. *May 1988.*

Blues for *bach*-heads

Welsh band T. *bach* have finally split following what are being described as irreconcilable creative differences. Formerly known as Thorazine *bach*, the band changed their name to try to find a younger fan base. But the change failed to have the desired effect, with steadily declining record sales and mounting audience indifference. Reggie Deakin, regarded as the creative powerhouse behind the band, has announced that he intends to pursue a solo career.

*

Financial Times. *November 1988.*

PET ROCK CRAZE SWEEPS UK

Stores all over the country are frantically trying to lay in supplies of Pet Rocks to cope with increased demand in the lead-up to Christmas. Business analysts continue to be astounded by the current craze, pointing out that the rocks in question are nothing more than pieces of granite with plaques attached on which owners can write the 'names' of their rocks. But they still sell for up to £20 each with demand continuing to outstrip supply.

The only person not taken aback by their success seems to be the man behind them, Edmund Crowe – also responsible for the rubber car tails phenomenon. In a rare statement, Crowe said, 'Everyone needs something to love – even if it is only a piece of rock.'

Following the success of his Pet Rocks, Crowe also intends to set up a number of related ventures. These will include a Pet Rock Summer School where owners can deposit their rocks when they go on holiday, a Pet Rock Sanatorium and a Pet Rock Insurance to protect their rocks against fire or theft.

*

Westchester Chronicle. *January 1991.*

Corky and Tinker Montcalm are delighted to announce the engagement of their daughter, Lia, to Rowdy Hepple of Amherst Avenue, W'chester, NY. Lia is a radio sex therapist in New York City, while her fiancé Rowdy is a sand and gravel supplier for the construction industry. Lia's father, Corky, needs no introduction, of course – a renowned Old Master copyist and humourist in oils, his work is highly sought after by collectors. His wife Tinker's pottery is also very popular among Westchester residents and available for purchase with generous discounts for bulk orders.

*

Helping Hands Model Agency Catalogue. Autumn 1993.

Model # 35. Barney Rees.

Barney has been with the agency for almost two years now, and his hands have been seen holding products such as electric razors, condiments and cutlery. At 36, Barney may be a little older than some of our other hand models; his hands, however, are in outstanding shape. Free from any signs of wear and tear, they have a natural grace and could easily belong to someone half his age. Barney is a bright, personable model with an outgoing personality and a light artistic bent.

*

'Hi, Lia.'

'Hi there. Who is this?'

'My name is Molly.'

'Hi there, Molly. What's your complicated problem?'

'It's my husband, Lia. He makes these . . . these terrible noises whenever we make love. At first, it was OK because he just used to make the one noise – kind of like a warthog at a waterhole. But then he started making these other animal noises. Honestly, Lia – you can't imagine. When I asked him what he was playing at, he said it was just for a little variety. So we carried on for a while with him a-brayin' and a-gibberin' away. But then – well, then I got to thinking that maybe I could use a little variety too.'

'OK. So where's the harm in that?'

'It's just that I don't think I can stand to be with him any more, Lia. Somehow this has made me want to explore my own sexuality. To try some of the other fish in the sea, if you know what I mean. But I feel held back in my marriage. Like it's become this strait-jacket to me.'

'Are you saying you want to leave your husband, Molly?'

'I just don't know . . . I wondered what you thought, Lia.'

'Well I think – I think you should do whatever you feel like doing, Molly. I mean, you've got to listen to your heart, haven't you?'

'Uh-huh. But this is more of a groin thing.'

'Never mind, Molly. The same rules apply.'

'They do? What? If it feels right, then do it. Isn't that what you always say?'

'That's exactly it, yes!'

'But what about the consequences?'

'Now you be true to yourself, Molly. That's the main thing – and just let those consequences take care of themselves.'

'Thanks, Lia. I feel a whole lot better now.'

★

Tatler. *June 1995.*

London's Most Eligible Bachelors

No. 27 – Edmund Crowe

With a personal fortune in excess of £12 million, Edmund Crowe represents a sizeable financial catch. As the man behind both the rubber car tails boom and the Pet Rock craze, Crowe has plainly taken to heart the old adage about no one going broke underestimating the taste of the public. Personally, though, he remains an enigma – remote and unapproachable and seldom seen in public. Said one dinner hostess, exasperated by Crowe's taciturn silences, 'It's like feeding a corpse, but less fulfilling.' A challenge certainly, but worth the effort?

Marks (out of 10) –
Financial status: 8
Mystery value: 5
Looks: 3.5
Pulling power: 4
Personality: Unquantifiable
Party animal: 0

*

Dressed in a white lab technician's coat, Barney stood in a studio scarcely bigger than a cupboard. A man appeared carrying a glass bottle the size of a small decanter and of a faintly familiar shape. He told Barney that he should stand holding the bottle up to the light, tilting it slightly, as if checking it for impurities. Then a second man appeared with a jug full of lemony liquid, which he poured down a spout into the bottle.

Although he couldn't say why exactly, Barney began to feel uneasy.

'Wait a minute,' he said. 'What's this?'

'That? It's a specimen bottle. This is an advert for a medical supplies catalogue. Weren't you told before?'

'No,' said Barney, 'I wasn't told that.'

'Would it have made any difference?'

Would it? Barney wondered. Had he sunk so low as this? Modelling specimen bottles for a medical supplies magazine? Aye, that was low, all right. What had gone wrong? Why hadn't anyone come along to put him back on track, to take all his woes away? Had they been held up along the way? But how could anyone be held up for this long? Surely they must arrive soon?

'Let's not hang about,' said the second man. 'We're on a tight budget. Are you ready?'

Unless, of course, they were never coming.

'Are you ready?'

'Yes,' said Barney. 'I'm all ready now.'

★

'Hello, Lia. My name is Claudette.'

'Hi, Claudette. Let me hear that complicated problem.'

'I have what I guess is more of a problem of conscience than anything else. I'm a divorced woman. My husband – he was a Moonie, but he lost his faith in the winter of 87. A few years ago now, my brother-in-law, well, he made a pass at me. You can imagine how upsetting that was for me. And afterwards I had . . . I suppose strictly speaking you'd have to classify it as a breakdown.'

'I'm sorry to hear that Claudette.'

'Yes. After I was released from hospital, I started to question my own personality. Also my own sexuality. I found I had these . . . these desires. I must say I was quite shocked by how strong they are.'

'What kind of desires, Claudette.'

'Lesbian desires, Lia. That's what they are. I haven't acted on them, you understand. Not so far. But recently I met this other woman. She's a divorcée too, like me. Been through a very tough time. She left her husband after he started making these – well, these disgusting noises. Anyway, I found myself feeling very attracted to her.'

'But that's great, Claudette.'

'I don't know, Lia . . . The thing is, I worry about having a relapse. The doctor said I was mentally very fragile, you know, and I had to steer clear of anything that was too stressful, or potentially disturbing to me. So what I'm wondering, I guess, is should I risk my equilibrium by giving in to these desires?'

'It's not a matter of giving in to those desires, Claudette. That's really not a helpful way of looking at them. No, it's more as if those desires express the real you. And to deny them is to cut off a very vital and fundamental part of yourself. So my advice would be, don't bottle them up. Take that stopper out – do you hear me now, Claudette? Go and join the party!'

★

Wall Street Journal. *March 1996.*

PET ROCK KING TO EXPAND

Edmund Crowe, the man behind the late 80s Pet Rock craze, as well as the rubber car tails phenomenon, has announced that he is to set up an office in New York. Mr Crowe, 40, says that while he will keep charge of his British interests, he intends to expand into the US market.

Renowned as a prime exponent of 'pure salesmanship', Crowe has already diversified into a number of different areas, including travel and condiments. But as Crowe has become steadily more successful, so the number of complaints about his management style have increased. Crowe was the subject of litigation from former employees in Britain alleging unreasonable behaviour, including random withdrawal of sickness benefits.

★

Barney stood and watched his father-in-law fiddle with various dials on his radio set. As he did so, there was a crackle. Then voices began to talk hurriedly in a language Barney did not understand. When the dial was turned, the voices disappeared and were followed by a further outbreak of crackling.

'You can talk to anyone anywhere in the world from here, you know.'

Barney struggled to show an interest. It was bad enough listening to his father-in-law's theories on police dog sterilization. That he should also be a radio ham struck him as being unnecessarily harsh.

He looked with distaste at the dank little shed with its banks of radio equipment, some in green metallic casing, some in khaki. Once again the dial was given another fractional turn.

Then, from out of the speaker, a male voice said quite clearly, 'I've got an Edwin for you.'

'Hello, Edwin,' said another voice – female this time. 'And what's your complicated problem?'

'Anyway, Barney,' said his father-in-law, 'you get the general idea.' His fingers reached for the off switch.

'Just leave it a moment, will you?' said Barney.

'See. I told you how interesting it was.'

'Are you still there, Edwin?' came the voice again.

'. . . Yes.'

'Oh, I thought we'd been cut off. How can I help you? Take your time.'

'Many years ago . . .' said the male voice '. . . many years ago now, I fell in love with this girl. When we were both very young. Our relationship didn't go on for long. Not long at all, in fact. But I've never been able to forget her, or to get her out of my mind. It's ridiculous, I know, but there it is. And I just wish . . .'

'What do you wish for, Edwin?'

'I wish my heart didn't feel so dark. So damaged.'

'Have you had relationships since then?'

'Only . . . Nothing of any importance.'

'And this girl, was she in love with you?'

'Maybe. At least I thought so. Once. But now I think I was just fooling myself. People do, don't they? All the time; they cling to these illusions. I always had this stupid idea that – that if she and I could lie in a wild-flower meadow somewhere, then everything would be all right.'

'I see . . . That's certainly romantic.'

'So what do you think I should do then?'

'I think you should try to see this girl, Edwin. Talk to her and explain how you feel. Then, who knows – maybe you'll be able to move on.'

'But what if she doesn't want to see me?'

'Well, perhaps you can manufacture a set of circumstances where you come into contact with her? Edwin? Can you still hear me?'

There was silence in the hut. Barney leant forward towards the radio set. He thought the signal must have faded, or drifted away. But then the woman's voice came again, a lot fainter this time, 'I'm sorry Edwin . . . I think I've lost you.'

★

Village Voice. *Arts Section. March 1999.*

REVIEW OF OLD FRIENDS/NEW FRIENDS: AN EXHIBITION OF PAINTINGS BY CORKY MONTCALM

This latest batch of paintings by the indefatigable Montcalm, self-appointed leader of the 'Pubist School', once again takes as its starting point Old Master nudes. But in characteristic fashion, Montcalm has added a number of what he terms his 'Corky configurations', subtle amendments to the originals, such as a squirrel here and a yachting cap there. The effect is both witty and revealing, offering a new perspective on well-known works, but also posing unsettling questions about ideas of completeness and contamination.

★

'It's Pete here, Lia.'

'Hi, Pete. And what's your complicated problem?'

'Don't you remember me, Lia?'

'Well, I get a lot of calls, Pete.'

'It's just that I called you a long time ago and asked your advice about my sister-in-law. You said I should talk to my wife about it and ask if she'd mind if I made a move on her. So I did.'

'And what happened Pete?'

'Bitch threw me out. Took the kids with her too. I'm on my own now – have been for quite a while, in fact. You know, I used to linger over my food because I had such a big boner, but now I do it because I don't have anywhere else to go. Except I visit this Divorced Men's Club once a week. Which is where I met this . . . this other man.'

'And you and he are having a relationship? That's terrific –'

'Hold on. I haven't finished yet. This other guy, most of the time he doesn't make a lot of sense. He just sits there making these kind of weird noises. But from what I could understand, he also called you up. To ask your advice. And now he's in as bad – in an even worse state than me.'

'So what's your question, Pete?'

'What I want to know is what gives you the right to pronounce on other people's lives? You don't know jack shit. It's like you're reciting from some manual of how you think people ought to behave, but you have no idea of how they feel or operate. All you do is go round making people even more screwed up than they were before.'

'Now, Pete, I'm sure you've heard the legal disclaimer we broadcast every week.'

'I don't want to sue anybody. I just want an explanation, that's all . . . Come on then. I'm listening.'

'I'm going to have to let you go, Pete. We've got literally hundreds of people waiting. I can't spend all my time talking to one caller. So goodbye, Pete. And good luck!'

*

Barney had begun to think that he was being followed. Although that was bad enough, there was worse to come. He strongly suspected that whoever – whatever – was following him was not necessarily of human extraction. Several times now he had heard as well as half seen this dark, lumbering shape hanging about at the end of his shadow. These clattery footsteps too, scratching away behind him wherever he went. His pursuer's appearance was far from clear. Yet an impression persisted of grey silvery skin with an unusual sheen to it, like the nap on a piece of velvet. He thought he saw whiskers too. Long and straight and thick as conductors' batons. Clattery footsteps . . . silvery skin . . . priapic whiskers . . . Abruptly, it came to Barney that he was being followed by a giant rat.

*

Lyndhurst Bugle. *October 2000.*

At an acrimonious meeting last Tuesday, local residents complained about the proposed improvements to Burcombe Grange. They claimed that these will be an eyesore and out of keeping with the tone of the New Forest. The new owner, 'Pet Rock King' Edmund Crowe, has announced that he intends to install a twelve-foot-perimeter fence around the property, topped with razor-wire. Other 'improvements' include installation of a helipad, a swimming pool and a specially created wild-flower meadow. Built in the 1880s in the then popular Victorian Gothic style, the house has been derelict for a number of years. Residents lambasted Crowe's attitude as 'arrogant and unhelpful'. Another meeting is scheduled to take place once final plans have been submitted.

*

Behind a small curtain Barney sat on a stool and waited. Today, he was advertising a new brand of hot sauce. The skin on his hand had been stained brown. Barney – or his hand – was playing the part of an old sheriff, soon to be toppled by a young ranchero with asbestos tonsils, newly arrived in town. Every so often a shout would come from the other side of the curtain, 'Activate the hand!'

As instructed, Barney would tip the bottle and start to pour the hot sauce on to the bowl of painted mush below. But it wasn't long before they hit problems. The hot sauce seemed to have developed a mind of its own. Again and again Barney tried. Yet all the time these tremors ran down his arm and sent long squiggles of sauce looping all over the floor. Little nerves twanging away. There had even been talk of hiring someone else to take his place. However, no one suitable was available; only the agency's hairier hands, normally used for advertising power tools and agricultural machinery.

'How was that?' Barney called out from behind his curtain.

'Terrible,' came the reply. 'Worse than before even.'

Barney felt sick, unsteady, not himself. At four o'clock, they stopped for tea. The director went into a huddle with his assistants. Barney sat on his stool and listened to them talking their stupid purposeless talk in low intense voices. Indecision was the only thing these people had any aptitude for; they hummed and hawed away like violinists.

After he'd finished his cup of tea, he stood up and walked towards them – to say that he felt better now and it was worth trying again. But when he was only a few feet away, he heard the director cry out in exasperation, 'How can I be expected to work with some buffoon with the shakes?'

Barney stopped. 'Shakes?' he said. 'What are you talking about? I haven't got the shakes.'

The director span round. 'Oh yes you have, chum. We're lodging a formal complaint about you. Won't be the first either – not from what I gather. You're a hand model with the shakes. That's no fucking use to anybody. We're letting you go.'

'Letting me go?'

'That right. Still, we don't want to be cruel about it – we'll pay you for today. Can't say fairer than that.'

Barney shut his eyes. Make him go away, he begged. Not just him, but the whole damn lot of them. Let a great broom come and sweep it all away. Bring on some endless black nothingness for a change.

But when he opened his eyes again he saw that everything was exactly the same as before.

'Could I have the money now?' he asked.

'What? Right now? I don't know about that. But don't you worry matey. I'll make sure it's sent to your home address.'

'It's just that I'm between addresses at present,' Barney explained. 'And I'd much rather pick it up in person, if –' Barney broke off and lowered his gaze to the floor, ' – if that's possible,' he said.

★

Police Gazette. *May 2001.*

We very much regret to announce the death of Desmond 'Des' Parnell, legendary Metropolitan Police dog handler, who died of a heart attack on 28 April. Beloved husband of Judy and doting father to Denise. As everyone who knew him can readily affirm Des was as devoted to police work as he was to his dogs. A man who placed a high premium on obedience in all walks of life, Des was often a controversial figure in the force – a visionary with ideas far in advance of his time.

His insistence on working with sterilized animals brought him into open conflict with superior officers at the commencement of his career. Neutering was something of an obsession with Des, and it led to his being derided for several years. Now, of course, it is general practice throughout the police dog world. A keen radio ham and keep-fit enthusiast, Des was known to have been depressed about the recent collapse of his daughter Denise's marriage. This strain is thought to have been a major contributory factor to his seizure.

★

'Hi, Lia. It's Molly here. Molly Sheen. I spoke to you some time ago about my complicated problem. Since then it's gotten even more complicated. Several years ago I left my husband, after he began making persistent animal noises, and decided to explore the singles scene. This I proceeded to do, deriving, I may say, a great deal of personal satisfaction from the experience. For a while I even had this lesbian affair with this other divorcée I met. A very warm and sensitive lady, if a little highly strung. But tragically, she suffered a relapse and had to be whisked away to a strap-down facility. Anyway, the thing is, Lia, I've met this man recently and we've really hit it off. First of all, it was purely a sexual thing. But sex like I've never experienced before! And now he's asked me to go away with him and start a new life in Alaska.'

'That's great, Molly. Well done you.'

'There's one catch, though. He's married.'

'I see. Did he tell you he was married?'

'Oh sure. He's very open, very straightforward. Frankly, I think his wife doesn't pay him enough attention. She sounds like one of those post-feminist media types. You know, always convinced that she knows best about everything. I think he feels emasculated by her.'

'So what are you going to do, Molly?'

'I just don't know! That's why I'm calling. "If it feels right, then do it" – that's what you always say, isn't it?'

'. . . That's what I used to say, Molly. I don't say it quite so much any more.'

'But you've got to take happiness when it's offered, haven't you, Lia? I mean, otherwise it can just slip away.'

'I . . . I guess you have.'

'That's right, Lia. You've got to live.'

*

Newcastle Evening Post. *June 2001.*

Durham police last night confirmed they are hunting felon Omar Montcalm, 28, who escaped from Durham Prison on Tuesday afternoon. Montcalm, who was serving a five-year sentence for arson and aggravated burglary, escaped while being taken to court to face a number of charges of assault on prison staff. After clubbing his guards unconscious, Montcalm then removed his handcuffs with an axe.

'This man is desperate as well as dangerous,' said a police spokesman. 'Under no circumstances should he be approached by members of the public.' He has a distinct tattoo on his left forearm consisting of the single word 'Discontent'.

★

Dear Mrs Lia Hepple, née Montcalm,

You asked us to look into your financial affairs, following the recent departure of your husband, Rowdy, from your marital home. I have to tell you that the news is not good. My understanding is that he has moved to Alaska with a divorced woman called Molly Sheen. However, he left no forwarding address, or record of his whereabouts. In his continued absence, and having closed his sole bank account prior to his departure, all his financial responsibilities revert to you.

These responsibilities, I regret to say, are considerable. As the house was in your joint names, you are now responsible for the payment of the mortgage. In addition, his gravel business has been running a considerable loss for a number of years, with consequent mounting debts. These debts also pass to you, through the joint account.

Furthermore, several court orders for late payments are outstanding – these should be settled without delay. Then there is the question of his taxes. I can find no record of any payment to the IRS within the last five years. If this is the case then we can expect further demands, along with accompanying late-payment liabilities.

We look forward to continuing to act for you in this matter. I understand you are planning to settle back in England in the near future and thus take the liberty of enclosing a bill for our services to date in expectation of prompt payment.

Yours sincerely,
Samuel Westbrook
Westbrook Attorneys
Westchester County

★

Lyndhurst Bugle. *September 2001.*

Owner Edmund Crowe has announced he intends to change the name of his house, Burcombe Grange. In future the house is to be known as 'Hope Springs'. No explanation was given for the change of name. The various building works and improvements are still ongoing.

★

The private detective was waiting in the café as arranged. He didn't look much like a private detective, Lia thought. More like a bank clerk with a gambling habit. He was drinking a milkshake through an unusually thick straw.

She sat down opposite him. 'Have you got some news for me?' she asked.

The private detective took his time unfastening his mouth from the straw.

'We've found him,' he said eventually.

'You have? How?'

'Ah, now that's the strange part. We were contacted ourselves. By someone who thought you would like to know where he was, but who wished to remain anonymous.'

'I wonder who that could be.'

'No idea.'

'And how is he?'

'To be honest, we don't know. In fact, that's the other strange part. What I mean is, we don't know for sure if he's there voluntarily, or –'

'Or what?' asked Lia.

Already the private detective had bent his head back towards his milkshake, his lips jutting forward in anticipation.

'Or being held against his will,' he said.

★

When it grew dark, Barney drove his car to a place under the Westway. He felt relatively safe beneath the giant concrete arches that held the road up. Safe from tempest, thunder, elemental discharge, or whatever else might rain down on his head.

Inside his wallet there was a £20 note along with almost £5 in change. Together with the money in his bank account, this made his total assets £287. That was it, apart from his car, which wasn't fit for anything other than scrap. The bodywork was worn right through in several places; a row of rubber tails hung limply from the back bumper. So much for warding off disaster. Fat lot of good they'd been. He had no home. No prospects. Nothing. All these years he had been waiting for someone to roll up and help him. But no one was coming – not any more. He knew that. What am I to do? he thought. What am I to do? I am completely fucked.

Barney spread sheets of newspaper over himself to keep warm and tilted his seat back to its furthest extremity. But he couldn't sleep, no matter how hard he tried. He picked up the topmost sheet of newspaper. It was one of the financial pages. The information meant nothing – just unfamiliar names and rows of meaningless figures.

He turned it over and found more of the same. Only this time there was a single photograph at the top of the page. Barney looked at the photograph, then at the caption below: 'Despite objections, petitions and the threat of sabotage from neighbours, work on Pet Rock King, Edmund Crowe's house, Hope Springs, in the New Forest, has finally been completed. Bachelor Crowe's business empire now includes car accessories, electrical goods, provincial newspapers, three publishing houses, two cable television channels and a travel company.'

Screwing the paper up in his hand, Barney opened the car door and hurled it as far away from him as he could. After that he did sleep, lulled into troubled slumber by the traffic roar from overhead.

But when he stepped outside in the morning, he saw that the wind had blown the sheet of newspaper back beside his feet.

★

White sheets covered the furniture. Dust had settled on the sheets and on the polished floors. It had settled in the folds of the curtains, along the window ledges and the radiators and on top of the chandeliers. Everything was new. Everything was unused. No meals had ever been cooked in the kitchen. The chairs had never been sat on. The curtains never drawn. The pictures never looked at. The beds never slept in. The baths never run. Nothing had been touched.

★

Mojo. September 2002.

Welsh prog rockers Thorazine *bach* have announced that they are re-forming. *bach*, as they were known to fans, had a cult following in the 1970s enjoying modest chart success with their concept album, *Arthur's Seat*. Following an unsuccessful name change to T. *bach*, the band split up in 1988. Frontman Reggie Deakin's solo career did not take off as hoped. His long-awaited solo album, *Blessed Arctic Sunchild*, sold so few copies that surplus stock was used as landfill on a number of construction projects.

Said a spokesman: 'The band lost a bit of impetus in the 1980s. But after an extended rest, they have rediscovered all their old enthusiasm.' The spokesman denied that this was a desperate money-making venture. 'No way is this a cynical move. Absolutely not. The boys feel they still have a tremendous amount left to offer.'

★

PART THREE

Barney

19

Hope Springs

Although the rest of the coach was full, the seat beside Barney remained empty. He had done his best to make sure it stayed that way by letting the top half of his body loll over the armrest while poking his tongue into the cavity between his teeth and his lower lip, thereby giving the impression that he had something large and inappropriate secreted within.

Periodically, Barney would move his lips about, as if in response to another pair of lips – invisible to everyone but himself – which were whispering elaborately lurid suggestions into his ear. Only by swivelling his left eye to its most outward extreme while keeping his right staring fixedly in front of him was he able to savour the looks of alarm from the other passengers – mainly made up of a large party of pensioners – as they hurried to look for seats elsewhere.

Then, just as the doors were shutting and Barney was congratulating himself on a job well done, one last passenger had got on. A pale, intense-looking child with braided hair and a scattering of freckles round the bridge of her nose. She moved purposefully down the aisle. It was too late for Barney to stick his former expression back in place. Without showing any signs of alarm – without, it seemed, registering his presence in any way – the girl sat down beside him.

Almost instantly, the coach started up. Motor churning, it nosed its way slowly out into Belgrave Road and headed down towards the river, picking up speed.

Beside him, the girl had started to read a book. There was something about her that Barney found disturbing. Perhaps it was her self-possession; he'd never cared for that in anyone apart from himself. At the same time he found himself unusually eager for distraction. To begin with he put on his headphones and listened to a selection of once-snarling subversives sobbing their way through a series of lushly orchestrated ballads. But this just depressed him further.

Taking off his headphones, Barney asked the girl what her book was about. At first she took no notice of him. He had to repeat his question. Whereupon she put the book down and said in a piping voice, 'It's about a harmonious couple whose idyllic life together is disrupted by the arrival of . . .' here she paused, as if for effect '. . . a wastrel.'

'. . . I see.'

'And what about you?' the girl asked. 'Are you a married man?'

'I was,' said Barney. 'Once.'

'What happened?'

'That's a long story.'

'Did something go wrong?'

'You could say . . . Mind your own business,' he said.

'Was your heart untrue? Or did you perhaps love someone else instead?'

'Look, just back off, OK?'

'I can see these things, you know. It's a gift.'

'Shut up,' said Barney.

'What did you say?'

'Shut up and read your fucking book.'

One of the pensioners – a woman – was making her way down the aisle. The girl touched her on the arm as she passed.

The woman stopped.

'Is everything all right, dear?'

'No,' said the girl. 'No, it isn't.'

'Oh dear. What's the matter?'

'This man told me to fuck off.'

'He never!'

'And I'm only ten, you know.' Wistfully, she repeated herself. 'Ten years old. This is my first time travelling alone.'

'But I assumed he was your father.'

'Him? He's not fit to be anyone's father.'

'Shame on you!' said the pensioner turning to Barney with a face full of reproach.

Barney stood up and pushed his way past them to the toilet. After fighting briefly with the toilet door, which hinged in such a manner that it could most effectively be opened by a horizontal blow from the head, he locked it gratefully behind him.

Unzipping his trousers and bending his knees to brace himself, Barney peed into the steel bowl. Even his urine looked somehow puny today; both in volume – no more than a small animal might manage after a brisk run on a hot afternoon – and in colour too: a watery malarial mustard. When he had finished he pushed the flush. A panel in the bottom of the steel bowl shot back and with a roar his puddle of urine disappeared, chased away by swirls of blue disinfectant.

Barney found himself sad to see it go. The strip light above the mirror was unforgiving. It aged him, gave his skin a flimsy, washed-out appearance. There no longer appeared to be enough blood going round in his system; the blue disinfectant seemed to have got in there instead.

When he returned the last few houses and light industrial units were disappearing, giving way to fields and hedgerows and long lines of flimsy trees bent over drainage ditches. Barney shut his eyes. But it made no difference; waves of misgivings continued bearing down on him in what looked very much like attack formation. He must try to stay calm – no matter how forcefully circumstances were trying to take his last few shreds of calmness away.

The trouble was that he had no idea what to think about. He didn't want to think about the past – certainly not. Nor did he have the slightest wish to think about the future. That only left the present. For all sorts of obvious reasons, he didn't want to think about this either.

Perhaps he dozed off – he couldn't be sure. All he knew was that when he opened his eyes, the coach had stopped at a junction. The note of its engine had dropped to a low shuddering rumble. By the side of the road was a large billboard. On it were two enormous pale hands, held open to greet all-comers. These hands stuck out of two cuffs; each ringed by the shadow of a sleeve.

Staring incuriously at the hoarding, Barney saw that the cufflinks bore the logo of a credit card company. Behind them was another, much larger, version of the logo. This larger logo was like a rising sun – a great burst of turquoise light.

He leant forward to look more closely.

However, it wasn't the logo that had caught his attention. It was the hands. He kept staring at them: at the alabaster sheen of the skin; the huge buffed nails; the cylindrical fingers as thick as pillars.

Then he stared at his own hands.

Now he saw it. The distinctive white moons at the base of his fingernails . . . The familiar pattern of whorls and ridges on the fingertips . . . They were the same! His own hands! Photographed, blown up, and held open to greet allcomers. Oh, this was unnecessarily harsh.

Barney reared back in his seat. He felt very frightened.

Ahead of him the road curved around the base of a small hill then re-emerged briefly, before taking a sharp right-hand bend into an unusually thick clump of bracken. According to his map Barney was now entering 'The New Forest' – an area that appeared to be characterized by a total absence of trees. Instead, the whole landscape was covered in bracken. In places, this bracken was crowned with bright purple flowers. In others, it was charred – presumably as a result of forest fires. Occasionally he passed rows of wooden brooms that had been provided for people to extinguish their forest fires – or else fan them into life.

The coach had dropped him off five miles short of his destination. In theory there was a local bus that would take him the rest of the way. In practice, though, as he had discovered, this bus ran only at weekly intervals. There was nothing else for him to do but start walking.

A few narrow-backed ponies grazed unconcernedly by the side

of the road. Above his head the sky was streaked with vermilion and Lincoln green, like a side of condemned bacon. He passed few houses. Those there were tended to be hidden down long lanes and had a carefully tended ramshackle look to them.

Slowly, the light began to fade. The temperature too was dropping. Soon it was only just possible to make out the road, a pale ribbon of tarmac disappearing off into the gathering darkness. Few cars went by; they paid no attention to Barney's outstretched hand. What possessions he had were in an old canvas bag. His feet were growing increasingly sore. At every step his shoes gave off a moist flapping sound, as if a tongue of material had become detached inside.

It was while Barney was bending down to see just how damaged they were that he smelled woodsmoke. Woodsmoke meant fire. Fire in turn might mean people.

He walked on.

He passed a sign to something called 'Drucilla's Private Zoo', and then, a mile or so later, entered a village. The village was set in a long, low valley. There were houses now on either side of the road. Mainly cottages, each with thatched roofs, low overhanging eaves and lights burning behind diamond-paned windows.

Despite his best efforts, Barney found himself thinking that it was like a vision of paradise from a children's book. Everything was so verdant, so manicured, so perfect – albeit with a brittle quality to its perfection, as if it could all be swept away in an instant. He felt that he had no business being in such a place. That he didn't belong here. As if he was simultaneously both invisible and a blot on the landscape.

Yet when Barney looked more closely, he saw that this wasn't really like paradise at all. In fact, it looked strangely suburban. There were four-wheel-drive vehicles parked outside each of the cottages, shining with a showroom sparkle. As for the houses themselves, they'd been spruced up in a manner that reminded him of the way in which hairdressers would once hold their hands over customers' heads after cutting their hair to make sure that everything was 'just so'.

Everything here was 'just so'. And yet at the same time it wasn't 'just so' at all. Several of these cottages had extensions built on to them – ill-fitting bits and pieces that looked as if they had been hacked off Moorish palaces, or Russian basilicas, or Turkish knocking shops. All painted in unnecessarily garish colours.

Their gardens too had been transformed with a similar disregard for taste or decency. Here again 'influences' had been drawn haphazardly from around the globe: Persian fountains, Japanese gravel that glinted like crystallized porridge oats, Balinese nuptial chambers constructed out of tin ducting and old tractor tyres.

Although not normally one to pay much attention to his surroundings, the utter unrepentant nastiness of it all struck Barney with some force. Television was responsible, he thought bitterly. Television had encouraged people to bugger up their surroundings in such a manner. His heart swelled with anger and jealousy. He could have done this; he felt sure that he could. He could have excelled at just this sort of buggering-up. All you needed was the doodling abilities of an average four-year-old, combined with an abnormally high opinion of yourself. On the first of these at least he couldn't be faulted. As for the second . . . well, once, of course. Very much so. But not so much any more.

In the middle of the village was a green, cordoned off with lengths of chain. On the far side of the green was a pub. Realizing that he needed a drink quite badly, Barney headed for the front door. It was very low. He had to stoop to go through. Inside, it was much as he had feared: absurdly low ceilings and pointless inglenooks. Like the houses outside, this too looked peculiarly contrived. Not so much the real thing as a semi-authentic re-creation of the real thing that had come in kit-form.

Some of these inglenooks had fruit machines in them, but not very many. The rest were crammed with witches'-coven furniture and hung with old farm implements. Why was it that England took such pride in its ancestral crones and yokels, he wondered, when most of them had either been drowned on ducking stools, or driven into workhouses?

The few customers moved about, half-crouched, their necks parallel to the floor.

'What will it be then?' asked the barman. He had a ruddy face and a gaping mouth that made him look as if he was about to catch a tennis ball in his teeth. Pinned on to the breast pocket of his short-sleeved shirt was a sign that read 'Kenneth'.

'Give me a pint of beer,' Barney told him affably enough.

'Passing through, are you?' the barman asked once the drink had been poured and set down. 'Stranger in these parts?'

Barney grunted by way of reply. He found he had formed an instant but hearty dislike of this barman. But he also found himself in the awkward position of not exactly wanting company, while not exactly not wanting it either. As a kind of compromise, he stared into his glass while his hands writhed pointlessly about in front of him. Sometimes, it seemed to him that his hands were trying to tell him something; sending out all manner of frantic messages. But whatever they were he couldn't tell. It was like watching a folk-dancing display in a foreign country of whose culture and traditions he knew nothing.

There was only one other person at the bar – a small, melancholy-looking man who sat on a stool in an attitude of coiled dejection. At any moment, it seemed, he might spring, infuriated, into the air like a little bantam cock. But for the time being, he just sat and drank.

'In fact,' Barney said to the barman, 'it's possible you might be able to help me. I'm looking for Edmund Crowe's house.'

The barman's mouth opened even more widely than before. 'Edmund Crowe?' he said.

'Yes, I believe he lives here.'

'Well, he has a house near by. What do you want to go there for?'

Desperation, Barney might have answered. Desperation and undeserved misfortune have brought me to this pass. Instead he said, 'I just do, that's all. Can you tell me where it is?'

'I think I could. Of course, Mr Algernon could tell you more precisely.'

'Who the hell's Mr Algernon?'

The barman nodded at the morose-looking man on the stool and lowered his voice. 'That's him. He's the butler for the Crowe household. Except he doesn't like to talk much – not when he's in his cups.'

Barney looked across at the butler, now throwing back his drink with a hectic fling of the wrist. 'Is he ever out of them?' he asked.

'Mmm. Mornings mostly. You'll find Mr Crowe's none too popular in these parts.'

'Why's that then?'

'He's made that house into even more of an eyesore than it was before. Then he built that fence and those security gates. Very arrogant, he is. Very stuck up. A lot of people here would like to give him a piece of their minds, believe me.'

After giving him directions to Edmund's house, the barman wished him goodnight. Outside, the moon was up. It looked un-usually low tonight, sending long, liverish rays slanting down over the thatched cottages with their ludicrous extensions and their debauched gardens.

Barney walked back across the green, over a bridge that crossed a stream and up a gravel drive with paling fencing on either side. The drive was much longer than he had anticipated. It seemed to go on for miles.

Feeling very tired, he flapped along, his shoes giving out louder, more disintegrating, noises than before. At the same time he heard – or thought he heard – these scratchy footsteps, following him up the gravel drive, lumbering along in his wake. He turned round, looking back down the drive and across the swell of darkened hills beyond.

Nothing.

Just when he thought that he couldn't be on the right road, that the idiot barman had given him faulty directions, he saw a white notice up ahead. It loomed out of the gathering darkness: HOPE SPRINGS. PRIVATE PROPERTY. KEEP OUT.

Beyond the sign were two stone gateposts, one on either side of a gravel drive. Between them was a set of gates – tall and topped with spikes. On either side of the gateposts, a high fence stretched away into the darkness. Set into the right-hand gatepost was the grille of an intercom with a button beside it. Barney was struck by the fact that the intercom looked brand new. Almost unused. He couldn't see the house beyond. Only a high wall and dark chimneys jutting above the trees on the other side of the gate.

He pressed the button.

Nothing happened.

He pressed it again.

This time an electronic crackle burst from the speaker.

After it had faded away a voice said, 'Who's there?'

Putting his lips very close to the grille, Barney said, 'My name is Barney Rees.'

'What do you want?'

'I've come to see Edmund Crowe.'

More crackling.

Then came a new voice – female this time.

'Not here,' it said.

'Not here?' repeated Barney.

It was the one possibility he had never even considered.

'Well, where is he then?'

'Not here,' repeated the voice.

'But when will he be back?'

'Not back . . . Never been here.'

Barney leant against the gatepost. He thought he might faint.

'You mean . . . you're telling me that Edmund Crowe has never been here?'

'Never,' confirmed the voice.

'But this is his house?'

'Correct.'

'So where is he then?'

'Don't know.'

'But – what am I supposed to do?' Barney asked.

'Not here,' said the voice again, and disappeared.

For the third time, Barney pressed the buzzer. But this time there was nothing. Nothing except a shush of static. Soon even this faded away.

It had grown very cold.

Barney began to shiver.

20

The Stars Look Down

Shortly before midnight the telephone rang. The housekeeper took the call. Immediately she summoned the private secretary, who then tried – unsuccessfully – to rouse the butler, Mr Algernon, who had returned to the house in an even worse mood than usual that evening and gone straight to bed. By the time the telephone call was over, the housekeeper had turned very pale. So had the private secretary. They were in a state of shock. Briefly, they clasped on to one another for support.

Despite the lateness of the hour, a meeting of the domestic staff was called – it was decided not to rouse the gardening staff; they could wait until the morning. At the meeting astonishment was expressed, followed by resentment. Finally, a glum resignation took hold of everyone present. They all agreed this was the worst, the most unexpected thing, that could possibly have happened.

Then they went to work.

Barney lay down in the bracken and did his best to make himself comfortable. His position in the lee of a large rock was the most secluded he had been able to find. But once he was lying down it proved even more uncomfortable than he had anticipated. What he'd hoped was a spongy dip turned out to be a shallow trench lined with pebbles and the crunchy carcasses of small animals. He wanted to cry, but he didn't dare. Like a camel whose hump is running dangerously low, he had to conserve his liquids.

Above his head, Barney could see stars. Not many – just a few of the brighter ones shining through the wash of cloud. They weren't twinkling benignly as they did in picture books – just glinting indifferently away, as if they couldn't care less about him.

Exhaustion and disbelief chased themselves round his system. Why is this happening to me? he kept wondering. Idly, despairingly, he sent his question marks twirling up into the night sky. But no reply was forthcoming. Maybe it will all be different in the morning, he kept telling himself. Maybe . . . And with this thought wedged as close to the front of his brain as he could possibly keep it, Barney slid into sleep.

He awoke to find that he had been bitten during the night. His arms and several inaccessible parts of his back itched. Gingerly, he touched his face. It appeared to be much bigger than usual. Likewise his hands; his fingers were all swollen; his wrists unnaturally thick. And all over his skin, the same tiny weals.

He was also very wet, he realized. Far from protecting him from moisture, the rock he had lain beside seemed – if anything – to have attracted it, like those packets of silica gel you found in camera cases and were warned never to eat.

Lying in his sodden trench, he scratched himself as best as he could and gave several experimental groans until he found one that suited his predicament best. Then he forced himself to stand up. He looked out across the low hills, each topped with fringes of heather, or bracken, or both. The cloud was unusually thick this morning, laid on in a kind of careless paste. He gave another groan, completely unforced and emerging from some deeper, darker part of him than all the others.

Barney looked inside his wallet. He now had exactly six pounds left. That, he calculated, might last him one more day at a pinch, if he decided to do without food and take his nutrients in liquid form.

What then?

Then nothing. There was no afterwards.

The house came to life. The sheets were taken off the furniture and shaken out. The curtains were drawn, the surfaces dusted; the gutters cleared, the floors swept and polished; the beds aired and made; the windows opened; the kitchens buffed and readied. The indoor-garden staff trimmed and watered the plants, while the outdoor-garden staff raked the paths and weeded the flower beds.

The private secretary liaised with the cook, the cook with the housekeeper, the housekeeper with the butler . . .

Everything began to stir.

All that day Barney stayed in the pub. He couldn't face going back outside. And even when all his money had gone, he still stayed there, perched up on a bar stool, exchanging tiny gobbets of small talk with Kenneth, loath to leave. When he did finally emerge he found that it was already getting dark. Shadows were falling, tumbling through the air, thumping down all around.

Once again Barney walked up over the bridge and then up the gravel drive with white paling fencing on either side. By the time he reached the 'Keep Out' sign and the gateposts, he felt fit to burst. Part of him wanted to turn round – to not put himself through further disappointment. None the less, he had to try; he had to do that. The intercom stood out in the darkness before him, bulbous and pale.

Barney found he could hardly bring himself to press the buzzer.

When he did so, a familiar voice squawked at him.

'Yes?'

Once more he put his lips close to the grille. 'My name is Barney Rees. I rang before. Yesterday. I don't suppose Edmund Crowe is here? By – by any chance?'

This time there was no reply at all.

So, he didn't even warrant that.

Right then . . .

Barney turned away.

As he did so, he heard a high-pitched creaking noise coming from behind him.

He turned back.

The gates, he saw, had begun to vibrate, as if with rage. They did this for several moments, slowly rising to a pitch of fury.

And then they started to open.

21

It Came from on High

Instantly, lights came on all around. There were lights in the flower beds, lights in the bushes and lights in the trees that lined the driveway leading up to the house.

Barney began to walk up the drive. At any moment he expected a voice to boom out and ask him what he was doing. Passing between the trees, he came to the house. His first impression was that it was very large. More like a school, or a nursing home, than a private residence. Someone had been buggering about here all right, no doubt about that at all, although in quite different ways to down in the village.

He could see patterned brickwork, diamond-paned windows, high chimneys and various jutting gables. Everything about the house was unusually pointed and spiky. There were columns on either side of the front door holding up a large porch, with a set of steps – as wide as a goods ramp – leading up to it.

At the bottom of the steps stood a group of figures. All of them were wearing white tunics.

As he walked towards the group of figures, Barney heard a whirring, clattering sound, as if the air all around had been tipped into a blender. Somehow this noise felt as if it was coming both from outside Barney's head and from inside it.

Then he saw that all the figures in white tunics had their heads tilted back and were looking up at the sky.

Barney also looked up.

At first he could see nothing. The clattering continued to grow louder. Then from over the tops of the trees came a light. This was far brighter than all the other lights – so bright that Barney couldn't tell what lay behind. It hovered above their heads for a while, then began to descend into a clearing.

As it did so, Barney was able to make out the shape of a fuselage – there was a large glass bubble on one end. Then he could see the whirring blades of a helicopter.

The noise was deafeningly loud. A pounding, sucking *whoomp*, *whoomp*, *whoomp* that pushed the air back and forth. The helicopter landed in the clearing. The blades continued to spin round, but more slowly now, decreasing in speed all the time. The moment they were still, the men and women in white tunics all rushed forward.

Then everyone stopped and seemed to sway back, as if caught by a sudden gust of wind. A figure had stepped down from the cockpit. Ducking beneath the rotor blades, this figure began walking quickly towards the house. One of the women in white tunics ran alongside. Barney could see her hands waving about as she spoke. He watched with mounting concern. Yet he found he couldn't look away. Abruptly, the figure stopped, turned and stared in Barney's direction.

As far as Barney could tell, Edmund's shape hadn't changed that much. Still it billowed out sharply from the waist despite the double-breasted overcoat he was wearing. Facially too, he didn't seem that different, although older, obviously. But there was something else. Something new. It had to do with his bearing. Edmund had a dark, brooding authority to him now that he'd never had before. At the same time, thought Barney, his complexion – at least in this light – suggested some sort of violent dyspepsia. He looked as if every meal he had ever eaten had disagreed with him.

As for how Barney must have looked to Edmund, he didn't want to think about that. Fortunately, he didn't have to not think about it for very long. Edmund strode up the steps to the now-open front door. As he did so, the woman he'd been talking to headed in Barney's direction. When she was about three feet away, she stopped and addressed him in a shrill voice, as if she were standing on the edge of a quarantine zone. 'I told Mr Crowe that you were here,' she said. 'That you had come.'

Barney started forward – he couldn't help himself. 'Yes? And?'

'He said –'

'What did he say?'

'He said you could stay.'

'He said that?'

The woman nodded, almost imperceptibly, so as not to ruffle her crisp white front. 'Yes,' she confirmed. 'You can stay.'

At that moment Barney would have happily prostrated himself before Edmund. And shed real tears of gratitude too. But it seemed he wasn't to be given the opportunity – not yet anyway. Instead, he was to be shown to his sleeping quarters, there to restore himself, dab at his swellings and sluice his cares away.

'Follow me,' said the woman in the white tunic.

She set off round the perimeter of the house, down a gravel path. Barney followed her. This path led into another garden – bigger than the one in front. Somewhere or other – possibly in a magazine, although not one of his usual periodicals – Barney had once seen pictures of the gardens at Versailles. These didn't seem so very different, he thought. The same avenues of box hedging with flower beds running between; the same arbours and pieces of classical statuary. They were smaller here, admittedly, but not by much.

They kept on walking, heading – as far as Barney could tell – towards the back of the house. In front of him was a fountain with the figure of a girl sitting on the edge of an oyster shell, her long stone legs dangling over the side.

'Where are we going?' he asked, more out of curiosity than anything else.

The woman in white didn't reply. Perhaps the staff were not permitted to talk to guests. Perhaps it was thought cheeky or disrespectful for them to do so. Well, fair enough, thought Barney, as he flapped along in her wake. While some people might regard such attitudes as outmoded, even barbaric, he had no complaints.

Still, the woman carried on. Down one formal avenue, and then another. Then down a narrow passageway lined with high hedges on both sides. At last she came to a door and went through it.

Barney did the same. Ahead of them was a stone staircase, the

steps dropping away at a sharp gradient. The staircase led down
into a long windowless corridor. The floor was covered in asphalt.
The walls gave off a dark, institutional gleam.

There was a strong smell of disinfectant.

At the end of the corridor was another door. The woman pushed
it open. Barney found he was looking into a large room with a low
ceiling. The walls were painted in the same faintly gleaming paint
as the corridor outside.

Inside, several men were sitting around on old iron beds. Some
of these men were playing cards. All had very pale faces and
flattened cheekbones.

They stared at Barney, but said nothing.

'Here you are,' said the woman.

'Who exactly are these people?' Barney asked.

Before she could reply, the penny dropped. This must be his
staff, his retinue. There were a lot of them; one for each extremity
presumably, plus several reservists for round-the-clock maintenance. Not that he required such devoted pampering. Never mind,
though. Never mind; he'd grow used to it in time.

The woman led Barney over to the far end of the room. There
was an empty bed here. An old-fashioned, iron-framed bed with
several blankets folded at one end and a single pillow at the other.

She pointed at the bed. 'For you,' she said.

'What do you mean, for me?'

'This is where you sleep.'

Barney felt as though he had been kicked very hard in the solar
plexus by a champion kick-boxer. 'Now just hold on – what's your
name?'

'Wendy.'

'Now you listen to me, Wendy –' Barney broke off. When
worked up, he had always been bad at ordering his thoughts. 'There
must have been some mistake,' he said.

The woman shook her head. 'No mistake.'

'Obviously you don't understand. I am an old – no, a valued,
friend of Edmund Crowe's. I have come here specially – to visit
him.'

'I know that.'

'Well, then, why have you brought me here?'

'Because he told me to,' she said.

The champion kick-boxer had landed another blow; this one even more carefully aimed than the last. Barney could hardly breathe.

'Edmund told you to bring me here?'

'Yes. So you can sleep. And then in the morning you can start work.'

'Work?' echoed Barney. He was aware that his voice sounded very small and far away. 'What sort of work?'

'With hands.'

'But I can't work with hands.'

'Why not?'

'Because I have very sensitive hands. Like an artist's,' Barney added. He wished he hadn't said 'like'.

'You must work,' she repeated. 'In the morning.'

And then she walked away.

The men took no further notice of him. They went back to playing cards and talking among themselves in a language Barney didn't understand. He sat on the bed. He felt very exposed. Very alone too.

As he sat there he began to shake. The tremors in his forearms were magnified several times over when they reached his fingers. His temples too had started to throb.

So this was Edmund's plan, was it? Revenge. Humiliation. A final settling of scores. Very well then.

Very well . . .

Two could play at that game, thought Barney, without having the faintest idea how.

Why was it, she thought, as her train emerged from under the glass canopy and out into an orange London dusk, why was it that the smallest move on her part carried with it these intimations of disaster? She felt as though she was walking across some high, swaying bridge with nothing but fraying ropes on either side. And if she put a single foot wrong, she might plunge into the chasm below.

It was dreadful to have to live life like this; with such anxiety nipping constantly at your heels. Such apprehension too. However much she tried to arrange her thoughts into proper shape and order, still these uncertainties came, battering at her self-possession, doing whatever they could to unsettle her.

Once she had been carefree, blind to fears, or consequences, or anything like that. Not any more, though. Now it didn't take much to ruffle her composure. Now she had to watch her step, try to protect herself from any upsets. Clutch herself tight and hope for the best.

And as for what lay ahead . . . As for that . . . She felt worried, suspicious, far from certain about what awaited her. Of course, she'd have to go. There was no real choice. No, there was nothing for it but to force down her doubts, polish her surface sparkle and soldier on.

Edmund looked out at his unfamiliar bedroom. At his furniture, his pictures, his bits and pieces. Except they weren't really his, of course – only in name. He might have been in a department store, or a show home. Someone else had bought everything; someone hired to imagine what might appeal to whatever taste he might possess.

There were times when Edmund felt that if he dropped a pebble into himself, the ripples might extend for ever, never reaching the shore. As if there was an emptiness inside him so vast that it could never be filled, only papered over.

He shut his eyes.

As he did so Barney's face rose up before him. Angrily, Edmund swiped it away. Barney? What was he doing here? Never mind; he couldn't think about him now. Apart from anything else there was another, quite different, image that Edmund wanted to fix in his mind's eye. With an effort he tugged it into place.

It wouldn't be long, he told himself. Not long now. Soon everything would be different.

22

Bugs

The Forester. *May 2003.*

The meeting of the local Music Society on Thursday, 11 April in the
Methodist church hall was well attended. What a treat we had as
our own Sylvia Winthrop brought us 'English Song throughout the
Ages', accompanied by her brother, Russell, on the piano. Despite
her recent appendectomy, Sylvia's golden voice filled the hall with
sweetest music. England, we were informed, was once known as
'the land without song', but we were thrilled with songs by such
greats as Handel, Vaughan Williams, Frederick Delius and Benjamin
Britten, rendered by Sylvia. So that cannot be said now.

In the morning Barney queued up with the others for his breakfast.
In the room next door two trestle tables had been laid out with
cutlery and mugs. He ate his food in silence.

Afterwards everyone trooped outside into the gardens, where a
foreman gave them all jobs to do. The foreman wore a workshirt
buttoned at the wrists, and his hair was cut in a toothed fringe,
possibly by pinking shears. Down the centre of his forehead he had
a wobbly cleft, like two clenched fists placed knuckle to knuckle.

When it came to Barney's turn, he explained that he needed to
see Edmund Crowe, without delay.

'Oh,' said the foreman, an unpleasantly scornful tone to his voice.
'You do, do you?'

'Without delay,' repeated Barney, quavering slightly.

But instead of paying proper heed to this, or any heed at all, the
foreman took hold of Barney by the shoulder and steered him down
one of the gravel paths. Here, hidden by a hedge, was a swimming

pool. In a changing room beside the pool was a bug-scoop. The scoop looked like a large butterfly net, a muslin-covered square on the end of a long pole.

'I want you to clean all the bugs out of the pool. Think you can manage that?'

'Why is everyone so fucking unfriendly round here?' Barney demanded.

'That's just the way it is.'

'At least – at least tell me your name.'

'My name,' said the man reluctantly, 'is Boomer.'

After Boomer had gone Barney stood and stared at the bug-scoop for a while. Unable to think of anything else to do, he picked it up. Throughout the morning he dipped and dragged and slid his scoop through the water. To begin with he was shaking so much that the scoop frothed up the surface of the water. But slowly he settled down. Meanwhile the clouds dissolved as the sun rose slowly – cumbersomely – into the sky.

The air felt thick and muggy.

Barney kept scooping away.

At lunchtime he was summoned back inside, then sent out again afterwards. In his absence, more insects had dropped into the water. They were in a mess of sticky tangled limbs, all wrapped around one another, so it was impossible to see which limb belonged to which insect. Some were already dead, but others clung to rafts of leaves. Feebly, they beat their wings and scissored their legs about.

Barney shook the scoop and several more fragile, long-legged creatures fell out onto the flagstones. Sodden to begin with, they shook themselves out and took to the air once more. Kneeling down, he looked at the bugs more closely, inspecting their water-logged limbs as they dried out; watching them disentangle them-selves, one from another. Another tangle of legs unglued themselves, took a few exploratory steps and then flew off.

As he watched this, Barney felt as if he had waved his hands over them and made them well again. This made him feel unexpectedly good. It struck him how various creatures cleaved to each other in the great chain of existence. Of course, a lot of fighting went on; a great deal of fighting. But there was a lot of cleaving too. His own situation wasn't so very different to these bugs', he realized. Like him, they had blundered into an element where they didn't belong, where they had no business being, and they needed a helping hand to set them back on track. Except that in his case there was no sign of a scoop to haul him back to safety.

I am misunderstood, Barney thought suddenly. Very misunderstood. Who by? Possibly by myself, he thought glumly.

'There you are.'

He looked up. Wendy, the woman in the white tunic, was standing on the other side of the pool. 'Come with me,' she said. 'To the house.'

'What for?'

'Come!'

All at once light seemed to stream to down on him, warm and enriching. 'Are you telling me that Edmund has finally come to his senses?'

'We must hurry.'

The measure of relief that Barney felt was surprisingly small. Far from sufficient to displace his sense of fury. No doubt that would go eventually. But it couldn't be whisked away, not just like that.

With reluctance, he set down the bug-scoop and they set off towards the house. Up the avenues of box hedging, past the fountain with the stone girl hanging her legs over the side of the oyster shell – and then into a part of the garden that Barney hadn't been into before.

'Hold on,' he said. 'What's this place?'

'This is the wild-flower meadow,' Wendy told him. 'Mr Crowe had it planted specially.'

They were standing by the edge of a field. Dotted among the long grass were wild flowers: poppies and cornflowers and buttercups and dog roses, all in different colours. A carpet of petals stretched away into the distance – red and blue and yellow and orange. Almost any colour you could think of.

Disarmed by the events of the morning, Barney found himself

thinking that this was one of the most beautiful sights he had ever seen. A breeze ruffled the grass and sent clouds of pollen drifting over the tops of the stalks. At the same time, the flowers lowered their heads and swayed reproachfully from side to side.

'Come on,' said Wendy.

'What's the rush?'

Barney dragged his eyes away. They set off again, turned a corner and the russet bulk of the house came into view with its patterned brickwork, its spires, its gables and its array of mullioned windows. In the daylight the house looked both darker and more forbidding than it had done at night, as if it had sucked all the light out of the surrounding air. Its countenance too appeared more blank, like a whole host of eyes – all of them without pupils.

This time they headed for another door, also round the back. The door led down into the kitchens. There was a series of long, low rooms with shiny stainless-steel work surfaces on either side of them. Everything – the machines, the saucepans, the utensils, the work surfaces – looked brand new, as if none of it had ever been used.

Passing through the kitchens, they entered a small room off the end. It had a single easy chair in it – again unused. Laid out on the chair was a suit of clothes – the jacket draped over the back, the trousers over the seat, a pair of empty legs dangling down. It looked as though whoever had once worn this suit had simply disappeared as soon as they had sat down, leaving nothing but these clothes behind. An unusually small person too, thought Barney in passing.

'Mr Algernon is sick,' said Wendy. 'He has a bad stomach.'

'You don't say.'

Barney felt a strong urge to be back beside the pool with his bug-scoop. There were insects there that required his help; they might well be lost without him.

'I can't imagine you've brought me here just to tell me this.'

'No.'

'Well, what then?'

Wendy pointed at the empty suit. 'Put it on,' she said.

'I don't understand,' Barney began – except he strongly suspected that he did understand. It was odd how often comprehension and incomprehension seemed to arrive together in a dead heat. Or rather, in a not-quite-dead heat. Always comprehension seemed to edge ahead, no matter how desperately you were rooting for incomprehension.

'There are visitors tonight for dinner,' she said. 'You must do the buttling.'

'No, not that,' said Barney. 'I can't.'

'You can.'

'Please –'

'You must.'

'Can't you find someone else?'

Wendy shook her head.

Barney looked down at the Hottentot costume lying over the chair. 'I assume this was Edmund's idea too?'

Wendy didn't reply – not directly. Instead she said, 'Come on, put the clothes on.'

What was it they said about action driving away thought? At least there was that much to be said for it. If only it could wipe it out completely, then it might really catch on.

Doing everything he could to disassociate himself from his own actions, Barney took off his own clothes and handed them to Wendy. She took these from him with a pair of invisible fire-tongs. The suit, as expected, was far too small. Only with a considerable effort was Barney able to fasten the buttons round his waist. The trousers ended shortly below his knees – not really like trousers at all; more like a pair of experimental culottes. As for the jacket, that was even worse. The narrowness of the shoulders effectively confined him to a few crabbed jerky movements. When Barney had finished dressing, he tried to stand up straight, but was unable to do so. His back was bent almost double.

Wendy watched all this with one hand cradling her chin. 'Mr Algernon, perhaps he is a little smaller,' she conceded. 'Even so, it will have to do.'

For the next fifteen minutes she instructed Barney on how he was to perform his duties at table. When the guests arrived – there were to be four of them apparently – he should hand round drinks. At dinner, he should serve the food from the left side to allow the diners to help themselves more easily.

'You clear, Barney?'

He nodded; he had no fight left in him.

Next, she took him through to await the arrival of the guests. Barney shuffled out of the kitchen, up another set of steps and through a door at the far end. This led into a great hallway that extended far into the distance. It had been built on two storeys. There were dark green marble columns holding up a series of vaulted grey stone arches.

Above them, stretching for the entire length of the room, was a balcony. This too was topped with more marble arches. Down the centre of the hallway, two rows of armoured figures stood facing one another across the polished floor, like dancing partners about to skip forward and link arms, all of them quite small and bandy-legged. From the ceiling bosses heraldic flags hung from short, horizontal poles.

There were dark wooden cabinets containing an extensive range of pewter plates, and at the far end of the hall was an enormous fireplace, encrusted – so far as Barney was able to tell – with even more heraldic rubbish. Here, pushed against the wall, were various stiff-backed sofas hung with tassles, and a table with bottles on it, along with dishes of eats.

Suddenly a distant bell jangled.

Wendy told him to stay where he was.

Barney did as he was told. He was aware that his breathing sounded unusually loud; hoarse and damp at the same time. Like an old horse. An old horse tethered in an underwater stable.

After a few minutes Wendy reappeared. Now she was at the head of a column of three people. There were two other women and a man. They came closer down the hallway. One of them – the man – walked with a heavy limp and had difficulty manoeuvring himself across the floor. He swung round into each step, poling himself forward on a walking stick.

Barney found himself thinking that this limping man looked peculiarly unconvincing – like someone applying for a disability pension with no real hope of success, yet determined to create an unforgettable impression.

When the guests reached the table, Wendy said, 'Mr Crowe is upstairs taking a business call. He will join you shortly. Would you care for a glass of champagne?'

All three said they would.

Closely supervised by Wendy, Barney poured out three glasses, set them on a tray and, still half crouched, handed them round. This first woman, he saw from his restricted viewpoint, appeared to be wearing some sort of canvas wigwam.

Her fingers – dusty looking, with flattened ends – hovered briefly over each of the bowls in turn.

'Now what have we here?' she said. 'And my . . . what are these little chaps? Little savoury fishes by the look of them.'

She was very white. Abnormally so: white hair, white lips and a white-powdered face, along with the creamy wigwam dress. The effect of all this whiteness was to make her look like a wraith, a zombie. Not just any old zombie either, but a kind of Dowager of the Undead. He also noticed – it was a very minor thing, but he noticed it none the less – that the woman was unable to pronounce her a's. They all came out sounding like u's.

'Could be,' he mumbled.

Barney could feel the woman's eyes upon him. He didn't like that. He began to walk back to the partial sanctuary of the table. But before he could take more than a couple of paces, the woman said, 'No, don't go – not quite yet.'

He stopped.

'Just turn around, would you?'

Barney turned around. He kept his head lowered.

'What's the matter?' Wendy asked in concern. 'He is not giving satisfaction?'

'It's a bit early to say, frankly. No, it's just –' The woman broke off and gave a disbelieving laugh. 'Just that this, this poor fellow looks strangely familiar.'

Again Barney glanced up.

Then down again.

Quickly.

'Tell me,' she said, 'are you from around these parts?'

He shook his head. Swung it grimly from side to side on an unnaturally low trajectory.

'Where from then?'

'London.'

Barney's lips appeared to have been anaesthetized, or even glued together.

'From London? Employed here as the beneficiary of some charitable scheme, no doubt.'

Don't say anything, Barney told himself. Just don't speak. Never speak again.

'Just raise your head for a moment.'

Slowly Barney did so.

The two of them were looking at one another now.

A pause followed.

This was followed by a gasp.

Then words emerged in a dry, crackling rush. 'Bunny? Is it really you?'

How should I know? Barney wondered. Was it really him? With all his heart he hoped not. The evidence, though, all pointed one way. He remembered how once, a long time ago, he had possessed a coat which he was particularly fond of. A tweed overcoat with red lining that he'd bought in a charity shop. What an excellent coat that had been. He remembered how, when he ran upstairs, this coat flapped out behind him, swinging from side to side, with the red of the lining producing a very dashing effect.

Barney found himself thinking how he must have looked in the coat – both from the front and the back. What a striking sight he must have presented. A picture of soaring intent. Up, up the stairs, he bounded – in his memory anyway – until he had reached the top and there was nowhere left for him to go. He wished he had a coat like that now. He would still have worn it well; he felt sure he would.

'Hello, Tinker,' he said.

'Bunny . . . My God . . . But what are you doing here?'

'That's a long story.'

'And with plenty of pitfalls along the way, I'll be bound. You remember my husband, don't you?'

The limping man lurched towards them, wielding his walking stick like the paddle of a canoe. Corky's face was more lined than before, his stomach more rounded. His manner, though, was no different. Still hale. Horribly hale.

'Hey, Barney! How's it going?'

'Obviously not well,' said Tinker helpfully. 'Not well at all.'

'That's quite a costume you're wearing there,' Corky went on. 'Have you been in a musical?'

Barney found he couldn't face looking at either Tinker or Corky for long. He dropped his eyes back to the floor.

'Ah,' said Tinker. 'I see you're staring at Corky's prosthesis, Bunny.'

'No, I'm not!' he protested.

'There's no need to be embarrassed. Is there, darling?'

'What about?'

'Your leg.'

'Which leg's that?'

'Why, the dud, of course.'

'Certainly not.'

'He lost it in an automobile accident.'

'In a five-car pile-up,' Corky explained proudly.

'They had to cut him out. It took hours and hours and hours . . .' said Tinker. She sounded as if she was about to swoon.

'Four and three quarters. Not counting the wait for the heavy lifting gear,' said Corky.

'You'd never guess Corky has a prosthesis, would you?'

Not if you'd had your eyes put out and your head wrapped in a sack, thought Barney.

'I chose it for him myself,' she added.

That at least came as no surprise. Where had she found it? Stolen it from a child probably.

'As you can see, though, I manage pretty well,' said Corky. 'Although I do have help.'

Here Corky indicated the other woman standing just behind him, a dumpy figure wearing what appeared to be an indoor anorak.

'You remember Squirrel Dorothy, don't you? Of course, she looks different without her tail.'

Squirrel Dorothy blushed at this.

'Goodness, it's a long time since I hung that up.'

'What – what are you doing here?' Barney forced himself to ask.

'It turns out that Edmund is a big fan of my work,' Corky explained. 'Old Masters, but with striking personal enhancements. He very kindly offered to mount an exhibition, a general overview of the whole Pubist School, with my work as the centrepiece. Naturally, Tinker's pottery will also be represented. Edmund called me up out of the blue and invited us to come and stay with him. What do you think of that?'

Barney didn't know what to think of it. All he knew was that this news made him feel even more unsettled than before.

'This calls for a toast,' said Corky.

'I don't think it would be appropriate for Bunny for join us,' said Tinker. 'On account of his ancillary status. But that's no reason for us not to enjoy ourselves.'

Barney refilled their glasses and set them on a tray. After giving Corky his, he shuffled back over to Tinker. So far, Barney had been relieved to find, he wasn't shaking too badly this evening.

Tinker reached out for the glass. Just before her dusty fingers closed around the rim, Barney allowed the tray to tilt fractionally to one side. This caused the glass to roll round on its base in a slow gyratory sort of way, then topple towards Tinker.

As he watched this Barney felt a ripple of satisfaction pass through his crook-backed form. It was the first pleasurable feeling he'd had in ages.

'Careful!' said Wendy.

She snatched the glass by its stem, returning it to an upright position before a drop could be spilled.

'Do try to be less clumsy, Bunny,' said Tinker. 'We could easily have had a small accident there.'

Again she looked at him, a challenging gleam in her eye.

'Let me go and see where Mr Crowe has got to,' said Wendy. 'He should have been here by now.'

23

The Art of Servility

'Mr Crowe, sir?'

'What is it?'

'Are you all right in there?'

'In where?'

'In the toilet, sir. The lavvy.'

'Why shouldn't I be all right?'

'Just that you've been in there a long time.'

'Have I?'

'Oh yes. A very long time. I thought maybe you'd had an accident.'

'No, no. No accident.'

'The guests are already here, sir.'

'Are they?'

'Yes. They are waiting downstairs.'

'Right,' said Edmund. 'Tell them I will be down in a minute.'

'Come here again, Bunny, will you. I'd like another of those little savoury fishes.'

Once more Tinker reached out her hand. Then she stopped, her hand frozen in mid-air.

Barney followed her gaze.

Edmund was walking towards them between the two rows of armoured figures. He wore a dark suit with an unusually long jacket and walked with his arms by his sides and his feet sticking out straight in front of him, like a pallbearer, or a figure at a march-past. I wasn't wrong about the dyspepsia, Barney thought. Or the authority, come to that. Especially the authority.

When Edmund reached them he stopped.

His presence was eerily unsettling. Judging from his expression, Edmund found everyone he looked upon to be lacking in some crucial way. He seemed to be holding enormous quantities of disapproval in check. But only with a big effort. At any moment, it could come spilling forth.

Edmund stared at them all in turn.

However, he stared at Barney for the longest. As he did so, Barney found that he had begun to shake – this time for real. Tremors passed along his shoulders and down his arms. Straightening up to his uppermost limit, he did his best to meet Edmund's gaze, making a reasonable job of it under the circumstances. Dimly, he was aware of a tearing sound coming from the back of his jacket.

Still no one said anything.

A bell rang for the second time, again muffled and coming from some way off.

Edmund half turned towards the sound of the bell, twisting stiffly from the hip.

'Go and answer that, will you, Wendy,' he said in a parched voice. 'I am expecting one other guest.'

While the guests made their way into the dining room, Barney returned to the kitchens. Among the gleaming surfaces, two chefs were at work, cooking and garnishing away. Once the food was ready, it was loaded on to a hoist which carried it upstairs.

By the time he returned to the dining room, the guests were all seated at a long table. The new arrival – a woman – had been seated on Edmund's right. Barney noticed nothing about her except for a general impression of glossiness and poise.

The dining room had been decorated in a similarly high gloomy style to the hall. There was more oak panelling on the walls and above it tapestries showing medieval scenes. On one an armoured figure on horseback rode across a wintry landscape towards a distant castle. The ceiling consisted of elaborately painted plasterwork and showed a golden maze with Latin inscriptions running down the various paths.

Edmund sat very upright in his gilded chair, his jacket still buttoned up. With a rumbling, grinding noise, the hoist roared into action. Soon afterwards a large silver dish appeared, wreathed in steam.

Barney took the dish round the table.

Tinker came first. She looked at him suspiciously as he bent forward, helping herself to food with sudden, darting movements in case he might try to tip it into her lap.

'This is a lovely place you've got here, Edmund,' she said, once her food was safely on her plate. 'Really lovely. Have you had it long?'

'Four years,' said Edmund, clearing his throat. 'Although I have only just moved in.'

'I think I read somewhere – in a gardening magazine possibly – that you have constructed a lovely wild-flower meadow here. Quite a passion of yours, I believe.'

'That's right,' said Edmund, unbending very slightly. 'I've tried to combine some of the more well-known wild flowers, such as columbine, wild thyme, nodding violets and woodbine, of course, along with some of the lesser-known ones, like musk-roses and eglantine.'

'Charming. Absolutely charming.'

'The house,' continued Edmund after another pause, 'was previously a catering college. Before that, it was a borstal. During the last war it was requisitioned by the army. They even say there's an ammunition dump round here somewhere.'

'Do they really? I adore ammunition,' said Tinker.

Silence – eventually broken by Squirrel Dorothy. 'This weather is unusually close for the time of year, isn't it?'

'They say there's going to be a storm soon.'

'That should clear the air.'

It would need to be one hell of a storm to do that, thought Barney. The atmosphere was extraordinarily tense. He continued round the table. Corky came next, then Squirrel Dorothy – then the new arrival.

Crouched low, arms extended to maximum length, he held out the dish. The woman took hold of the serving spoons. When she had finished helping herself to food, she set the spoons back down on the dish.

'Thank you,' she said.

Was it this passing courtesy that made Barney look up? He had no idea. Besides, by then it was too late. He felt himself rearing back. The woman also reared back in her chair – this in a way that might have been overdone, yet wasn't somehow.

Her eyes narrowed, and then widened to their furthest extremes. Somewhere inside Barney's head he could hear a voice chiming away – 'No, not this, not this, not this. Anything but this . . .'

At the same time he realized that all his limbs had become locked together. He had to unglue himself, like the waterlogged bugs, before he could carry on serving. It was only when he had finished taking the dish round that Barney allowed himself to look back at Lia. In appearance, at least, she wasn't so different, he decided. Her skin was the same pale olive colour; her neck perhaps longer – more slender – than he remembered. Her hair had changed colour, though. Now it was tawnier. This saddened him somewhat, although he didn't know why it should.

No, as with Edmund, it was more her manner that had changed. Also the way she carried herself. There was something very guarded about her. Even fearful, as if she'd tamped herself down. Her voice sounded more modulated than before, as if this too had been crammed inside narrow tracks.

'Now tell me, Edmund,' said Corky, 'are you still involved in your Pet Rocks scheme?'

'Very much so.'

'What a brilliant idea! Jesus, I thought I was on to a good thing, with my Pubism and my Corky configurations. But whatever made you think up something like that?'

'Everybody needs something to love,' said Edmund in a voice completely devoid of inflection.

'OK, maybe so. But a Pet Rock for Chrissake! Who could have imagined anyone would be so screwed up that they'd want to talk to a lump of stone? I mean, that just blows me away. And your rubber car tails too – convincing people that they'd be less likely to be struck by lightning if they hung one from their bumper. Brilliant! You really do have a genius for exploi– for homing in on people's insecurities.'

'Thank you.'

'But how did you develop such a knack?'

'I've really no idea.'

Barney saw that Edmund ate – in so far as he ate anything – with very precise, careful gestures. As if he might be undone, or burst apart, at any moment. On a couple of occasions he seemed about to talk to Lia. However, nothing audible emerged.

Amid Barney's fury and shame, it struck him that Edmund had no ability to set anyone at their ease. None at all. Indeed, the longer the meal went on, the more uncomfortable – even agonized – he seemed to become. At one point Barney saw Lia looking over at him. There was an expression of concern on her face – but also an imploring look too. He wasn't sure what, if anything, to make of this.

When the first course was finished, Barney collected up the plates and put them into the hoist. It rumbled down to the basement. Several minutes later it returned, carrying the main course. Conversation remained on the same halting, constantly-on-the-verge-of-petering-out level as before.

After the main course was cleared away, dessert was served – a frothy mound of fruit and cream. It was while serving the dessert that Barney realized his own movements were not quite as constricted as they had been before. He had no time to ponder this puzzling development.

Edmund was the last to be served. Barney moved towards him. Blindly – semi-blindly – he thrust the bowl forward.

As Edmund started to help himself, something unforeseen happened. Barney saw to his surprise that his hands appeared to be getting smaller. It was as if a veil was being drawn over them. Or rather, two separate veils, both moving at the same steady pace.

He blinked, assuming that this would help clear the hallucination away. But when he opened his eyes again, even more of his hands had disappeared.

He gave a gasp of bewilderment.

'What's the matter?' said Edmund sharply.

'Look what's happening to me.'

'What are you talking about?'

He saw Edmund look down, and then frown. 'What's going on?'

'I'm disappearing,' Barney told him. 'Being eaten up.'

'How can you be?'

'*Look at me!*'

Barney was aware that everyone had fallen quiet. They were all staring at him – Lia included.

Now his hands had almost vanished. Everything else was going too; everything plucky and noteworthy. Soon – very soon – there would be nothing left at all.

'Haven't you made me suffer enough?' Barney moaned.

'Steady on,' said Corky. 'Just hang in there, boy.'

'How can I?' Barney cried. 'Not when I'm being rubbed out. Piece by faded piece.'

Wendy stepped forward.

'Stop it, there's nothing wrong. See.'

Barney felt this back being grabbed. Then came a sharp pull. To his astonishment, his hands promptly reappeared. Pink. Restored. Apparently undamaged.

'How did you do that?' he asked.

'Your jacket is split, that's all.'

'Do you know, I think she's right,' said Tinker. 'The seam has split all the way down the back. That must have made the arms fall forward over Bunny's hands. A perfectly simple explanation, as I always assumed there would be.'

Barney looked down at his hands. Despite being pleased to see them again, he still felt very insubstantial. Very unsound.

Silence fell again.

Edmund cleared his throat. 'Wendy, I think that you had better take Barney away,' he said. 'To recuperate.'

'Recuperate him right away?' Wendy asked.

'This moment,' Edmund confirmed.

'Poor Bunny,' said Tinker as he was being led off. 'He tried his best. At least I assume he did. But he's just not up to it.'

Wendy took Barney back downstairs to the parlour. He sat slumped in the easy chair. 'I told you I shouldn't have worn that bloody suit.'

Wendy shrugged. 'Mr Algernon never had problems.'

'But.the man's half my size.'

'Not once.'

Barney was in no mood to argue. Not only did he feel insubstantial, but also exhausted. He couldn't even face changing his clothes, or going to find a drink.

After a while Wendy went back upstairs to clear the dishes away. Barney stayed where he was. At one stage – he didn't know when – he was dimly aware of a dark figure standing outside the parlour looking in at him.

Barney didn't look round.

Soon the figure went away.

24

Bedtime Interlude

Edmund lay on his bed, shaking. Waves of emotion coursed through him, back and forth. His blood was pounding. His wattles vibrated wildly, his hands trembled. Adhesive sweat cascaded through his pores.

There could be no doubt about it: he was in surge.

At dinner, he'd hardly been able to speak. Tiny hands had fastened themselves round his windpipe. Presumably that was nerves. Not that he'd ever had any aptitude for small talk. But this had been far worse than that. No topic, however tiny or inconsequential, had alighted on his tongue. All his channels were blocked.

Blocked!

Self-consciousness had come over him like never before. That and a sense of his own ridiculousness. Every movement, every attempt at conversation, had been a torture to him.

Oh! Oh! Oh!

Edmund balled his fists and pounded the bedclothes. What must Lia have thought? There was no way of telling; she'd scarcely uttered anything all evening. Indeed, she looked almost as awkward – as uncomfortable – as him. What was he to make of this? He had no idea. What could he do? His heart was already out of its box. Halfway out anyway. The temptation to put it back again and fasten the lock even more tightly than before was very strong.

Yet what if there was a prospect of happiness hanging there, within reach. What then? He must try to grasp it. He must do that. But what if it all went wrong? He couldn't stand the disappointment – not again. And what about Barney? Damn Barney! Damn him for everything.

No, thought Edmund. No, he mustn't slip back. Not now. Not after such anticipation, such preparation. Whatever happened, he must not falter.

Barney tried to stretch out in his iron crib. He held up his hands and watched them jumping and twitching before him. Then he put them back down by his sides. How he wished she hadn't seen him like this. Laid so low. It struck him that Lia was the only person who had ever understood him; the only person who appreciated his attributes and his complexities.

He was still raking over this thought when another one came along. Briefly, Barney wondered if he was falling victim to the curse of introspection – he very much hoped not; he would do anything to avoid that. None the less, he couldn't help seeing how he had used himself up by seducing – no, not seducing – bedding Lia all those years ago. He'd had to dig deep into himself in order to do that. Much too deep. In the process vital essences had been washed away. Ever since, he had been running on diminished resources. Yes, that was where it had all gone wrong.

He must see her as soon as possible and explain this.

The door to the dormitory opened. A figure stood there, silhouetted in the moonlight. From the size of the silhouette, and from its smudged and yet curiously purposeful air, Barney guessed that it belonged to Boomer. He was breathing hard as if he'd just been running, or at any rate exerting himself in some way. Beside him was a large square shape, apparently a crate of some kind. With some difficulty – it was obviously heavy – Boomer dragged this crate across the floor and pushed it underneath his bed.

Lia sat on the edge of her bed. Whatever she had been expecting, it wasn't this. Seeing Edmund suffused with hectic khaki flushes, hardly able to talk. That upset her more than she could say. And Barney too. Possibly he was in an even worse state – although frankly there wasn't a lot in it.

What was going on?

She had no idea. Once, she thought she'd known all the answers.

But now she realized she'd known nothing. Nothing at all. All she'd done was hold up a shield of phoney certainties. Behind it, though, she was as unsure of herself as any of the people she tried to help, whose problems – whose lives – she battened on to, in the hope that their uncertainties would deflect attention from her own.

There was a knock on the door.

After a moment's hesitation, she called out, 'Come in.'

Wendy the housekeeper entered at a restless clip.

'I have a message for you from Mr Crowe.'

'Yes?'

'He would like to see you tomorrow morning. Eleven o'clock.'

'All right.'

'But not in the house.'

'Ah. Where then?'

'I will give you directions.'

25

Wild Flowers

Overnight, yet more insects had fallen into the swimming pool. Barney scooped them out and shook them on to the paving slabs. When he had finished a circuit of the pool, he knelt and watched them with as much fascination as the first time. The insects were wrapped in a warm and sticky embrace. All cleaving away, springing apart and taking to the air once more. They didn't seem to mind it much – provided they were able to escape in the end. Even then, some would head straight back into the pool. They never learned from their mistakes, of course. But then again, who did?

That's quite enough of that, Barney told himself. Yet saving these creatures gave him more of a sense of achievement than he would have thought possible. It took his mind off the previous night too.

'What are you doing?'

Barney turned round. Boomer was standing behind him.

'Nothing,' he said defensively.

'That's what I thought. Come with me then, I have another job for you.'

With a pang of regret, Barney set down the bug-scoop. He followed Boomer along the network of paths until they reached a hut where the garden equipment was kept. Here Barney was told that he should spray the wild-flower meadow with fertilizer. But first of all he had to watch carefully to see just how the fertilizer was mixed up.

Taking a plastic bottle from a shelf, Boomer tipped some of the contents into a container. Next, he took the container through to a smaller, inner room. The ceiling was lower in here, the air heavier. Running along one wall was a narrow lid. Boomer lifted up the lid.

Beneath it were two holes. From deep within the holes came the sound of bubbling.

'What's that?' asked Barney.

'Faecal matter,' said Boomer, a note of solemnity – almost reverence – in his voice. 'All the waste here is recycled,' he explained. 'For manuring purposes.'

Lowering a bucket into the right-hand hole, he pulled it back up and tipped the contents into the container. This container had straps on it like a rucksack. Boomer attached a spray gun to the bottom of the container and told Barney how to build up the pressure by pumping on the handle at the side.

Then they went to the wild-flower meadow. Once again, Barney found himself struck by the beauty of it; by all the wild flowers, swaying and bobbing away on their thin stalks; by all the different colours, so bright and yet so delicate. However, he didn't have time to dwell on beauty for long. Boomer started showing him how best to apply the fertilizer to the wild flowers. All he had to do was make sure that they got a good soaking. Then, when the container was empty, he should mix up another batch and carry on where he had left off.

'Do you understand me?'

'Of course I understand you,' Barney told him irritably. 'Any damn fool could do that.'

The beginnings of a smile flickered round Boomer's mouth. 'OK, I'll leave you to it then.'

As soon as he had gone, Barney began walking through the meadow, pumping the handle up and down, spraying as he went. There were even more flowers here than he had realized. A lot of them were hidden away in the grass. He had to part the stalks and aim the spray closer to the ground to make sure they all were properly covered.

He finished the first container of liquid manure with surprising speed. Those wild flowers really soaked up their nutrients; they couldn't get enough of them. However, he filled the container up again easily enough, mixing together the solution from the bottle with a bucketful of treacly muck from the right-hand pit.

And on he went, spraying away. The worst part of it was the acrid smell, which stung his nose and made his eyes water. How did he feel? Barney asked himself, as he pumped away on the handle. Not exactly good, obviously, but not exactly bad either. His anger hadn't gone away – not remotely; it had simply been put to one side for the time being. At any moment it could be summoned back.

It was only when Barney reached the middle of the wild-flower meadow that he saw there was a structure there. A small round bower, like a summer house, made entirely of hedging. An arch was set into the hedging.

He looked inside.

In front of him was a stone bench. Nothing else. Barney went inside and sat on the bench. But not for long. After a few moments he jumped up with a strange sense that he had no business being there.

Outside, he kept pumping away, the fertilizer fanning out around him in a hazy arc. He hadn't been doing this for more than a couple of minutes when he saw Edmund approaching through a curtain of spray. Edmund had his head down and from this angle his bottom looked even bigger than usual. He swung his arms back and forth as if trying to generate extra propulsion.

As if to prove the ease with which Barney's anger could be summoned, it flooded instantly back. His immediate reaction was to tackle Edmund – to give him one of the few remaining pieces of his mind. But something – again he couldn't say what – made him stay where he was. Far from coming to see him, as Barney had assumed, Edmund was clearly oblivious to his presence. Still with his head down, still sawing his arms back and forth, he passed through the arch without mishap.

Barney stopped spraying and prepared to move to a new patch of meadow.

Then he heard a voice.

'Hello, Barney.'

Lia was standing there. She had her hair tied back. Her arms were crossed over her chest, each hand cupping an elbow.

'What are you doing?' she asked, giving him an appraising look.

'Noth– just spraying,' he told her. 'Where are you off to?'

'To see Edmund.'

He didn't care to hear this. But before he could register proper disapproval, Lia said, 'How are you, Barney?'

'Me?'

'Yes, you. How have you been?'

'Up and down,' he said truthfully. 'More down than up recently,' he added.

'Why is that?'

'Well, a number of reasons.'

'Emotional factors?'

'Mmm . . . Financial ones too.'

'Have you got into difficulties, Barney?'

There was an edge of something here – sternness, possibly – that Barney found he didn't care for. He'd forgotten how judgemental Lia could be when threatened; how eagerly she climbed on to her high horse.

'You could say that,' he allowed.

'I see.'

But why then was he so unmanned by her? Or was it re-manned? Barney saw that he'd been right the night before; that there was a slight tarnishing now to her surface gloss – but somehow this only made her more attractive to him. Perhaps it was the evidence of vulnerability that shone through. He'd always had a soft spot for that.

Barney drew his free hand across his brow. He wasn't hot, but he was definitely flustered. What was happening to him? Whatever it was, he didn't care for it. There seemed something pretty low about being privy to insights that he couldn't properly recognize as his own.

'Tell me about yourself, Barney.'

'Why do you want to know?'

'I'm curious.'

'It's not easy to explain.'

'Just try.'

'Sometimes I think I'm being followed by a giant rat,' he said quietly.

'Do you think that might be drink related?' Lia asked.

'I suppose it might be.' Barney looked down at his clanking assortment of pipes and plungers. 'I don't know . . . It's just that – nothing feels real any more.'

Although it wasn't a bright day – another grey summer morning – Lia had her eyes screwed up, as if peering into the sun, or else coming to an important decision.

'Doesn't it, Barney?'

'No,' he said. 'No, it doesn't.'

Lia continued to look at him. Again he felt as if there was something both scrutinizing and imploring in her expression.

'Anyway,' he said, 'what's been happening to you?'

'Oh, we don't need to go into that.'

'Don't we?'

'Not now. I have to go. I have to see Edmund.'

'Some other time then.'

'Yes. Some other time.'

Barney watched as she made her way through the drooping grass towards the round bower. He knew that the correct thing to do would be to walk away and let Edmund and Lia talk on their own. However, it wasn't simply because it was the incorrect thing to do that he began to walk – slowly and silently – towards the round bower himself.

About three feet away, he stopped. He'd imagined that he would be able to hear perfectly well what was going on inside, but in fact he could hear nothing. Perhaps they weren't actually saying anything? Or perhaps the hedging was thicker and more insulating than he had thought?

He crept closer.

Still nothing.

Barney began to feel oddly panic-stricken. What was going on? Then he heard Lia say, 'Oh, Edmund,' in a slightly exasperated sort of way, and he had a vision, which he didn't much care for, of her putting her hand on Edmund's wrist.

221

The next few exchanges were inaudible. Barney came closer.

'For me?' he heard Lia say. 'But, Edmund – you can't have done.'

The hedge closed in once more. Either that or the fertilizer spray had clogged up Barney's ears. Without having any idea why, he found his eyes had begun to water.

'. . . care for you,' Edmund was saying, thickly.

All at once Barney found himself wishing fervently for another blackout. But still Edmund went on in the same clumsy yet relentless way. 'More than care.'

'More than care? What – what do you mean?'

'Only you,' said Edmund. 'Only you. Ever – and always.'

Then nothing.

Then came Lia again. Her voice faltering now. 'Edmund. I'm sorry.'

'What about?'

'I can't . . . It's just too much.'

'Too much what?'

'Too much everything. Too much time . . . Too much feeling . . .'

'Please – just listen to me.'

'No – no. I can't. I'm very sorry, Edmund.'

Lia emerged from the round bower and strode quickly away, not glancing to left or right, her arms crossed over her chest even more tightly than before. From inside the bower Barney could hear an unnatural sucking sound, like someone fighting for breath.

Cautiously, he crept away and prepared to resume his spraying. He hadn't gone far when Edmund appeared, walking towards him, with his head down as before. Barney found himself torn over whether to run or stand his ground. In a spirit of valiant paralysis he decided to stay where he was.

So far at least Edmund hadn't even seen him.

But then Edmund did look up. Immediately, he raised his hand to his cheek as if a bubble of dust had just burst there. Then he seemed to stagger and put out a hand to steady himself, although there was nothing for him to hold on to. Still, he carried on, though. The pit of Barney's stomach felt a good two feet lower than usual.

When he was about three feet away, Edmund stopped and raised a hand. Then he spoke. 'Barney, what have you done?'

'Me? I haven't done anything.'

'Yes. Yes, you have. This is all your fault.'

'Oh for God's sake . . .' Barney wheeled around.

He had intended to walk away. However, he didn't – mainly because his feet had become stuck. Now he was convinced he was hallucinating. He had to be. Behind him, the wild-flower meadow wasn't there any more. Nothing was left. Nothing except for an empty expanse of blackened vegetation. A stubble of irradiated stalks, with this acrid, muddy cloud hanging over them.

Everything was dead.

'What's happened?' he asked.

'You've killed my beautiful wild-flower meadow,' said Edmund.

'But I can't have done.'

Barney looked down at the spray gun in his hands. He lifted it to his nose, and sniffed. The acrid smell was much stronger now. So strong that it had made his eyes water. Surely fertilizer wasn't supposed to smell quite so – so chemical as this?

What had that Boomer been playing at?

Looking up, Barney seemed to see himself reflected in the curve of Edmund's eyeball. This massively distended head on top of a wavering tadpole body. He saw something else too that he didn't want to see: the weight of disappointment banked up behind Edmund's eyes.

'Who are you to come here and spoil everything?' Edmund was saying. 'Why? Why? Everything I've planned for so long.'

'Who am I?' cried Barney.

Who am I?

He leant back. Above his head the acrid cloud swayed about, as if loosely tethered to the ground below. Barney too wanted to reach out for something – someone – to hold on to. To keep himself upright. But there was only Edmund, and he couldn't reach out for him.

26

Man Descending a Staircase

The Forester. *June 2001.*

The artist exhibiting at our May meeting was the well-known painter Shelagh Bowden, who titled her work *Pets in Oils*. The club members had chosen a horse as the subject to be depicted, with the horse very kindly provided by Drucilla's Private Zoo. As Shelagh painted away, her ability was obvious; expertly mixing her colours from a limited palette. In her thanks to Shelagh, Chairperson Yvonne Fox said, 'Her freedom expressed the freedom of the horse.' A sentiment endorsed by us all. The craft competition, a floating arrangement, was won for the third successive month by Kenneth and Erica Dexter.

The next exhibition, entitled 'Pubism and Its Peers', has generously been supported by new local resident Edmund Crowe. It will feature the works of Corky Montcalm and his potter wife, Tinker. Corky Montcalm's paintings look at first like mere copies of Old Master nudes, but include a number of witty personal embellishments of his own. See if you can spot them! Tinker Montcalm's work is renowned for both its decorative and functional elements. It is suitable for either mounting or for home entertaining. Due to the size of the works, this exhibition will not be held in the village hall but in a former stable on Mr Crowe's estate, which is being converted specially.

Arrangements for the annual St Swithin's Day fête will be announced shortly.

In so far as Barney had a plan it was to confront Boomer at the first opportunity and bust his head open with whatever heavy object he could find. But first he had to find him. There was no sign of Boomer at supper, nor in the dormitory afterwards. Barney lay down for a while on his bed trying to pretend that he was relaxing. But he could only pretend for so long. Especially when his head was spinning round this badly. It wasn't just seeing Lia that had shaken him up. So had destroying the wild-flower meadow. Upsetting or angering Edmund was of no consequence, of course. None whatsoever. No, it was the fact that he had obliterated something he had found beautiful.

He felt bad about that.

As Barney lay there another plan took root. He must talk to Lia; take up where they had left off – as well as fill himself in on the hedge-obstructed gaps in her conversation with Edmund. Yes, he must talk to Lia. He had forgotten just what a close and natural rapport he shared with her.

Swinging his legs off the bed, Barney stood up and waited for a while, hoping that his head might stop spinning a little less hectically now that he'd reached a resolution. Next, he made his way through the kitchens until he reached another staircase, leading up into the Great Hall. He pushed open the door. Moonlight gleamed off the marble surfaces. Down the centre of the hallway the two rows of armoured figures stood facing one another, still awaiting their cue to spring forward and link arms.

At the far end of these figures was another staircase – an absurdly grand, baronial affair that curved in a wide sweep up to the first floor. As he began to climb the stairs, Barney had the odd sensation that he was sleepwalking, although he knew that he wasn't. He was awake – wide awake – but he still felt as if he was moving through thickened gravity. He had no idea where Lia's bedroom was, but perhaps fortune would show him the way.

Halfway up the stairs was a landing. Off to one side of the landing was one of the balconies that looked down into the Great Hall. This balcony – he could see it quite clearly – was smaller than some of the others; more of a minstrels' gallery.

Barney stopped.

He thought he heard something, but he couldn't be sure.

He stood and waited.

Now there were definitely voices. They were hushed, but growing louder. Two figures came into view at the top of the stairs. One of these figures was in shadow and therefore invisible – apart from a general impression of bulkiness.

The second, however, was neither in shadow, nor invisible. It was Lia. Her feet were bare. A small length of ankle was visible beneath the hem of her garment – pale and slim. There was something about this length of bare ankle that made Barney's heart swell and feel very tender at the same time.

As he watched the two of them embraced.

The bulky man kissed Lia on the cheek. Then he began to descend the staircase. Barney shrank against the wall. His heart was pumping wildly. Footsteps continued to come closer. The figure was so close now that Barney could almost put out his hand and touch him.

Still, the figure was in shadow. But as it walked across the landing it had to pass through a narrow puddle of light. This it proceeded to do, half turning in Barney's direction as it did so.

Grey light seemed to slide up its body. First legs, then trunk.

And then the face.

Barney stepped forward. The shock was considerable.

'*You!*' he exclaimed.

Lia walked slowly back down the landing to her bedroom. She wished she hadn't been so harsh to Edmund, storming out and leaving him on his own like that. But how else was she supposed to react? Learning that he'd been dreaming of this for so long? Planning it for years? Was it any wonder she had panicked?

Even so, she wished she hadn't been so harsh.

'Barney. What are you doing here?'

'Never mind *me*. What do you think *you're* up to?'

'None of your business.'

'I'll be the judge of that.'

'Seeing someone, if you must know.'

'You were seeing Lia, weren't you?'

'If you knew, then why bother to ask?'

'I – I demand to know what you were doing?'

'Oh, you demand it, do you?'

'Yes,' said Barney breathlessly. 'I do.'

'All right then. I'll tell you . . . But first, I want to ask you something, Barney. Fair enough?'

'I suppose so.'

'Don't you recognize me?'

'What are you on about? Of course I recognize you.'

'No, not as I am now . . .'

'Eh?'

'As I used to be.'

At this, the figure stepped away from Barney and into the minstrels' gallery, facing out over the Great Hall below. He seemed to shrug up his shoulders, almost up to the level of his ears, and then to speak. Or rather to declaim in a low, harsh voice.

> But then I sigh, and, with a piece of scripture
> Tell them that God bids us do good for evil:
> And thus I clothe my naked villainy
> With old odd ends, stol'n out of holy writ;
> And seem a saint, when I most play the devil.

He stopped.

'Any wiser now?'

'Don't – don't rush me.'

Although Barney had never been much of a reader, there was something oddly familiar about this passage. About both the words and the delivery, although he couldn't think why. But never mind that. It was the association with Lia that troubled Barney the most.

He therefore repeated his question. 'What were you doing with Lia?'

'Why shouldn't I see her? After all –'

'After all, what?'

'After all, Barney. She is my sister.'

227

Barney found that his head was now going round faster than ever, possibly at its fastest-ever recorded speed. 'Christ alive!' he said weakly.

'Now you're getting warmer.'

'You must be Omar.'

'I was Omar. Once. But I never liked the name, and so I changed it to Boomer. Besides, I had some trouble with the police.'

'What sort of trouble?'

'Mainly arson. Also car theft, narcotics, extortion, racketeering, grand larceny, underage drinking –'

'I see,' said Barney, a note of admiration stealing reluctantly into his voice.

'Hold on, I haven't finished yet. Illegal transportation of minors, smuggling. Then there's possession of deadly weapons, of course.'

'Boy, you really have gone off the rails. What went wrong?'

'A lot of it relates back to my childhood, Barney. Basically – to simplify – I'm just a bundle of grievances.'

'You are?' said Barney uneasily. 'Well, I hope you don't want to talk to me about them.'

'Why not?'

'Because I can't stand listening to other people's problems at the best of times. And right now I've got far too many of my own.'

'There's no need to be like that.'

'Yes, there is, believe me. Every need.'

Boomer began to laugh. A rich chortle that rolled round the minstrels' gallery and out into the Great Hall.

'I got you good with the wild-flower meadow, didn't I?'

'I suppose so,' Barney conceded. 'What was that stuff you made me spray it with? Wasn't fertilizer, that's for sure.'

'No, no. Quite the reverse, actually. It was Agent Orange. They used it in the Vietnam War as a defoliant. Stops anything growing for at least three generations. I suppose they must have cleared the bracken with it here. Yeah . . . I got you good there, all right.'

'But why? What have I ever done to you?'

'To begin with, I thought you might be an undercover cop. Even a private detective. There's a reward on my head, you see.'

'Is there? How much for?'

'Never mind about that, Barney. Then Lia told me who you were, just now. That's when I realized I'd seen you before – a long time ago.'

'I remember seeing you in your little karate suit.'

'There you are! At an age when I should have been learning how to relate to people, I was being taught how to paralyse them with one swing of my foot. And to memorize all of Richard III's speeches. I ask you, is it any wonder I'm so fucked up?'

'I guess not,' Barney agreed. 'So how come you're here?'

'I'd escaped from prison after one of my – my episodes, when this guy traces me. At first I assume he's going to turn me in. Then he explains that he's acting for Edmund Crowe and offers me a job here.'

'But why would Edmund want to offer you a job?'

'Don't you get it, Barney? He wanted to use me as bait to lure my sister to the house.'

'I see,' said Barney, although he was far from sure that he did. Or wanted to.

'And that's not all,' said Boomer. 'In case that didn't do the trick he also got my parents to come, on the pretext of offering them both an exhibition. This is like a regular reunion, isn't it? Especially with you turning up out of the blue. Anyway, we'd best not hang round here for too long.'

'I was hoping to see Lia.'

'Not tonight, Barney. She's feeling a bit shaken up. Just let her rest.'

'I wouldn't want to upset her any more.'

'That's the spirit.'

Together, they descended the remainder of the staircase and crossed the Great Hall. Barney headed for the door that he'd come through earlier. Boomer, however, veered off towards the main entrance.

'Where are you going?' Barney asked.

'I've got some stuff to attend to,' Boomer told him.

In the moonlight the cleft down his forehead was unusually prominent.

'What sort of stuff?'

'Oh . . . Just stuff.'

'You don't want to be any more specific than that?'

'No, I don't. Not yet, Barney. All I can say is, there's going to be quite a bit of action round here soon. I can guarantee you that. I'm attuned, you see.'

'Attuned to what?'

'To anarchy!'

'I see. And when do you think this anarchy might be happening?'

'Won't be long now.'

'I shall look forward to that,' said Barney sincerely.

'Well, this is where we part company. Goodnight, Barney. You sleep well.'

'Night then.'

Barney stood and watched as Boomer vanished into the shadows.

27
The Deep Pocket

The next day, due to the weather and the fact that no one wanted to swim, Barney was taken off his pool duties and put on to raking leaves instead. He dragged his rake across the grass, pausing every so often to clean the accumulated leaves and petals out of the spikes.

Low cloud filled the horizon. At the far end of the lawn was a belt of trees. Barney threw the rake out on another flailing trajectory, pulling it back with one loosely clawed hand this time, by way of variety.

'Hiya, Barney.'

Corky was standing by the edge of the lawn, leaning on his stick at a heavy tilt. 'How you doing?'

'Not – not too bad.'

'Good man.'

'Tell me, Corky, do you know where Lia is?'

'She's helping Tinker and Squirrel Dorothy unload the artworks. They've just arrived. I'd lend a hand myself, but I'm not much help. Not with my leg and all.'

Barney carried on raking.

'So you jacked in the magazine then?' he said semi-conversationally.

'Had to, I'm afraid. But, you know, Barney, mere pornography could never contain me.'

'It couldn't?'

'No way. Why, even art can barely manage it. Still, at least I have my configurations.'

'What happened to all the squirrels?'

'At the club? Apart from Squirrel Dorothy, you mean? A surprising number went into geriatric nursing. And interior design, of course. That was always a great favourite. So, you reckon you're bearing up OK then, Barney?'

'I think so. Just about.'

'Funny . . . That's not what I heard.'

Barney stopped raking. 'It isn't?'

'Oh no,' said Corky. 'Quite the reverse.'

'How do you mean?'

'I heard you'd screwed up big time.'

'Who told you that?'

'Can't rightly remember. I can remember the gist of it, though. You touch something, it turns to shit. Yup,' said Corky brightly, 'that's what I heard.'

'Jesus, show a bit of fucking sensitivity, can't you?'

'I don't want to be tactless or anything, Barney.'

'No? Well – well make more of an effort then.'

'It's just this medication I'm on. Makes me say things.'

'Things you don't mean?'

'No . . . I wouldn't say that.'

'Oh.'

As Barney was about to start raking once more, he heard a voice saying, 'Ah, there you are.'

Wendy had appeared behind Corky. Barney had never been so pleased to see her.

'Will you come with me?' she said.

They left Corky where he was. Once again Barney followed her back up to the house. This time, though, they didn't go inside. A car was parked in the drive. An Austin Allegro, painted in vivid pea green.

Barney stopped in his tracks when he saw it.

'Where did that come from?' he asked in unfeigned surprise.

'It is Mr Crowe's. He had it restored specially. He wants you to drive him.'

'Drive him where?'

'He didn't say.'

Barney looked inside the car. There was a flat, grey, circular object sitting on the driver's seat. Wendy opened the door, lifted this object off the seat and held it out towards him.

'What?' said Barney.

She continued holding it out towards him.

'Oh no . . . Not that.'

'You must, Barney.'

'Must?'

'I'm sorry.'

He was shocked to see a look of sympathy in Wendy's eyes.

'So am I,' he said.

Taking the chauffeur's cap, Barney put it on top of his head.

'What happens now?'

'Just wait in the car. Mr Crowe will come.'

Barney sat in the driver's seat. He hadn't been there for more than a couple of minutes when Edmund came out. He was wearing the same long double-breasted overcoat he'd been wearing when he had arrived in the helicopter. From the look of Edmund's skin, his general pallor, his inner tubes were knotted even more tightly than usual today.

Without saying anything, he got in the back of the car. Once he was settled, he said, 'Just drive, will you, Barney. I'll give you directions as we go along.'

They drove down the drive, out through the electronic gates and towards the village. The car ran smoothly if heavily, pulling a little over to the right. When they reached the village green Barney was told to turn left and carry on until he received further instructions.

The road unwound before him, past the trench that he had slept in and might soon return to, and out into open country. Barney glanced in the rear-view mirror. Edmund was sitting on the back seat, his head turned, gazing out of the window, one hand resting lightly on his knee.

Barney's eyes flickered back to the road. Then to the mirror again. Edmund's mouth moved about as if practising words to say, or releasing noxious gases from his stomach. Meanwhile his other hand drifted upwards and slid into his overcoat.

What did he have hidden in there? Barney wondered.

Whatever it was, Edmund half took it out of his pocket – his hand appearing briefly from within the folds of his coat. Then he seemed to think better of it, and slid his hand back again. Again Barney's eyes switched back to the road. Then back to Edmund again.

Once again Edmund's hand had crept up to his coat pocket.

All at once Barney realized what was happening. Edmund meant to kill him. Yes! That was it. He would be taken to a secluded spot and shot. So that was what this was all about – it had to be. How could he have been so naïve, so trusting, not to see this coming?

Barney's hands began to shake.

'Careful!' shouted Edmund.

They had drifted out into the middle of the road. Another car was heading straight towards them. Barney could see the driver's eyes filling with alarm as the two vehicles closed in on one another. He swung the car back to the left-hand side. The other car hurtled by, its horn hooting frantically; its driver's face now fully inflated.

'What are you playing at?'

'It's this stupid steering wheel,' said Barney, gripping it by its two uppermost corners and struggling to aim the car in a more-or-less straight line.

'Just concentrate, Barney.'

'What do you want from me?'

'Just keep driving. Like I said. When you reach the next cross-roads, go straight over.'

They were passing between yet more bracken-covered hills. One or two of these hills were dotted about with the incinerated stumps of trees. In places, sand had blown across the road in a series of loose arcs. Standing on the verges were several more of the narrow-backed ponies that Barney had seen when he had first arrived. They had their heads down and were nibbling at the gorse. There were no houses about, not even corrugated-iron shacks.

Up ahead was the crossroads Edmund had mentioned. Barney slowed as they approached the junction. He looked at the sign on the far side of the road.

'But that says "Dead End",' he said. He could hear the fear in his voice.

'Take no notice of that.'

Shortly after crossing the junction they crossed a cattle-grid. The tarmac gave way to a rutted track. The Allegro bounced and rolled from side to side, gorse scratching at the paintwork.

'Are you sure you know where we're going, Edmund?'

'Just carry on.'

A hundred yards further on, the track broadened briefly into a complicated arrangement of ruts.

And then it stopped altogether.

'This is where we get out,' said Edmund. 'No need to lock the car.'

They were in a clearing. With a certain amount of relief, Barney saw that it was a picnic area. A number of benches and tables were dotted about. He looked around for any other cars.

There weren't any.

'Why don't we sit down,' said Edmund.

Barney headed for the nearest table.

'No, not there, Barney. Over here.' Edmund walked over to a table on the far side of the clearing. It was set on its own, almost concealed by sprays of yellow flowers. 'Yes,' he said looking around, 'this'll do.'

Edmund sat down. After a brief pause intended to signal the possibility of disobedience rather than its actual manifestation, Barney sat opposite him. He took off his chauffeur's cap and dropped it on the table. 'I expect you're wondering why I've brought you here,' said Edmund.

'Not especially.' Barney was determined to hang on to some shred of nonchalance for as long as possible. He dropped his head and watched pieces of litter blow lazily round his feet. He liked litter, he decided; it was a shame there wasn't more about. He looked up to see Edmund staring at him in a particularly hard and unforgiving way. 'All right,' said Barney. 'What do you want of me?'

Instead of replying, Edmund's hand once again drifted up to his coat pocket.

'No – don't.'

'Don't what?'

'Don't do that. Have a heart. Please.'

Edmund's hand stayed where it was. Then he patted his coat pocket several times, apparently for reassurance. As he did so, Barney began to speak, very rapidly. 'Just don't think I'm going to make it easy for you. Because I won't.'

'I – I beg your pardon?'

'No, no, no,' Barney went on, even more rapidly now. 'Far too late for that. You can't get away with this. Even though I may have sunk pretty low. Look what's become of me. I was a king at the Roundhouse – at least a very big fish in a small pond. But then you came along and pulled the plug out. How do you think that felt? My God, you've no idea what it's like out there. How cold the water is; how easy it is to go under. I didn't know what hit me. It was horrible. Oh, I'm sure that my – my plight is of no consequence to someone like you. But you can't just treat me like dirt and then dispose of me like . . .' – momentarily, he lost his thread, then regained it – 'more dirt. There are laws, even for people like me. Anyway, what do you think it's like being in my shoes? Have a guess. Not much fun. Not being forced to throw myself on your mercy. No, not very much fun at all. You – you plantation-owner, you!'

When he had finished Barney saw that Edmund was looking at him in the same pitiless way as before. To which some incredulity had possibly been added.

'What are you talking about?'

'What am I talking about?'

'Yes.'

Abruptly, all Barney's certainties fell away. 'I don't know,' he said helplessly. 'What *am* I talking about?'

'I've no idea.'

'You haven't?'

'None at all.'

'Oh . . .'

Barney gripped the edge of the table. As he did so a car with a caravan attached to the back of it pulled into the clearing. People spilled out. Adults as well as children.

'As a matter of fact,' said Edmund, his voice thickening now much as it had done when he'd been inside the round bower, 'I brought you here, Barney, because . . . because I wanted to ask you a favour.'

Despite being greatly taken aback by this, Barney was determined not to show any signs of surprise. 'What sort of favour?' he asked.

Edmund swallowed; a manoeuvre which entailed his lifting his chin sharply up, then setting it down just as sharply. 'That's not very easy for me to explain . . . Do you remember you and me driving out for a drink in the country, however many years ago?'

'No,' said Barney. 'Well, vaguely.'

'You told me about your father being decapitated by a dumper truck.'

'Did I?'

'And about how you'd worked in a circus with Stripey the Tiger after you'd escaped from the orphanage.'

'I don't fully recall.'

'And that you found it hard to give yourself to any one woman.'

'Where exactly are we going with this?' Barney demanded.

'You said then that people would do anything to feel earthed – to feel anchored to reality. Do you remember that?'

'. . . Maybe.'

'That was what gave me the idea for my rubber car tails.'

'Didn't you ever consider cutting me in on some of the profits?'

'No,' said Edmund. 'No, I didn't.'

The adults and children who had spilled out of the car had now started setting up a picnic on a table. They had bottles and cans in a cold-box, paper plates and napkins. Barney could see bright slices of meat spread across cream-coloured plates. Although not remotely hungry, he found himself distracted by these slices of pink meat.

When Edmund next spoke his words came out even more slowly than before. 'Barney?'

'Yes?'

'I want you to talk to Lia for me.'

'To Lia?'

'You've always been good at that sort of thing.'

'What sort of thing is that?'

'Talking to women.'

Before Barney could acknowledge the truth of this, Edmund went on, 'Whereas I'm not, you see. In fact, I just don't seem to be able to do it.'

'What happens?'

'I seize up.'

'Do you really?' said Barney, his interest awakened now. 'I thought that might have got better.'

'So did I,' said Edmund. 'So did I. But it hasn't.'

'What exactly did you want me to talk to Lia about?' Barney asked.

'I'm just coming to that. You know, Barney – you and me – we're not so very different. Obviously, there's a difference in our material status. And our social status,' Edmund added unnecessarily. 'But maybe things haven't worked out quite the way either of us hoped.'

Barney realized that his initial fear that Edmund was going to shoot him had been succeeded by quite a strong sense of disappointment that this was not going to happen.

'How do you mean?'

Edmund nodded towards the people on the other side of the clearing who had sat down to their picnic. 'Families, children . . . All of that . . . Never came our way, did they?'

Barney too looked over at the picnicking family, now tucking into their pink luncheon meat. 'No,' he agreed. 'No, they didn't.'

'No point just standing round hoping for happiness to land in your lap, is there?'

'I suppose not.'

'You've got to do something about it,' said Edmund. 'Directly or indirectly.'

A flock of birds flew overhead, cawing boisterously. When they had gone Barney asked, 'What did you have in mind?'

Edmund seemed to gather himself in, in preparation for hurling himself forward. 'I want you to tell Lia how I feel about her,' he said.

It was a while before Barney spoke. 'I don't know about that.'

'My mind is full of dry things, Barney. There's no – no poetry in me.'

'Even so . . . I mean, what do you want me to say?'

As if by way of reply, Edmund's hand started climbing back up to his inside pocket.

'Now wait a minute,' said Barney in sudden panic. 'I haven't said no yet.'

Edmund's hand continued to climb upwards.

'Hold on, all right? Just hold on. You haven't even said what's in it for me.'

Edmund, however, took no notice of what Barney was saying. His hand was sliding into his coat. He reached inside his pocket and took out several folded sheets of paper. Barney saw that these pieces of paper were covered in writing.

He looked at them in surprise. 'What are those?'

'I've made some notes,' said Edmund.

Nothing Stirred

Five elderly men lay huddled together in the back of a yellow van. All of them had colourless skin and long colourless hair hanging down over their chests. All wore the same colourless denim shirts with frayed hems and metal buttons worn smooth with handling. All five had their eyes closed and their hands folded over their bellies.

At lengthy intervals their bellies rose and fell as they breathed in and out. Another man stood outside the back door of the van. He was bald apart from tiny twists of hair that stuck out around the crown of his head like shrivelled pipe-cleaners.

'Goodnight, boys,' he said softly, and then closed the door.

An Unusual Proposal

'Are you still in there, Barney?'

'Yeah.'

'What are you doing?'

'Just think– none of your business.'

'Well, you can't stay in there all day, you know.'

'Why not?'

'Lots of reasons. Also, I have a message from Edmund. He wants you to go down to the old stables right away.'

'What for?'

'He didn't say.'

'All right. I'm just coming.'

'Well, hurry it up,' said Boomer.

Barney folded Edmund's notes and put them away. Then he stood up. Although he hadn't done anything apart from sit on the toilet for some time, as a kind of sop to convention he pulled the chain.

Barney walked around Corky and Tinker's exhibition. Several large pictures were hanging on the walls, and pieces of gnarled and shapeless pottery were displayed in specially hired glass cases.

There was no one about.

He looked at the largest of all the pictures. It showed a woman lying naked on her side on a divan bed, facing directly outwards. The woman, Barney recognized without difficulty, was Lia. Something brown and furry was protruding from beneath her thigh. A squirrel's tail. Behind Lia and the divan was a curtain, partly opened. Peering through the gap in the curtain was a small figure – possibly kneeling, or truncated in some way – with an expression of mischievous glee on his face. This figure he also recognized. It was Corky.

Barney gazed at the painting. However vile it was – and it was certainly that, with ample amounts of misplaced pride taken in the level of vileness – he was forced to admit that it was a pretty good likeness of Lia. Corky had caught the directness of her gaze, but also that tremor of uncertainty. The defiant unselfconsciousness about her body, yet with something peculiarly naked about her nakedness.

There was a crunch of gravel outside.

Lia came in.

'Hello, Barney. I gather you wanted to see me.'

Briefly, Barney feigned immersion in the painting.

'That's right,' he said carefully. 'I thought we could have our chat.'

'What chat was that?'

'The one we talked about having earlier.'

'Oh yes . . . Fine.'

Lia was more at ease than when Barney had seen her before. Bubblier too, although he couldn't help feeling that this could give out without warning. Although she no longer had her arms crossed, there seemed to be shadowy imprints across her chest indicating where they might go.

'Was there anything in particular you wanted to talk about, Barney?' she asked.

Shifting his feet about, Barney could hear Edmund's notes rustling in his pocket. 'As a matter of fact, there was,' he said. Now that he was actually here Barney realized he had given very little thought to how he might proceed. 'I have this friend . . .' he began.

Lia, he saw, had tilted very slightly to one side and was looking at him quizzically. 'You have a friend, Barney?'

'That's right.'

'Male or female?'

'Male.'

'Do I know him?'

'That's – that's not important.'

This was proving harder than Barney had anticipated.

'I see,' said Lia, sounding understandably puzzled now. 'What about this friend of yours?'

'I'm just coming to that ... He has what you might call a complicated problem.'

'Oh, Barney, I can't help you there.'

'But I thought that's what you did for a living.'

'I used to, but not any more. I'm afraid my listeners didn't derive very much benefit from my advice.'

'You mean, they didn't follow it?'

'No,' said Lia. 'That was the trouble. They did.'

Abruptly, Barney had another insight. How he wished this would stop; it only made matters worse. None the less, he saw how Lia had tried to keep her life in a series of sealed compartments, to try to stop herself from being engulfed by chaos. Hadn't worked, though. You could never fix the lids on tightly enough. Besides, a lot of this chaos emanated from Lia herself. Without meaning to, she pumped the stuff out in darkish clouds.

'I have this friend,' he began again.

'Do we have to talk about this friend of yours, Barney? He doesn't sound very interesting.'

'He improves,' said Barney slowly, 'with knowing.'

'I wish you'd tell me what his name is. To make matters easier.'

'I'd rather not do that.'

'Why ever not?'

'For – for personal reasons,' he improvised. 'Yes, that's right. For personal reasons.'

'Oh,' said Lia abruptly. 'I see ...'

'You do?' said Barney in some relief.

'I think so. You have this "friend", Barney,' Lia said, laying an undue amount of stress on the inverted commas.

'That's what I've been trying to tell you.'

'I'm sorry. I was a bit slow on the uptake.'

After a moment of disquiet Barney plunged on. 'This friend of mine has always had feelings for you. Strong feelings. But he's never properly been able to express them himself.'

'Your "friend", Barney?'

'Precisely.'

Finally, it seemed, they were getting somewhere.

'My friend had always hoped, in his heart of hearts, that you and he might make a life together,' he went on. 'Because – because he loves you. Very deeply. However, having a nervous disposition – along with a raft of other impediments – he asked me to talk to you instead.'

Any relief Barney felt at having got this far was offset by the sight of Lia wringing her hands together. He had never seen anyone do this before.

'Barney . . . I don't know what to say.'

'Take your time,' he said considerately. 'Bound to be a bit of a shock.'

'It's certainly that all right.'

Now Lia had begun to pace about. 'This is very difficult for me,' she said.

'It's not easy for me either, believe me,' Barney reminded her.

'No, no. I see that. Does your "friend" expect an answer, Barney?'

'Not immediately, no. But I'm sure he'd like to be put out of his misery.'

Still she kept pacing about, taking smaller, tighter steps now. 'Oh, Barney,' she said. 'I didn't mean to hurt anyone.'

What did she mean by this? Barney's train of thought, he realized, had now split into several different sections, none of which he appeared to be fully in control of any more.

'I don't suppose you did,' he said.

'You know I've always liked you, Barney.'

'Well, I should hope so!'

'It's just that coming here has shaken me up. Seeing you, and Edmund.'

'Edmund, yes . . .' Cautiously, Barney inched forward. 'What about Edmund?' he said.

'He looks so unhappy. Haven't you noticed?'

'Probably just indigestion.'

'I'm not so sure about that. Do you mind if I ask you a question, Barney?'

'If you want.'

'If it's within your power to make a person happy, do you think you have a duty to try?'

'I don't know about duty,' Barney replied, thinking that here at least he was on firm ground. 'I don't think you should do it purely for charitable reasons. Surely it depends on what you feel for that particular person.'

'Yes, you're right, of course. Except that's not easy for me to say. Or admit to. It's been so long, for a start, and my judgement is not what it was, you see. Maybe it was never up to much in the first place. To go back to your "friend", Barney. I'm afraid that if I had feelings for anyone then they wouldn't be for him.'

'Ah. They wouldn't?'

'No.'

'Fair enough.'

'I must say you're taking it very well.'

Barney gave an artless shrug of his own devising. As he did so, he heard a crunch of gravel from outside. 'Who do you have feelings for then?' he asked.

There were shadows lengthening through the room. One of them shaded the top half of Lia's face.

'Can't you guess, Barney?'

'No,' he said quite genuinely. 'No, I can't.'

'For – for a friend of your "friend's",' she said.

It was at this point that Barney realized he had lost hold of all the threads of their conversation. Every single one. It wasn't just Lia who was pumping out darkish clouds of confusion. He was chock-full of the stuff himself.

He tried to recap. Clearly Edmund was the 'friend' he had been referring to. Any fool could see that. So who on earth was this other friend of his? Who could that possibly be? After all, there weren't many candidates . . .

Lia was standing with one foot extended, balancing on a heel tip.

'Maybe I haven't explained myself very well.'

'No, no, no . . .'

'You do understand, don't you, Barney?'

245

'I think I do. So why don't you tell him directly?'

'Tell who?'

'Why, this friend of my friend's. Obviously.'

'I panic too easily,' said Lia. 'After all, it's been such a long time, hasn't it? Also, there are sensitivity issues.'

'I'll say there are.'

Barney was trying to put his thoughts into some sort of order, while simultaneously dissuading his internal organs from embarking on a lap of honour. Standing there, trembling a little, a quote came to him that he had heard once. Something about it being the things in life that you didn't do that you regretted most, and not the things you did do. Who had said that? Probably someone serving a lengthy prison sentence. Still, he thought . . . still there was a lot in it.

'Come away with me,' he said suddenly.

'What was that, Barney?'

'Come away with me.'

Lia had stepped forward, out of shadow. She didn't look shocked – he wouldn't have minded that – so much as dumbfounded, which he found he did mind a lot.

'I don't follow you, Barney.'

'I know I haven't got anything' – hurriedly, he corrected himself – 'much to offer. But the two of us, we'll manage somehow.'

'But, Barney,' said Lia, 'what about Edmund?'

'Edmund? But . . . ?' Barney felt both his lungs about to ignite simultaneously. 'Screw Edmund!' he bellowed. 'Just forget all about Edmund.'

Again, he was aware of the sound of gravel crunching outside. Also a low, anguished moan.

'You can't mean that?' said Lia.

'Oh yes I do,' said Barney. 'I mean it more than I've ever meant anything before in my life. Let's leave tomorrow morning. We musn't stay here a moment longer than necessary.'

Lia continued to look at him. Her brow clouded, her arms crossed over her chest.

'Barney, I don't think you've properly understood –'

But before she could go on, another voice said, 'Hello, you two. Am I breaking anything up?'

Tinker had entered the room.

Silently, she glided across the floor towards them, even whiter and more powder-caked than usual.

'You're not breaking anything up,' said Lia quickly.

'Thank goodness for that. I wouldn't have been able to forgive myself – not if I'd broken anything up. Are you all right, Bunny? Your skin looks flushed, or even flayed.'

'I'm fine.'

'That's a relief. The exhibition is looking very impressive, don't you think? All our works together, en masse, for the first time. Such a shame nobody has been to see it. I mean, I know the official opening isn't until tomorrow, but you'd have thought some people wouldn't have been able to contain their curiosity.'

As excellent as he was already feeling, Barney found he still had room in his system for another dose of pleasure.

'Nobody at all has been to see it?' he asked.

'Not so far,' Tinker admitted. 'But I've no doubt they'll come in the end.'

30

Scratchy Footsteps

'You're in a very good mood tonight,' said Kenneth.

'Maybe I am.'

Barney bent forward and took another sip of his beer.

'Had some good news, have you?'

'You could say that.'

Apart from everything else, when Barney had returned to the dormitory after his talk with Lia, he'd found a brown envelope on the bed. Inside was £65 in cash – money for the work he had already done. Also in there was a security card allowing him to pass unhindered in and out of Hope Springs.

'Another one?' asked Kenneth.

By way of a reply, Barney aquaplaned his glass across the bar.

'So Edmund Crowe has finally arrived, has he? Finally deigned to honour us with his presence.'

'He's not that bad,' said Barney. 'Once you get to know him.'

'You won't find many here who'll agree with you,' said Kenneth with unusual venom. 'No, country people have their pride, you know. They can't be bought off with sops and bribes. Well, not that easily. You coming to the fête tomorrow?'

'What fête is that?'

'Our annual St Swithin's Day Fête. There's a party afterwards in the Village Hall.'

'Not a chance,' said Barney. 'I'll be long gone by then. In fact, this is my last night here.'

'Sorry to hear that. Let's hope the weather stays fine. They say that if it rains on St Swithin's Day, it will rain for the next forty days and forty nights.'

'Do they really?'

When Barney left the pub, he narrowly avoided being run down by a yellow van which swerved in his direction, then passed just a few inches away, a plume of exhaust fountaining out behind.

'Maniac!' he shouted, and as a kind of futile afterthought shook his fist at the disappearing van.

Barney walked across the green, over the stream and back up the drive. It had started to rain. Nothing, however, could dampen his mood. He was feeling better than he had done in years. As a way of celebrating this, he began to sing, 'He was driving ninety miles an hour down a dead-end street. That's how fast he was going. Ninety miles an hour down a dead-end street.'

Ahead of him the 'Keep Out' sign loomed out of the darkness.

As Barney fitted his security card into its slot, he heard a dry clattering sound coming from just behind him. Like large rodent claws scratching along the road. Large brown rodent teeth too, nibbling away . . .

He began to sing again – more loudly than before. 'Ninety miles an hour! Down a dead-end street!'

Boomer was standing outside the dormitory. Dimly Barney registered that Boomer seemed strangely put out – even embarrassed – to see him.

'There you are, Barney. Had a good evening?'

'A good evening,' he said, 'and a very good day.'

'I don't want to spoil your mood.'

'I don't see how you could do that.'

'I'm afraid I've got some bad news, Barney.'

'Bad news?'

'Yes. You've got to leave here.'

'Who says so?'

'Edmund Crowe.'

'Edmund? But why?'

'He didn't give a reason. He just said he wants you out of here first thing in the morning.'

'Just me?' said Barney.

'Just you.'

Although Barney had been planning to leave in the morning, there was a world of difference between going voluntarily and being sacked. He took this very badly.

'That's not fair.'

'Fair?' repeated Boomer, more ruminatively than Barney might have expected. 'But what is fair?'

'Never mind that. I'm not having this.'

'But what can you do, Barney?' Boomer was right. What could he do? 'I'm sorry.'

'Yes,' said Barney. 'Me too.'

'The timing could hardly be worse.'

'Couldn't it? How do you mean?'

'Well,' said Boomer, 'it looks like you're going to miss all the fun.'

Rain continued to fall throughout the night, growing steadily heavier. It fell on the surrounding hills, filling up the ditch that Barney had slept in. It fell on the pub and the village green, cascading off the cottages and washing away several of their decorative features. At Hope Springs it saturated the formal gardens, flooded the pathways, caused the swimming pool to overflow and turned the blasted remains of the wild-flower meadow into a sodden expanse of orange mud.

31
The Eye of the Storm

As Barney climbed the front steps of the house, he noticed that the sky had turned from dark grey to a thunderous black, with an unusually oppressive, velveteen quality to the blackness. The rain was falling, heavier than ever. Raindrops, some as big as grapes, splattered all around.

He rang the bell. From inside he could hear a series of jangles, retreating into the distance.

The door opened.

Wendy was standing in front of him, dressed in her white tunic.

'I've come to collect Lia,' he told her.

'Lia?' said Wendy.

'That's right.'

'Collect Lia?' she repeated.

'Yes – collect Lia,' said Barney reflecting that a less patient person might well be showing signs of irritation by now. 'Tell her I'm here, will you?'

'I'm sorry. I can't do that, Barney.'

'Why not?'

'Because she's gone.'

'What, she's just stepped out for a breath of fresh air?' said Barney, tilting his face towards the rain and the blackened sky beyond. When he glanced back he saw that Wendy was shaking her head.

'I don't mean that.'

'What do you mean then?'

'I mean she's gone.'

'But how can she be gone?'

'She must have left first thing, without telling anyone.'

'Oh . . . You mean, she didn't leave a message, or anything?'

Again, Wendy shook her head. 'Nothing,' she said. 'She just went.'

'Oh . . . Well, what about Edmund then? I want to see him.'

'That's not possible either. He won't see anyone. Those are his instructions.'

Barney's whole body felt like the aftermath of an archery twang; as if it had been stretched to its furthermost limits, then let go, with the resulting arrow landing nowhere near its intended target.

'That's it then,' he said.

They stood facing one another across the open doorway. The rain continued to lash down. A worryingly sympathetic expression came over Wendy's face.

'Goodbye, Barney,' she said.

He walked down the steps and away from the front door. He headed down to the dormitory. There was no one about.

As he packed his canvas bag, he saw that his hands had begun to shake again. Once he had packed he checked to see how much money he had left. Barney was fumbling through his pockets when he realized he still had the keys to the Allegro.

After all that he'd been put through, the theft of a car seemed like a very minor matter. The Allegro was still where he'd left it after his drive with Edmund. He opened up the garage doors and then started up the engine. Outside, the ground was so wet that the wheels spun around several times before they found a grip.

The car sprang forward.

Barney drove down the drive, through the village – now all but invisible behind a curtain of rain – and out on to the same road he had taken with Edmund. The wipers couldn't cope. No sooner had they shovelled one lot of water away than another lot took its place. A clap of thunder almost lifted him out of the driver's seat. It was followed soon afterwards by another loud clap, this one coming from closer by.

When it had subsided, Barney eased up on the accelerator. He opened the door and looked out to see if he was still driving on tarmac. That at least was still the case – he could see the black ribbon of road stretching and disappearing into the deluge.

He carried on, keeping the wheels as straight as possible. He must be nearing the crossroads just by the picnic site by now, he thought, but it was impossible to tell. Visibility was down to a few feet. There were deep puddles on the road that threw up waves of water on either side as he drove through them. He could hear the water churning away beneath his wheels. Meanwhile gusts of rain buffeted back and forth.

The car began to veer to the right. He fought to pull it back over again. Once he had done so, he stopped the car and turned the engine off. Then he began to beat his fists against the square steering wheel. Then he beat them against his head. Everything inside was foggy, confused. If he'd had a stick to hand, he would have beaten himself with the wrong end of it; that at least would have been appropriate.

After he had finished hitting himself he sat and listened to the rain hammering on the roof. Feelings of sadness and regret washed through him. Disbelief too; at having to endure such adversity. I've never been so low as this, he thought. Never. Oh, I've been down, of course. But not so bruised. So deflated.

What else? Eh? What else? What else could be thrown at him?

Then came another clap of thunder, this one louder than the one before, followed by a sharp crackling sound.

When Barney looked through the windscreen, he saw that the car was now surrounded by a shimmering blue light. It enveloped the chassis, swaying and rippling away. His immediate reaction was to open the car door again and run for cover. Just as he was about to jump out, he stopped himself.

Something wasn't right. He shut the door.

The bracken appeared to be hissing at him. It wasn't just the bracken. All around, the ground was sizzling. As he watched, the blue light continued to dance over the car, hugging it and rolling up the bonnet in a thin blue wave. There was nothing Barney could do but sit and watch this blue wave rolling towards him. It slid up the windscreen, furling gently as it did so. And then it passed through the glass, straight through him and out the other side.

All the while the car continued pulsing with light. Barney found that he too was pulsing. The light matched his heartbeat – growing and diminishing with every thump, as if he was connected up to a distress beacon.

Then the light went away.

Barney twisted round to see if it had rolled on elsewhere, but as far as he could tell it had disappeared. There was a faint smell of burning plastic and a metallic taste in his mouth as if he'd been sucking on a rivet. His tongue, he found, had become stuck to the roof of his mouth.

He put up his hand to touch his head. It was still there – that was something. And yet somehow his head felt different. His vision too. Everthing looked sharper and brighter than it had before.

Barney sat there for a moment, trying to collect himself. Then, for the third time, he opened the car door. Slowly, he lowered his foot to the ground, thinking as he did so that an enormous electric shock might well leap through him and reduce him to a heap of ashes.

The bracken had stopped hissing. The rain continued to fall, although nothing like as heavily as before. Barney stood and listened. There was no sound either. No giant rat clattering behind him. Nothing apart from the patter of the raindrops.

He raised his hand in front of him. He held it there for a moment and then he raised his other hand and held it alongside. They were both quite still.

Steady as a gunfighter's.

What's happened to me? Barney wondered.

The answer arrived with surprising speed. I've been struck by lightning, he realized. Christ, that's what's happened! I've been struck by fucking lightning . . .

He went round to the back of the Allegro. A row of blackened and charred car tails hung limply from the back bumper. Some were giving off thin wisps of smoke. The sky was growing lighter now. Clouds were parting before the sun, being drawn ceremoniously aside. As they did so, Barney felt that clouds inside his head were also being drawn aside with the same degree of ceremony.

When he climbed back in the car and turned the key in the

ignition, the engine coughed once or twice, then burst into life. Wrenching the steering wheel round, Barney headed back the way he had come.

He put his foot to the floor.

There was a pause at this – as if the car, instead of merely obeying instructions, had decided to chew them over first, in case they could possibly be challenged, or ignored, or referred elsewhere. Apparently concluding that they couldn't, the Allegro began to pick up speed.

32

Hosed Clean

'Stand aside!'

'Barney!' said Wendy in obvious surprise.

'Stand aside,' he said again. 'I must see Edmund.'

'But what's happened to you, Barney? Your clothes? And your hair?'

'I was struck by lightning,' he said, more stiffly than he might have wished.

'By lightning? Are you sure?'

'Of course I'm sure. Now, let me through. I won't say it again.'

Wendy continued to look at him in the same impassive way as before, as if assessing his weight for postage purposes. Then she gave an almost imperceptible nod, and stepped aside.

Barney rushed past into the Great Hall and through the avenue of armoured figures. There was no sign of Edmund here, nor in the dining room. He took the stairs two at a time, running past the minstrels' gallery, then stopping on the top landing.

'Edmund!' he shouted.

Nothing.

He ran down the corridor, opening doors and looking inside. All the rooms were empty.

'Edmund!' he yelled again. 'Where are you?'

At the end of the corridor was another door. Its wooden frame was carved with roses, or bindweed, or creeping tendrils of some sort, plaited together and snaking upwards.

He pushed the door open.

Edmund was sitting on the bed with his back towards him, a hunched figure staring out at the muddy streams sweeping between the rows of box hedging.

'Ah, there you are.'

Edmund turned around. 'Barney? What are you doing here? You were meant to leave.'

'I did leave,' Barney told him. 'I stole the Allegro, as a matter of fact. But then I came back.'

'Why did you do that?'

'Because we need to talk.'

'I don't think so,' said Edmund quietly.

'Yes, yes. We must talk.'

'What about?'

'About Lia.'

'No point,' said Edmund. 'No point.'

'Why not?'

'Because she's gone.'

'Why didn't you try to stop her?'

'I couldn't. She left without telling me.'

'You too, eh? That figures.'

Edmund continued to look at Barney. His eyebrows, Barney noticed, had begun to inch together.

'What's happened to you, Barney?'

'Why do you ask?'

Edmund continued to scrutinize him, more intently than usual. 'Just that you seem different somehow.'

Barney reached up and touched his head again. It felt as if everything inside had been clarified, hosed clean. 'I *am* different,' he told Edmund.

'What's brought that about?'

'Well, I've been struck by lightning.'

'By lightning? Are you sure?'

'Don't you start. Would I make it up?'

'But what about the rubber car tails?'

'Absolutely useless,' said Barney. 'Made no difference whatsoever. Besides, you can't go through life trying to protect yourself from random hammer-blows.'

'You can't?' said Edmund in obvious surprise. 'Why ever not?'

'Because if you do you just end up like –'

'Like what?'

'Like us. Like all of us.'

Edmund's eyebrows lifted some way up his forehead. Then they began to descend again.

'Just go away, Barney,' he said. 'It's all over. You betrayed me.'

'Now let's not get technical here. There was a bit of a mix-up, that's all.'

'A mix-up? Is that what you call it?' Edmund went back to staring out of the window. Barney followed Edmund's gaze. The sun, he noticed, was struggling to emerge from a bank of cloud. 'Anyway,' said Edmund, sighing. 'There's nothing to be said. Leave me alone. It's too late now. Just too late . . .'

Barney continued gazing out of the window, at the waterlogged gardens and the muddy rivulets racing down the narrow pathways. As he did so, the movement of the water seemed to gather up his newly clarified thoughts, knotting them together and carrying them forward in one sensibly amalgamated channel.

'Not necessarily,' he said.

33

A Partial Reprise

On the village green the fête was in progress. Tarpaulins had been erected over a number of stalls selling country produce. There were jams, chutneys and oddly knobbled fruit, along with artworks made from hazel twigs. People were drifting about from one stall to another. On the other side of the road children's races were taking place along the grass verges.

Barney stopped the car and scanned the crowd.

There was no sign of Lia.

Then he drove past the pub and parked outside a low corrugated-iron building – a tin tabernacle left over from the days of Methodists and Pentecostalists, and now used as the Village Hall. Barney waited by the car, hoping against hope that Lia might make a dramatic reappearance.

While he was standing there, a yellow van drew up alongside, its engine clattering away. A man emerged, carrying an old-fashioned doctor's bag, and walked into the corrugated-iron building. This must be the man who'd tried to run him down on the previous evening, he reckoned. Of all the insults that had been aimed Barney's way, this was far from being the worst. Even so, it was one of the more recent, and, combined with the disappointment of not finding Lia, it left him keen to exact retribution. Barney went inside the hall. It was beginning to fill up with people. He saw that the man had stepped up onto a small stage at the far end of the hall and was disappearing through a curtain. When Barney did the same, he found himself in a short corridor with a door at the far end and another door to his left.

The door on his left was pulled to, though not shut.

Inside a light was burning. It was very dim, like a child's nightlight.

Five elderly men were lying stretched out in chairs. Barney's first thought was that he must have stumbled into a makeshift morgue. All the men had the same colourless skin and long colourless hair like roughly bleached flax.

The air was very still.

Out of curiosity – nothing more – Barney felt one of the men's pulses. He was just able to detect a faint tremor.

'Hey! What are you doing with my boys?'

The man with the doctor's bag was standing in the doorway.

'I'm not doing anything with them,' said Barney. 'I thought they were dead.'

'Dead? They're not dead. They're just snoozing. Anyway, who the hell are you?'

'You tried to run me down last night.'

The man shook his head. 'If I'd tried to run you down, you'd have been run down.'

As Barney struggled to think of a suitable reply to this, his eyes crept upwards to the man's hairline, or what was left of it. To the line of tiny shrivelled dreadlocks studded around the crown of his head.

'Don't do that,' said the man sharply.

'Do what?'

'Stare like that. At my hair.'

'You haven't got much hair to stare at.'

'I've got enough.'

'Yeah? Where do you keep it then?'

'Now just hold on . . .'

Throughout this exchange, Barney had been aware of feelings of unease building inside him. He moved his head experimentally from side to side. The other man, he saw, was doing the same.

'What did you say your name was?' the man asked.

'I didn't.'

'Well, what is it?'

'No,' said Barney, 'you go first.'

The other man appeared equally reluctant to say who he was. They continued to face one another. Meanwhile, stretched out on their chairs, the five recumbent figures slumbered away.

'I'm not sure about this,' said the man. 'I don't know . . . I'm getting a weird feeling here.'

Barney realized that he too had a weird feeling without knowing why. The man, he noticed, had flecks of brown in the whites of his eyes. Still they stared at one another.

Then the man spoke.

'Barney? Is it really you?'

'Possibly,' Barney acknowledged. 'Possibly . . . Ron?' he said weakly.

The other man spread his arms wide. 'That's me. Still me. Heh-heh-heh. Well, what do you know? So how have you been, Barney?'

As with all such inquiries, it was hard to know just where to start. 'Well, recently I was struck by lightning.'

'By lightning? Are you sure?'

'Why must everyone doubt me the whole ti–' Barney began – but stopped himself short; he would deal with his own grievances later. 'But, Ron, what are you doing here, with these – these terrible old people?'

Ronald chuckled. 'Don't you recognize them, Barney?'

'Why should I do that? Mainly I like to hang with a younger crowd, you know.'

'But, Barney, it's *bach*.'

'*bach*?'

'Thorazine *bach*. They re-formed.'

Barney found that the metallic rivet taste had come back into his mouth.

'They did? I thought they were dead.'

'Only most, not all. We lost one along the way. And Reggie here has to have his medication very carefully controlled, in case he –'

'In case he what?'

'. . . Reverts.'

'But, Ron, how do you fit in here?'

'I'm their manager. Have been for the last couple of years. To be honest, no one else was that keen to take them on. But I thought

I'd give it a go and, you know, all things considered, it's worked out pretty well.'

Again, Barney looked down at the five comatose men. They hadn't stirred. From his medical bag, Ronald took five large syringes.

'You watch, Barney. I always like this bit.'

Ronald went round each of the five figures, plunging the syringes into their arms. Some jerked away in an unconscious gesture of self-preservation. But others – no more awake – stretched out their arms towards him, as if an unconscious craving for the needle penetrated the shuttered depths of their minds.

Nothing happened for a while. Then, very slowly, the men began to stir. They opened their eyes and rubbed their faces in a cautious, experimental way. One or two of them looked about, blinking, their eyes completely devoid of curiosity.

'Ron, isn't it cruel? Keeping them like this?'

'It's not cruel. They're perfectly happy.'

'But just look at the state of them.'

'You've got to remember they're all getting on a bit now, Barney. They spend a lot of time asleep. Actually, it's more like a form of hibernation. Their whole metabolism slows right down, almost to zero, and they only need to eat once every few days. But you just wait. In a few minutes' time they'll be raring to go. They do all the old favourites, you know. Of course, we don't do the cannon effects any more – the boys can't take any sudden shocks.' Ronald went round each of the five members of Thorazine *bach*, rubbing their hands and slapping them on the cheeks. 'All right, guys? Ten minutes. Now then, Barney, you haven't told me what you're doing here, deep in the forest.'

Barney gave Ronald a highly abridged account of what had brought him there. When he had finished Ronald said, 'So you've been staying with Edmund Crowe? I've always admired him.'

'You have? I never knew that, Ron.'

'Very much so.'

The sound of chanting could now be heard in the hall. Half-hearted, but real enough. *'bach! bach! bach!'*

Feet too were being stamped. Again, Ronald tried to rouse the band, but with little success. The musicians gazed back at him with vacant, watery eyes. Ronald looked at his watch and shook his head. The remains of his dreadlocks shuddered slightly.

'Barney, would you mind going and telling everyone that the band will be a few minutes late?'

'Go where?' said Barney.

'Out front. On to the stage.'

'I don't know about that.'

'Why not?'

'Because – I was struck by lightning earlier, you know, Ron.'

'Uh-huh, you already told me.'

'I couldn't remember if I had.'

'No, you definitely mentioned it. Be a pal would you, Barney?'

It seemed he had little choice in the matter. Barney left Ronald and the five prostrate members of Thorazine *bach* where they were, made his way back down the corridor and out through the curtain on to the makeshift stage.

There was a polite ripple of applause at his appearance.

He walked to the microphone and looked out at the upturned faces. The Village Hall was about two thirds full – no more than that. Even so, it was a larger audience than Barney had appeared in front of for a very long time.

He tapped the microphone, and said, 'I'm afraid there will be a slight delay.'

A good-humoured groan went up.

'Nothing serious. Just that the band members need some medical attention, so that they can . . .' – here he paused and swallowed – 'walk,' he concluded.

As he was speaking, Barney became aware that his hands had crept up from his sides. They were now in front of his face, moving around, independently of instructions. It wasn't clear if anyone in the audience had noticed this. Possibly they thought it was a piece of mime, or the prelude to a paper-folding display. Barney found he didn't care much what they thought. He saw that his hands were on particularly fluent form tonight, waving and curling about in the air.

He felt taken aback by all these shifting, floating shapes. But it seemed to him that these movements weren't just frantic and full of unfocused yearning. Not his usual repertoire of desperate gestures. Instead, they were clear and purposeful – and, what's more, his own. They belonged to him. Despite everything, Barney felt pleased with himself for mounting such a display – at the same time as feeling sad that it should come now, when it was all too late.

As Barney peered through the horizontal slats of his fingers, he noticed Kenneth the barman staring up at him, his mouth more agape than Barney could have believed possible. Other faces were also looking up at him, scarcely any less agape. Among them, he saw, was Lia's.

34
Thunder Roars

With a final flourish Barney brought his hands back down to his sides, then jumped down from the stage. People parted before him. When he reached Lia, he took hold of her arm.

'Barney? What are you doing here?'

'I thought you'd gone,' he said.

'My car broke down. The engine was waterlogged.'

'Oh, it broke down, did it? That's good.'

'Why should it be good?' Lia was asking.

But before Barney could answer her, there was a commotion by the curtain. To a chorus of cheers, Thorazine *bach* now took the stage. Five ashen men walking in line as if they were tied together with invisible thread. Each with the same glazed expression and ghostly pallor. From the side of the stage, Ronald kept a protective eye on them.

The band members paid no attention to the cheers of the crowd. It wasn't even clear if they were aware of them. They seemed to need all their concentration for hanging their instruments around their necks and working out which direction they were supposed to face.

And then, as if responding en masse to some silent clarion call, Thorazine *bach* began to play. A jumble of different sounds emerged – each entirely free of melody, rhythm or beat, and yet each with its own distinctively insipid tone. It was like having diluted water poured in your ears, thought Barney. When they came to the end of the first number, more applause rang out. After lengthy retuning, the band began to play again. As they did so, Barney was aware of a distant and far-from-welcome familiarity about what he was hearing. He realized it was an extract from 'Arthur's Seat'. Dopey, mutton-headed Arthur roused at last from his bed of clay, come to save his countrymen in time of need.

He glanced over at Lia. Her mouth too was open. She clutched at his sleeve. 'What's going on, Barney?'

'I can't explain here. Let's go outside.'

When they were standing outside the Village Hall overlooking the green, Barney said, 'Why did you leave like that?'

'Because it was all too much. Edmund . . . you . . . I just couldn't cope with it.'

'Hmm,' said Barney. 'Hmm . . . You can't keep running away from everything, you know.'

'What are you talking about?'

'This is no way to carry on.'

'Isn't it?' said Lia.

'Definitely not,' said Barney. 'Look at where it gets you. Look at us, we're already more than halfway round the track and we're all still behaving as if we're stuck on the first lap.' He paused, feeling like a medium who has helped himself to another medium's ectoplasm by mistake. Still, it was good stuff this; no point wasting it. He ploughed on, aware of Lia looking at him in astonishment. 'You can't just leave Edmund there like that. If you have feelings for him, as you put it, then for God's sake let the poor bugger know. Otherwise he's going to spend the rest of his life floating about in this . . . this black haze. And that's not fun at all,' he added with sudden passion. 'Not for anyone.'

'What's got into you, Barney?'

'I was struck – no,' he said. 'No, never mind. I'll tell you later. The only important thing to know is that I am no longer responsible for my own behaviour.'

'You're not, Barney?'

'No,' he said. 'At least, I don't think so.'

Fortunately, any further conversation was prevented by a loud bang.

'What's that?' Lia asked.

'I don't know. More thunder maybe?'

Except it didn't sound like thunder, Barney realized. Somehow

it sounded more man-made than that. Soon afterwards Ronald
came out. Barney introduced him to Lia, but Ronald hardly took
any notice. He was preoccupied.

And then came another explosion – even louder this time.

'I thought you said you didn't do the cannon effects any more,
Ron?'

'We don't,' said Ronald.

'Then what are those bangs?'

'No idea. Anyway, they're not coming from inside the hall.
They're from outside.'

As if to confirm this, there was a third explosion. A great bang
that seemed to split the clouds apart. Showers of sparks rained
down through the night sky. People started to stream out of the
tin tabernacle, all gazing upwards. Thorazine *bach*, meanwhile,
continued to chug tunelessly away inside.

'Aren't they coming from Edmund's place?' said Lia.

'I think so,' said Barney.

'What could it be, do you think?'

What could it be?

Barney came to a sudden decision. 'Come with me. You too,
Ron.'

'But what about my boys?' Ronald protested.

'They won't notice anything. Besides, this is important.'

'How important?'

'Just come!'

The three of them ran over to the Allegro. Barney started up the
engine and moved off in the direction of Edmund's drive. The long
ribbon of gravel unrolled before them.

Barney pushed his foot down.

When they reached the gateposts they saw that the gates were
wide open and the lights in the bushes turned on. At the bottom of
the steps leading up to the front door of the house a crowd of angry
villagers had gathered. Standing on top of the steps was Edmund.

Edmund's face, Barney saw, was rigid with tension.

There was another explosion – from very close at hand. The air
seemed to ripple and fold in on itself. When the sound died away,

the villagers began shouting at Edmund and moving closer to the bottom of the steps.

'This could turn ugly,' said Ronald, twisting round and looking out of the car window. 'I know the signs.'

'I think you're right, Ron. There's a lot of resentment towards Edmund round here. Won't take much for it to boil over.'

'So what do we do, Barney?'

Still, Barney found his mind was quite clear.

'OK, everyone,' he said. 'Time for action.'

The three of them left the car and started to walk towards the steps and the crowd of angry villagers gathered below. Edmund was staring in their direction. His expression hadn't changed; his face was just as rigid as before.

Yet as they drew closer, Barney saw that Edmund's hand had begun to make a strange gesture. Palm down, moving rapidly back and forth; slowly, hesitantly, at first, but with increasing frequency – even desperation.

'What's Edmund doing?' Lia asked.

Something stirred inside Barney. He looked again; he needed to be sure. All the while Edmund's hand continued to move. Back and forth, back and forth . . .

A lot of what had happened to Barney in the past was lost – gone for ever – and no bad thing either. However, he remembered this all right. But then how could he forget it? Edmund was making the 'Help, my encampment is in danger' gypsy hand-signal that Barney had taught him all those years ago.

35
Blinding Flashes

Barney, Lia and Ronald continued making their way towards the front steps.

'Who have we here?' called out a voice from the crowd of villagers.

'Yeah, who the hell are you?'

'You tell them, Ron,' said Barney.

'We're Mr Crowe's fucking security,' said Ronald. 'That's who.'

They had almost reached the foot of the steps when there was another explosion. A white light ascended above the trees and burst into a blinding magnesium flash. It was as if night had suddenly been banished and daylight had swept in.

Everyone threw up their arms to protect their eyes.

While the light was still hanging in the sky, Barney began to run. He ran round to the converted stable where Tinker and Corky were having their exhibition. It had been a long time since he had run anywhere and his body took a while to settle into a rhythm – although not as long as he might have expected.

As Barney was heading towards the door, a muffled roar came from within. Immediately afterwards, the entire building disintegrated in front of him; as if it had burst apart at the seams. Slates, bricks and pieces of wood flew everywhere. With them came a wave of intense heat, fanning outwards.

Barney pitched forward on to the ground, holding his hands over his head. When he lifted his head he saw shreds of canvas hanging from the trees; some alight, some still in jagged pieces of frame, others flapping free. The remains of the Pubist Old Masters with their Corky configurations. One picture, more or less intact, was balanced on top of a burning bush.

There too, standing off to one side and watching as the debris settled, was the bulky figure of Boomer.

'Hey, Barney! So you decided to stay after all. See, I told you I'd got something planned. Bet you never expected this, though.'

'No,' said Barney truthfully. 'No, I can't say I did.'

'It's my curtain call, my farewell to arms. A temporary farewell, anyway. I found this old World War Two ammunition dump in the grounds. They've got some really combustible stuff in there, believe me. Well, you can see for yourself – made short work of this lot.'

'But, Boomer, you've destroyed the entire Pubist overview.'

'That's right. The whole damn lot. It's my gesture to humanity, Barney. Remember I told you I was a bundle of grievances? Well, this is my way of getting my own back. We all have to resolve our own issues in our own particular way – and this is mine.'

'Is anyone hurt?'

'Don't fuss so. Everything will work out in the end.'

'I'm not so sure about that.'

'Have faith, Barney. One hell of a bang, wasn't it? Even better than I expected. Anyway, I don't think I'd better hang about for much longer. My work here is done. Time for me to light out once more. Maybe our paths will cross again. Who knows? But remember me, won't you?'

'I'll do that,' Barney promised.

As Boomer was about to go, he stopped. He hunched up his shoulders and adopted a rasping voice. 'And when I have my need, I must away,' he said. 'For this will out, and here I must not stay.'

Then he turned and ran into the trees. A pale bounding shape growing fainter and fainter until he was swallowed up in the darkness.

Edmund made his way through the rubble to where Lia was standing. Between the two of them, sprawled on the ground, was a groaning figure, and beside it a shiny, spherical-shaped object. Edmund had no difficulty in identifying the groaning figure – it was

Tinker – and scarcely any less difficulty identifying the spherical-shaped object lying beside her.

As he bent down to pick it up, he recognized the little contorted face and the knotted limbs around it. All squeezing, all throttling away ... So, this was 'Nowhere to Turn' – the same piece of pottery that Tinker had shown him at the Nutkin Club. When Edmund looked down at Tinker he saw there was a spherical-shaped indentation in the centre of her forehead. The explosion must have propelled the piece of clay with sufficient velocity and accuracy to knock her unconscious.

Greatly encouraged as well as emboldened by this, and seeing it as a sign that the Fates were with him at last, Edmund stepped over Tinker's prostrate form and walked towards Lia. Drawing closer, he felt an indefinable hope circling inside him.

As soon as Boomer had gone, Barney found that he was so tired he could barely stand up any more. It had been a long day. A very long day. He'd been intending to go back to the dormitory – to rest there. Yet even this felt like too big an effort. Instead, he found a patch of grass without any debris on it, lay down and instantly fell asleep.

36

Two Voices

'So you didn't go after all?'

'I was going to, Edmund, but the road was flooded. I couldn't get through. And then I saw Barney and he said I should come back.'

'Barney said that?'

'He said that it wasn't fair leaving you like this. That I should tell you one way or the other how I felt.'

'You're sure Barney said that?'

'He seems different, doesn't he?'

'He certainly does.'

'I'm sorry, Edmund – about just running off. But I didn't know what else to do. I suppose I panicked.'

'Well, that's understandable.'

'I suppose I've made so many mistakes in my life that I couldn't face making another one. And I was frightened of being carried away by my feelings. So I just shut myself away.'

'Nothing . . .' Edmund found he had to clear his throat before he could carry on. 'Nothing necessarily wrong with that either.'

'Yes, there is. Lots wrong with it.'

'You do have feelings then? For me?'

'What do you think?'

'I've no idea,' said Edmund. 'I don't know anything any more. Or rather I do know one thing. I know that I love you. That I always have done. Obviously, I wish I wasn't so dark, so withdrawn. So awkward. But that's just the way I am, and try as I might there doesn't seem an awful lot –' Abruptly, and with no warning whatsoever, he stopped. Bugger, he said to himself with even more vehemence than usual. Bugger, Bugger . . . But he couldn't give up. Not now – not after all this time.

Edmund opened his mouth. Mercifully, words did come out. Not necessarily the words he had intended, but perfectly serviceable words in their own way.

'I want to have full sexual intercourse with you,' he said.

Lia looked at him. Something twitched at the corner of her mouth.

'All in good time, Edmund. All in good time. Right now, though, for God's sake shut up and kiss me.'

37

The Open Road

Daylight . . .

Barney opened his eyes. Immediately, his heart sank. There, just a few inches from his face, was an animal. It was roughly three feet long, with a glossy black snout, two protruding teeth and a white stripe running down its forehead.

The animal looked at him for a while. Then it turned around and waddled away. How could he have been so foolish as to think that his head had really been swept clean? Purged of confusion, of trepidation and delirium tremens and giant rats. Just another delusion – that's all it had been.

Just another delusion.

Barney stood up, brushed himself down, then walked past the remains of the stable and back to the house.

Edmund and Lia were coming down the steps. Barney saw that Edmund's face looked less dark and overhanging than usual. Lia too looked different – not as tightly reined-in or as poised as before.

'What are you doing, Barney?' said Edmund.

'Just getting ready to leave.'

'Leave? You know, you're welcome to stay on. As a guest.'

'I don't think I will, thanks. Time to move on.'

'Do you have anywhere in mind?'

'Not – not especially, no . . .'

Throughout this exchange the giant rat continued to skip lightly around the perimeter of Barney's vision. And now there was something else too. He glanced over, and saw that the first giant rat had been joined by a second. Then, to his dismay, he saw a third.

'Are you all right, Barney?' Lia asked.

'Can I ask you something?'

'Anything you like.'

Barney lowered his head until the rats were out of his eyeline. 'Do you see those animals over there?'

'What animals, Barney?'

He shook his head. 'Doesn't matter.'

'Oh, those animals,' said Lia.

'What? You mean you can see them too?'

'Of course I can. They're honey badgers. My brother must have released them from Drucilla's Zoo before he left.'

'Honey badgers?' said Barney. 'I see.'

So he hadn't been hallucinating after all. Barney put his head back. The clouds had gone. The sun was shining. He sniffed the air. A smell of mingled woodsmoke and gunpowder came to him on the breeze.

'And how about you?' Barney asked Lia. 'What are you doing?'

She looked at him briefly before she spoke. 'I thought I might stay around here for a while,' she said.

'That's good.'

Barney made himself focus on a completely nondescript patch of lawn. Giving a very plausible impression, he reckoned, of someone with a world of his own to be lost in. He kept his gaze fixed there as Lia said, 'I want to thank you, Barney. For everything.'

'Yes,' agreed Edmund in a voice thicker and yet less throttled-sounding than usual. 'I don't know what we would have done without you.'

Barney waved his hand in a dismissive sort of way, then let it hang there for a moment.

'Why not take the car?' Edmund indicated the Allegro. 'And, Barney, before you go, there's something else . . .'

Barney saw that Edmund was holding something out towards him. A piece of paper. Or rather several pieces of paper. For a moment he wondered if Edmund wanted him to deliver another speech on his behalf. Surely he couldn't be that desperate? Not now. But these pieces of paper didn't have handwriting on them – just printing. Printing and numbers.

'No, no, I couldn't possibly,' he might have said. However, he didn't say that; he didn't say anything. He didn't trust himself to. He just took the bundle of notes and stuffed them into his pocket.

'Goodbye then, Barney.'

Lia embraced him – tightly – for a moment, while Edmund stood alongside, patting him on the shoulder. Afterwards Barney started up the Allegro, grasped the steering wheel and pulled away.

He drove out of the village on the same road he had taken before. There were still puddles of water in the dips and hollows. Narrow-backed ponies sloshed through them to reach dry clumps of grass.

He hadn't gone far – a couple of miles at the most – when the engine began to falter. It coughed – once, twice – and then died. Barney pulled into the side of the road.

He turned the key in the ignition.

Nothing happened.

The petrol gauge showed the tank was still half full. Barney opened the bonnet and peered inside. Although he didn't know much about engines, he knew they weren't supposed to look like this. Instead of the usual array of shining pipes and gaskets, there was just a large mass of solidified grey metal. The lightning must have done that, he supposed. The Allegro had kept going for as long as necessary, and then given up the ghost. Very well, he thought. I came here on foot, and I shall leave on foot too.

Barney began to walk. The road stretched out in front of him, threading its way between the bracken-covered hills. Around his head was a faint buzzing sound. The air was fresher now than before. What am I going to do? he wondered. Where am I going to go? He had no idea. But he wouldn't worry about that – not just now.

It really was a fine day, the sky a pale, duck-egg blue threaded with the loose white weave of vapour trails. He looked down, watching one foot stepping out in front of the other, carrying him along. Still insects clustered around his head. All of them cleaving and fighting away. The same cycle endlessly repeated, with only occasional spanners being thrown into the works.

He could also hear a light clattering coming from behind. When he turned round he saw that a column of honey badgers was following in his wake. In loose formation, they shuffled along. Their snouts down, their tails erect, their feet splayed, their heads waving from side to side, like a line of unsynchronized bandsmen. Barney thought he saw them clearly enough – without being absolutely sure about it. But what did it matter if they were there or not? It didn't, he decided. Not at this moment anyway. Right at this moment nothing mattered at all.